the
windsurf
girl

M. A. Meadowcroft

M. A. MEADOWCROFT

Matador
9 Priory Business Park
Kibworth Beauchamp
Leicestershire LE8 0RX, UK
Tel: (+44) 116 279 2299
Fax: (+44) 116 279 2277
Email: books@troubador.co.uk
Web: www.troubador.co.uk/matador

ISBN 978 1783063 697

British Library Cataloguing in Publication Data.
A catalogue record for this book is available from the British Library.

Typeset in Aldine401 BT Roman by Troubador Publishing Ltd
Printed and bound in the UK by TJ International, Padstow, Cornwall

Matador is an imprint of Troubador Publishing Ltd

For my children
Georgie, Rosie, Beth and Tom

1

A strong south-easterly came sweeping in across the bay, whipping the sea into a frenzy and dispersing the holidaymakers as effectively as a sudden downpour of rain. Couples with young children, not yet restricted by the academic year, despaired of the fickle weather for, instead of avoiding the crowds and basking in some late summer sun, they found themselves cooped up in bed and breakfasts with their fractious offspring. Equally despairing landladies commiserated with each other in the village shop and vowed, yet again, to remove the words *children welcome* from their neatly embossed cards, as the big black clouds heaved their way across the sky to Warbleton.

Fran was feeling none of the despondency that emanated from the village shop. In fact, a quite delicious sense of anticipation had been with her since early morning, when the first strong gusts of wind came whistling over the sand dunes to the beach huts. From a distance, the six deeply-weathered huts gave every appearance of Lego houses which a bored child had discarded. There was no promenade neatness, no name plaques or brightly coloured doors, but the interiors belied the stark simplicity of the creosoted boards. Fran's hut stood slightly apart from the rest, facing squarely into the south-east wind. Light poured in through the tiny windows, bringing the essence of the sea and marsh with it. Bright red geranium plants balanced precariously on wooden windowsills that the first owner of the beach hut had enthusiastically hewn out of driftwood; blue and white checked curtains picked out splashes of blue in the cushions that were scattered everywhere, and a tiny teapot with an anxious-looking black and white cow painted on it perched on a pot-bellied stove.

Fran looked out of the window, her eyes following the shoreline to the point where the windsurfer usually launched his board. If her intuition was correct, it could only be a matter of minutes before he appeared, for all the weather conditions that normally heralded his appearance were evident. Since early dawn, fishing trawlers had been racing for the estuary trying to outrun the storm, and boats due out on the morning tide stayed securely tethered to their moorings in the harbour. Down by the bathing beach, where only yesterday the holidaymakers had been splashing about in the sea, the red flag was flying. Even the old rowing boat, manned by a third generation Cuthbert to ferry people across the estuary, was nowhere to be seen. Yes, she knew with certainty that the windsurfer would appear, to use the sea as a dance floor and partner the wind and waves in complete harmony.

Simon, staggering against the wind in his totally unsuitable attire, arrived just in time to see Fran emerge from the beach hut wrapped in a woolly fleece and scarf. He shouted her name, but the sound disappeared immediately, lost in the crash and suck of the waves. He tried to run but the soft sand made him feel unbalanced and stupid, and it was only when she stood still to look along the beach to Dunsmere that he was able to catch up with her.

'Fran, what the hell are you striding off across the beach for when I know you heard me calling?' he snapped.

He watched as she turned, giving him a look so reminiscent of their childhood, that he felt he was a fourteen year old kid again, bullying his little sister.

'I didn't hear you calling you idiot! How could I in this wind. Anyway why are you here?' The answer was obvious, but she certainly had no intention of making things easier for him.

After such unusual exertion Simon was red-faced and out of breath and suddenly Fran wanted to laugh. Poor Simon, he really couldn't cope with family dramas, she thought. Even when they were children he used to hide if their parents had one of their flaming rows.

'I don't know what you're smiling about,' he said. 'You can't bury yourself in the beach hut and pretend nothing has happened.'

Fran's smile quickly turned to a glare. 'Pretend nothing has happened? You insensitive idiot! Do you really think I'm doing that?'

'Look here, Fran, Mum and Dad can't handle this. Malcolm's on the phone every night asking them to make you see sense. And then there's Grace.'

Mention of Grace reminded Fran that she could never really be free of Malcolm even if her worst suspicions were realised.

'Grace is fine,' she said, glancing back towards the beach hut where Grace was having her morning sleep, 'but if you think you can manipulate me through her, forget it. She's better off without an adulterous father.'

'I say, Fran, that's a bit steep. He might have had one silly little fling but you can't jeopardise a marriage because of that.'

Fran looked at him in disgust. She had never thought of her rather overweight blond brother as being the type to attract women, and had been amazed when the lovely Annabel married him. Now he was intimating that affairs were a part of marriage.

The wind had picked up to a good force six; spindrift was streaking off the crests of the waves reminding Fran of the first flurries of snow.

'Stupid bastard,' exclaimed Simon.

Fran turned just in time to see the windsurfer head out to sea through the mounting surf.

'Idiot, windsurfing in these conditions. Irresponsible, that's what I call it.'

Fran knew it was the holidaymakers who were the irresponsible ones. There were always a few every summer who pressed their white bodies into inflatables and drifted out to sea. She wondered for the hundredth time how she could have been landed with such a pompous brother. Even as children their worlds encompassed different things, especially in Warbleton. Fran used to spend hours on the estuary messing about in any little boat she could lay her hands on, but Simon preferred to be dressed in whites on a tennis court or, more latterly, propping up the bar in a golf club after a token round of golf.

Their words were being snatched away by the wind, making conversation difficult and Fran suddenly felt like laughing again. Simon looked so uncomfortable standing on a tussock of grass arguing with her, his blond hair flying back off his brow, revealing the early but progressive stages of balding, and his eyes screwed up against the wind and sand were red-rimmed and watering.

'Annabel's up at the cottage,' he said. 'We're both here to sort this mess out, so the very least you can do is come and have a chat with us.'

Two hundred yards out to sea, the windsurfer was performing some thrilling manoeuvres amongst the waves. The horizon, which yesterday was a clear pencil line, had completely disappeared, smudged into oblivion by the mist and spray. Fran watched as he effortlessly landed another perfect backward loop and wished Simon was in London, or anywhere, other than Warbleton. Unfortunately, past clashes with him had left her in no doubt that he would stay there remonstrating with her, despite his discomfort, until she agreed to his request. She was also pretty certain his decision to act as the family go-between had more to do with self-preservation than brotherly love. Malcolm's share tips were far too lucrative to be jeopardised by her romantic idealism.

'Okay, Simon,' she said in defeat. 'Tell Annabel we'll be with you at about four.'

'I'll pick you up in the Porsche. Wait until you see her Fran, she's a beaut.'

'Thanks, but I'd prefer to walk.'

Simon looked at her in disbelief, then turned and staggered back over the sand dunes, waving his arms at a few marauding seagulls which swept low over his head, mistaking him for one of the many holidaymakers who fed them titbits.

Tom had woken late that morning to the sound of the south-east wind pummelling the reed beds surrounding his cottage. Even after ten years of chasing the wind, he still felt an adrenalin rush when he knew it was pitching towards gale force. During the night his sleep had been fitful, disturbed by the rattle of ill-fitting windows and dreams of a dark-haired woman.

The cottage looked no more than a shadow in the landscape. Years of salt winds had turned the whitewashed walls to ochre and pushed the chimney to an impossible angle. Even the garden blended unobtrusively into its surroundings, being just a wild patch of earth given over to the seeds that landed there to germinate undisturbed. As he watched the seabirds flying low over the moving sea of rushes, Tom contemplated the day ahead. After a hectic summer, it was rather pleasant to think the day was his own, with just the challenge of perfecting a few windsurfing manoeuvres ahead of him, and the exciting prospect of meeting the dark-haired woman from the beach hut who flatteringly seemed mesmerised by his windsurfing. His only immediate decision, once he'd devoured two boiled eggs and numerous slices of toast, was whether to zip himself into a summer or winter wetsuit. Having been used to the balmy sea temperatures of the Mediterranean, he erred on the side of caution.

The North Sea in a force six could be as daunting as any of the top windsurfing locations around the world and it needed all his natural skills to survive. Trying to watch two figures having a heated debate on the beach was almost suicidal, but he really did want to know who the plump blond chap was.

When he looked again she was alone, standing framed by the bleak marshland, with only a little red scarf flying round her neck to brighten the dull hue of the landscape. He gybed down the face of a wave and headed back to shore, making as straight a line as he could to the point on the beach where Fran stood watching him. Suddenly, she turned and walked back towards the beach hut. Through the spray he briefly glimpsed the bright interior before she disappeared and the door closed.

Watercolour Cottage had been the family holiday home for as long as Fran could remember, although 'family holiday home' was perhaps an inappropriate word to use. From an early age, she and Simon were bundled off to it for the whole of the summer holidays, to be looked after by grateful friends and relatives who were allowed to use the cottage in exchange for keeping an eye on the two children. Occasionally their parents joined them for a week, but more often than not the whole summer went by with no visit and just a few phone calls.

As soon as she reached the gate that led up the stone flagged path to the front door Fran regretted having complied with Simon's wishes. She should have told him to mind his own business and drive his pretentious Porsche back to London. She kissed the top of Grace's head, took a deep breath and then walked purposefully up the path. The flowerbeds flanking the path were awash with Japanese Anemones as they always had been when the summer holidays were drawing to a close. The sight of them was so evocative that she felt again the intensity of her childhood anguish at leaving Warbleton.

Fran opened the back door and heard the unmistakable sound of Lydia's loud, almost hysterical laughter. She couldn't possibly imagine why Annabel's sister was in Warbleton, when she'd frequently voiced her dislike of the place.

Annabel got out of her chair in one elegant movement.

'Fran sweetie, we're so pleased you've come to talk to us about this horrid mess,' she said, oozing sympathy and understanding.

From most people, Fran would have dismissed this slightly extravagant display of concern, but with Annabel she knew it came from the heart. She hugged her, then directed a smile at Lydia and asked what had brought her to Warbleton.

Lydia shrugged her shoulders and said she was bored.

'Don't be ridiculous! How could anyone be bored in London? said Simon. 'Now, what's it to be? Gin and tonics all round?'

'Isn't it rather early in the afternoon for alcohol?'

'Fran, darling,' said Annabel, 'I think you need a bit of Dutch courage to help you through this, and we're certainly not going to let you drink alone. Yes, pour us all a nice stiff gin, Simon, with plenty of ice, and don't forget to put lemon in,' she shouted after him as he retreated to the kitchen.

Fran sat on the edge of a chair by the bay window. She lifted Grace onto the wide windowsill and held her there so she could see the little boats in the estuary being tossed about at their moorings by the unremitting wind.

'I do find it odd,' said Annabel in a whisper, 'that Simon

is concerning himself with all of this. He's not normally so selfless.'

'And I hate to say it but I'm certain he doesn't have my best interests at heart. There's always been an enormous shortage of brotherly love from him,' Fran informed her wryly.

Within a couple of minutes Simon was back in the room with four cut glass tumblers on a tray. Fran knew each one would have at least a treble measure of gin in it.

'Help yourselves,' he said. He cleared his throat and gave Fran one of his, *'I'm your big brother listen to me'* looks.

'Without beating about the bush, Malcolm desperately wants to put things right between you. I'm his emissary so to speak because he knows you won't talk to him. I have to say, Fran, that Mum and Dad, and Annabel and I, think you're making a mountain out of a molehill.'

Fran felt her shoulders tense with anger.

'Excuse me,' Annabel broke in, 'you and your parents might think that, but I don't.'

Simon gave her a withering look.

'We don't even know if he slept with the girl,' he said turning to Fran. 'It's all assumption, and you flew off down here without giving him the chance to explain anything.'

'Why did he take her to Moscow in that underhand way if it was a bona fide trip where a linguist was necessary?' Fran said hotly. 'And I'll bet you anything Sandra doesn't speak Russian! She's been his secretary for over a year and he's never spoken of her linguistic talents before.'

'For goodness sake Fran, I don't know, but I'm sure there's a perfectly good explanation,' he said loftily.

'If that's so, then why did I get a phone call from his

office asking me where he was? When I told them he was still in Moscow they said he'd been expected back two days before. Can you imagine how that made me feel? Well, I'll tell you, a complete idiot. I didn't even know where my husband was.'

Fran's raised voice made Grace give a little startled cry. Mortified to be the cause of her distress she swiftly took her in her arms whispering reassurances.

Simon began to look agitated. 'Just go home and give Malcolm the chance to explain things properly, won't you? He's only human, and he works bloody hard. Perhaps he just needed a few days on his own.'

'But he wasn't on his own, Sandra answered the phone in his room, it was seven in the morning and when he spoke to me he was on the defensive immediately. I'm not stupid, Simon, it wasn't difficult to put two and two together.'

'And perhaps come up with six,' said Lydia coolly.

They all looked at her.

'She could have gone into his room for any number of reasons. Why do people still assume sex is on the agenda if two business colleagues who happen to be of the opposite sex go away together? Very outdated, if you ask me,' she drawled, taking an exaggeratedly slow sip of her drink.

'There you are,' said Simon, as if everything had been neatly resolved by Lydia's statement.

Fran wondered if she should throw into the equation certain instances in the past that had only now begun to play on her mind; unaccountable flight delays, business meetings that went on into the early hours of the morning, and numerous other discrepancies of time and place. Had she been naively trusting? One thing she knew for certain was that she had to stay away from Malcolm and London for as long as she could. The thought of walking through the busy streets to the park every day, where hundreds of people like herself walked aimlessly with dogs and prams, filled her with gloom.

'Tell Malcolm I'll be back in two weeks to talk things through with him. I desperately need some time away from London. Did you know that I haven't stayed in the beach hut once since I married Malcolm?'

'Good thing too,' muttered Simon.

Annabel glared at him. 'Come back with us tomorrow,' she said gently, 'you'll be bored to tears with nothing to do but look at the sea and sky.'

Fran laughed at this typical Annabel comment.

'At least stay here tonight,' said Simon. 'It's ridiculous sleeping in a hut when you could be nice and comfortable here.'

Fran knew the whole family had doubted her sanity when she'd bought the beach hut in Warbleton. If her inheritance money from her grandmother had been spent on an expensive holiday, or totally self-indulgent spending spree in Harrods or Harvey Nichols it wouldn't have raised an eyebrow.

'Do stay Fran, we can all go over to The Reed and Whistle for a drink tonight,' said Lydia.

Fran lifted Grace off the windowsill. She had been completely mesmerised again by the little bobbing boats, and wriggled furiously in Fran's arms.

'But who will look after Grace?' she said, trying to distract her with the sea-glass necklace she wore round her neck.

'Darling, we'll take it in turns,' said Annabel. 'Now off you go and collect your night things from the beach hut. I'm going to stay here in the warm with Lydia and catch up on some gossip.'

Walking back to the beach hut with Grace half asleep in her arms, Fran felt that she had allowed herself to be manipulated by Simon. Her one comforting thought was that she had traded her return for two weeks in Warbleton, and there was nowhere in the world that she would rather be right now.

The last thing Fran had ever wanted was to live and work in London. She'd gone straight to horticultural college from school and then spent a year going to all the top windsurfing locations around the world. It had been an amazing time.

It was a July night when her father picked her up from the airport. She was full of ideas for her career, and excited about discussing them with her parents. Afterwards she wondered how a year away could make her forget the sort of people her parents were. That night over supper she started talking about her plans to set up a florist shop in Southfleet. Her father gave her one of his indulgent smiles and told her he'd sorted out a brilliant job for her whilst she'd been away, using his valuable contacts, and hoped she wouldn't embarrass him by turning it down.

'Wonderful opening for you, Fran,' he'd said. 'Green World is the biggest plant display company in London, they supply all the top firms.'

She didn't know if going along with her father's wishes

was a sign of weakness or strength. She only knew she hated to disappoint him, and if accepting the job he'd arranged would keep him happy, then why not? She would revert to her original plan after that.

So she found herself working in London, trailing around office buildings, organising displays of new plants and replacing dead ones. Malcolm had appeared one day from behind a massive yucca. She had always hated yuccas, with their sleek, lizard-like appearance. She couldn't remember much about their conversation, but he was charming and witty, and quite handsome in a blond Brad Pitt sort of way. He seemed wise and kind, and she had been swept off her feet by his demonstrative love. Her parents thought he was wonderful, such an improvement on the slightly tongue-tied farmers' sons she had met at college, and occasionally risked bringing back home to meet them. For the first time in her life Fran felt her parents were proud of her. She basked in their approval. After a whirlwind romance, Malcolm asked her to marry him and she accepted. Their baby daughter arrived on a cold January night exactly a year after they were married. Malcolm wanted to name her Portia.

'Why Grace?' he had asked.

'Because today is Tuesday, and Tuesday's child is full of grace.' As soon as the words came out she felt stupid.

'Shame it wasn't a boy,' he said, looking at the tiny baby in Fran's arms, 'Call her whatever you like.'

꙰

It was just after eight by the time Fran, Simon and Lydia

made the short walk from Watercolour Cottage across the village green to The Reed and Whistle. It was already heaving at the seams with friday-night drinkers, which meant having to weave their way through the scrum of warm, pressing bodies to get to the marble-topped bar. Now that the summer invasion of visitors had almost come to an end, the locals were appearing again. Some of them sat on old church pews by the inglenook fireplace that always had a blazing log fire in it once the first hint of autumn descended on the village. The local doctor, dentist and vet dropped in at least five times a week, once the height of the holiday season had passed. The vicar called in every night to mingle with the locals, and even managed fairly frequent lunchtime sessions too. He had decided from the early days when he was a curate that it was an excellent way of getting to know the more flamboyant members of his parish, and a wonderful excuse to enjoy a few pints of beer whilst ministering to his flock.

The endless skies and landscape attracted artists and poets like a magnet and the locals mingled happily with them. Even the holidaymakers were grudgingly accepted for they brought much needed revenue to the little village, but the wealthy London set who had started to invade Warbleton managed to antagonise the whole community. They inflated house prices, took over the pub every weekend throughout the summer, and walked about the village as if they owned it. Many of them were now beginning to appear during the winter months too. They monopolised the giant fireplace when they came into the pub for lunchtime drinks, speaking in loud, intrusive voices to each other, or bellowing down mobile phones as if their business was so important that the whole world needed to know about it.

From early childhood, Fran had blended into the village and its surroundings as easily as the migrant swallows. Her tiny figure marching across the village green to the vets with an injured bird or animal under her arm, was a frequent sight throughout the summer months. Simon, however, was viewed in quite a different way. Fran always felt guiltily uncomfortable appearing in the pub with him and her sister-in-law, and now, with Lydia in tow, she knew they epitomised the London set the locals despised.

Lydia draped herself over a barstool and sized up the males in the room for any likely conquests. Fran immediately recognised the signs; she was going about her usual mating ritual. Lydia reminded Fran of certain women throughout the ages who had been the downfall of powerful men. Her long blonde hair, big blue eyes and perfect figure were the initial attraction, but it was her infinite sexuality that ensnared them.

'Lydia, you're not in a London bar now,' she said, laughing. 'Stop looking at the males in here as though you're planning a naughty night for them all.'

'For goodness' sake, Fran, they're just a lot of country yokels, not my type at all,' she replied.

'Here's the champers,' said Simon, passing them glasses that were full to the brim.

Great, thought Fran, *hardly an appropriate drink for The Reed and Whistle*, but then Simon rarely drank anything else in London, so she knew he wasn't going to change his habits just because he was in Suffolk. He was already chatting up Phoebe, the landlord's daughter. Fran looked at him slouched against the bar in his ankle length camel-haired overcoat and stupid trilby hat. She never failed to wonder at his total inability to step outside of his own blinkered world.

⚭

Jack Henshaw parked his car outside the pub next to a sign that said '*No Parking*'.

Being the village vet and much loved by everyone, no one cared where his old Citroen ground to a halt. He loved the feel of the warm, smoky air on his face as he pushed open the door, and silently thanked the landlord for resisting the modern trend of piped music and fruit machines.

He worked his way around the drinking groups with amazing agility for a tall, stocky man, and nearly made it to the bar without mishap but just caught the top of his head on one of the thick beams that supported the low ceiling.

'You'd think after all these years I'd know when to duck, wouldn't you?' he said, giving Fran a kiss on the cheek. 'Now, how's the windsurfing going?'

'I wish life was still that simple,' she replied. Seeing Jack always took her back to her childhood, accompanied by the knowledge that it could never be recaptured in any form. Take Christmas, for instance; everyone said that once you had a child Christmas was wonderful and magical again, but it wasn't. It was just more complicated because both sets of grandparents wanted to see their beloved grandchild, and with one set of grandparents divorced, it made the whole thing into an impossible juggling act. Anyway, Christmas wasn't for a few months yet, so she wasn't even going to begin thinking about it.

She found the temptation to reminisce whenever she saw Jack quite impossible to resist.

'Do you remember all those animals I kept bringing to you?' she said.

Jack wasn't likely to forget. Once she'd even brought him a hedgehog that had decided to go into early hibernation. It was quite a relief at the end of the holidays when Fran disappeared back to London and the wild animals had to go back to fending for themselves.

Jack smiled his lovely warm smile and said, 'Are you staying on that stuff, or do you want something different?'

'Something different would definitely be good. In fact a pint of Adnams is probably just what I need.'

Fran looked at Lydia and saw that she was gazing intently across the bar to the far corner of the room. Sitting at a small table, squashed just to one side of a well-worn dartboard, were the objects of Lydia's interest.

'Who are the two men over there?' asked Fran. 'Lydia can't keep her eyes off them!'

'Now there's an interesting young man,' said Jack.

'Which one?'

'Well, I don't know the dark-haired chap, although I've seen him in here a couple of times just recently. I'm referring to George.'

At that moment, George looked across the room and gave Jack a friendly wave.

'He's just landed the job of head ranger over at Dunsmere,' said Jack, waving back. 'He got a first at

Cambridge, qualified as a vet, but then couldn't cope with the human element, and I can't say I blame him. If only the animals could come to the surgery on their own!'

'I think his friend's the windsurfer I've seen out in the bay a couple of times.'

'Well, they're heading this way so we'll find out in a minute,' replied Jack.

Tom had been watching Fran from the moment she entered the pub, and had already decided that the blond chap was neither her husband nor lover. Close up she was as pretty as he had imagined her to be when he'd first seen her on the shoreline. He briefly wondered if she was of Irish ancestry as her black curly hair and blue eyes were a rare mixture.

When everyone had been introduced Fran turned to Tom and shyly asked him if he was the windsurfer who had been out in the bay that morning.

'I was out this morning,' he said smiling at her. 'Have you ever had a go at it?'

'I know it sounds incredibly corny but I used to live for windsurfing,' she confessed, 'but since having my little girl I've hardly been out at all.'

Mention of the child made Tom glance at her left hand. There was no mistaking the gold band on her third finger. He suddenly experienced the dreadful anticlimax of a child who sees the most wonderful present that could possibly be imagined, only to find it has been given to someone else.

'If it's windy again tomorrow, why don't you use my kit?' he offered.

'I'd love to if someone could look after Grace.'

Lydia eased herself off the bar stool and put her arm affectionately around Fran. 'If you're looking for a babysitter, I'm your girl,' she said.

Fran was instantly suspicious. It certainly wasn't in Lydia's character to be helpful, or to be interested in looking after small children.

'Are you sure, Lydia?'

'Of course I am. I think I'll stay on here for a few days and enjoy this bracing Suffolk air.'

George suggested that she bring Grace over to the nature reserve to look at some young otters he was caring for.

'Oh, how absolutely lovely.' Lydia gave George a wide, inviting smile. 'I can't wait.'

So Fran agreed to the windsurfing rendezvous at high tide the next day, and then hastened back to Watercolour Cottage, hoping Annabel hadn't downed too many gins.

As soon as Fran left, Lydia turned to Jack and began a little game of seduction with him. It might be fun to ensnare a country vet.

'Be warned,' whispered Tom to George, 'girls like Lydia are trouble.'

'I shouldn't really be going for her at all,' confessed George. 'I think I've been making progress with Phoebe recently. Nothing definite, but we always have a good chat when I come in for a pint at lunchtime.' He looked across at the landlord's daughter just as she was giving a particularly flirtatious smile to Simon.

'Don't you just hate those London types?' he said.

Tom pointed out to him that Lydia was one of those types.

✤

A rush of warm air greeted Fran as she opened the door to Watercolour Cottage.

Annabel always turned the heating up as soon as she arrived, and only conceded to having it turned off during a rare heat wave. Although Annabel was centre stage of the London scene Fran adored her. You knew where you were with Annabel, which was certainly more than could be said for most of the people she was forced to mix with in London.

'Guess who's just been on the phone, sweetie?' she said.

'Oh, Annabel I'm so sorry you've been drawn into all of this. What did Malcolm have to say?'

'Now, don't you go worrying about Malcolm, I've sorted him out, but I did say you'd give him a call in the morning.'

Fran sighed. 'You are a gem,' she said sincerely. 'You'd better get over to the Reed and Whistle and rein in Lydia, though. I think she's about to seduce a game-keeper, a windsurfer, and quite probably a vet, too!'

'Sounds like fun,' said Annabel. They looked at each other and laughed.

✤

Over in The Reed and Whistle Simon was having a splendid time. Phoebe's looks epitomised his fantasy of a country barmaid. He thought he might come to Warbleton more often if she continued to look at him in that saucy way, with her breasts nicely escaping from a top obviously one size too small. He loved her sultry, nut-brown eyes and pouting red lips. He had always found something erotic about women who wore red lipstick, assuming they must all be a little bit naughty.

'Care for a drop of this?' he invited, waving the champagne bottle at her.

Annabel wasn't in the least bit surprised to see Simon drooling over a woman with a bottle of champagne in his hand. She was used to his flirtatious habits. She made her way to the bar and suddenly found herself face to face with the vicar. She had never quite been able to reconcile herself to the fact that James Green was a vicar. He was too big and tall and, she supposed, too handsome in a rugged way, to be a vicar, although she hadn't really given much consideration to what a vicar should look like.

'Hello, Annabel,' he said, 'having a little holiday are you?'

'Goodness no,' she replied. 'It gets much too cold up here at this time of year for me. The heating system in the cottage is most unreliable and the wind whistles through all the windows. No double glazing you know.'

'Is Fran staying?'

The beach hut sprang into Annabel's mind, completely exposed to the elements and isolated. It made her shudder just to think about spending a night there.

'Fran has taken leave of her senses, and is going to sleep in the beach hut with Grace for two weeks. Perhaps you could say something to her Vicar. It can't be safe in such a remote spot.'

'I think living in London poses a far greater threat to one's safety than being in a beach hut in Warbleton.'

Annabel felt slightly insulted by this remark. Was he

insinuating that they lived in some undesirable part of the capital?

'We don't have any problems in Notting Hill,' she replied stiffly, and then made her way to the bar where Simon was generously filling up Phoebe's glass again. She looked at the two men standing next to Lydia, and could understand her attraction to them, although she thought their clothes left much to be desired. Both were wearing jeans, but whilst George sported a sort of lumberjack top Tom was wearing a short-sleeved tee-shirt. *Mad*, she thought, *on a freezing cold night like this*. Annabel had draped a little fur wrap over her shoulders before coming out. The last thing she wanted was to go sniffing back to London with a wretched cold.

George had managed to prise Lydia away from Jack when Annabel joined the group at the bar, and decided for once he was going to work fast.

'Fancy coming back for a night-cap?' he said. He desperately tried to remember what state his tiny coastguard cottage was in. He knew there were definitely piles of unwashed dishes in the sink, but that was perfectly acceptable in a bachelor pad. Would Flash have sneaked upstairs and be lying on his bed? No point in worrying about the bedroom, he'd never managed to work that fast on a first date. His confused thoughts had barely taken shape before Lydia declined the invitation.

'I'm obviously losing my touch,' he said to Tom as they left the pub at closing time.

'Leave well alone. Just trust me that girl's trouble,' warned Tom.

2

George woke up the next morning to the sound of a cockerel heralding dawn with impressive enthusiasm. He had experienced a dreadfully disturbed night, with Lydia and Fran entering his dreams like jumbled colours in a skein of wool. He was pretty certain Phoebe had been in there somewhere, too, for he seemed to remember a bright pouting mouth.

He mulled things over as he sat drinking his second coffee of the day, and for once was completely oblivious to the unfolding charms of the marsh as it awakened to a new day. He had obviously drunk more pints of beer last night than he'd realised, for his head felt heavy and the coffee only seemed to aggravate his dry mouth. He needed to get out of the house and try and clear his mind in the cold morning air. He wondered why he didn't feel more upbeat, but he knew if he had a fling with Lydia, Phoebe would almost definitely hear about it. If only she'd stop playing hard to get. He was sure she flirted with every male customer that came into the pub just to wind him up.

Fran was pretty gorgeous, too. There was something disarmingly innocent and yet wild about her. It was probably her amazing curly black hair that created the impression of wildness, and the blue eyes that spoke of innocence; but then he thought of Lydia's blue eyes and the association seemed ridiculous because there was certainly nothing innocent about *her* eyes. Thank heavens Fran was married with a child in tow. At least that narrowed the possibilities down to just two women.

He went out of the cottage, took a deep breath, and gazed across the marsh to the shingle coastline and the sea's far horizon. The air was full of the haunting cries of seabirds, giving the marsh a greater loneliness. Many people thought it bleak, but George loved its solitude. He daily thanked some divine providence that had made him wake up one morning and decide that antiseptic surgeries and neurotic pet owners were going to be a thing of the past. The fact that his decision coincided with an advert in one of the veterinary magazines for a head warden at Dunsmere seemed like a small miracle. It was a favourite holiday destination of his parents, and he and his brother had been taken to the small campsite on the edge of the marsh throughout their childhood.

By the time George was walking to the village shop for his loaf of freshly baked bread, the marsh lay dreaming under a watery sun. The sea had stilled its turbulence during the night as the wind died and, shifting to the east, became no more than a whisper. *No windsurfing for Tom and Fran today,* he thought, and wondered if Lydia would still call in to see him.

He left the marsh to go up a track that led to the centre of the village. There was no one about at this hour of the morning, apart from a few dog walkers. Most of the cottages that lined the narrow street still had their curtains drawn, but when he reached the place where it dipped away to reveal a glimpse of the harbour, he could see lots of activity. Most of the shops were in the lower part of the street and revealed the influence the holiday trade had made on the village. Apart from one, they were all gift shops offering trinkets and china ornaments, the sort of items any sane person would never normally dream of buying. George was convinced that holidays had a very strange effect on people. He remembered watching a programme on television only a few nights ago where people wearing silly hats and clutching toy donkeys were being squashed onto a departing flight from Malaga.

The last in the group of shops belonged to Mrs. Kennard, and it certainly had nothing displayed on its shelves to attract the average holidaymaker, apart from food. She ran it with terrifying efficiency and never kept paper boys or shop assistants for more than a few weeks. Unbeknown to even her closest friends, she did have a few weaknesses; she loved a nice stiff whisky and a handsome man.

George arrived at the shop just as she was opening up for the morning bread delivery.

'Good morning, George,' she said, giving him a coquettish smile that sat strangely on her severe, slightly masculine face.

He exchanged the usual pleasantries with her and was just about to leave, juggling a few groceries in an inadequate brown bag, when Phoebe appeared. He suddenly remembered with startling clarity the part she had played in his dream.

'Thank goodness that awful wind's dropped,' she said.

'I don't expect Tom will be too pleased, he was planning on having a session with Fran today.'

Phoebe looked puzzled, so Tom explained that the session was all to do with windsurfing.

'Is there any chance of you having the night off, Phoebe? It's about time you came round and tried out my cooking.'

George mentally cursed himself for asking Phoebe out in such an ineloquent way. He despaired at his reversal to adolescence when he was in the company of attractive women. After a few pints it all seemed so easy, but in the cold light of day, trying to get a date with Phoebe was a daunting prospect.

'You've obviously got a bad memory,' she said. 'I'm never behind the bar on a Monday night.'

'Can I take that as a yes?' he said with a grin.

Phoebe gave him a gorgeous smile and asked what time the cordon bleu meal was going to be ready.

As George walked back to his cottage, he felt that divine providence had intervened in his life yet again. Bumping into Phoebe had made his decision for him. He would forget about Lydia. All he had to do now was decide what on earth to cook.

⁂

Simon and Annabel had made an early departure that morning and were already motoring down the A12 at the time when George and Phoebe were having their tete-a-tete outside the village shop.

'I can't think what's possessed Lydia to stay on at the cottage, it seems very unlike her to want to hide away in the country,' said Simon.

'How can you be so lacking in perception? She's staying

in Warbleton because there are several men there that she wants to go to bed with.'

'And then there's Fran, embarrassing the family by hiding away in that appalling beach hut. I don't know what Mum and Dad are going to say when I return minus daughter and granddaughter. They think she must be suffering from post-natal depression, and so do I. Malcolm's such a super chap.'

'If you don't shut up, I shall be leaving you,' said Annabel, 'and as for Malcolm being a super chap, that is entirely a matter of opinion, and one I don't share with you.'

Entering London barely two hours later, they joined the rush hour crawl to get to Notting Hill. Simon breathed a sigh of relief and immediately felt stimulated by the hustle and bustle of urban life.

'Shall we drop in and see Malcolm? He probably won't have left for the office yet and we can give him the latest on Fran.'

'Do we have to?' said Annabel. 'I only spoke to him on the phone last night.'

'I think it's the decent thing to do,' he replied pompously.

Just as they pulled level with Malcolm's house, the front door opened and a tall, slim woman appeared. Malcolm was briefly visible, framed in the doorway in a blue silk dressing gown, before the door closed and Sandra made her way down the front path. Simon put his foot hard on the accelerator and shot off.

'Was that entirely necessary?' asked Annabel.

'We don't want it to look as though we're spying on him.'

'Are you going to tell Fran, or shall I? That was Sandra, his PA, the girl this whole problem is about.'

'I know it was Sandra. Listen, Annabel, it's nothing to do with us, and we shouldn't draw any conclusions from what we saw.'

'If it's nothing to do with us, why have we just spent the last two days in Suffolk? Does family loyalty mean nothing to you?'

'We both like our lifestyle, so don't jeopardise it.'

Annabel looked at him suspiciously. 'What on earth do you mean by that?' she said.

'It's nothing for you to get worked up about. I just don't want to upset Malcolm, and if Fran was a bit more realistic about life we wouldn't be in this mess.'

Malcolm shut the front door behind Sandra and walked back through the hall. He noticed that the vases were empty of their usual kaleidoscope of colours. Fran's displays had always rather embarrassed him when friends came for supper as they gave every appearance of flowers plucked straight from the hedgerow, but right now he missed their wild cheerfulness.

In the early days of their relationship, when he'd been keen to please her, they had gone to Great Dixter, a stately home and garden in the folds of the Sussex countryside. Fran told him people travelled miles to see the wild flower meadows there, and raved about the beauty of their simplicity. He thought long grass interspersed with buttercups and daisies and equally uninspiring flowers quite ridiculous. Manicured lawns with nice borders would have been far more appropriate. As he turned away from the empty vases to go back upstairs and have a shower, he heard a handful of letters being pushed through the letterbox. There was one addressed to Fran. He placed the letter on the hall table, but then decided to open it himself. The content, from a firm of solicitors in Southfleet, was short and to the point.

Dear Mrs. Reeve,

I have been requested by Sir Matthew Miller of Starston Hall, Southfleet, to inform all occupants of beach huts on the land legally known as Dunsmere Marsh, that the aforementioned land is to be sold. The land in the first instance is to be offered to the owners of the beach huts. If the owners are unable to meet the required price the land will be sold and the owners reimbursed for the beach huts at a price to be agreed by an arbitrator.

A meeting has been arranged for Wednesday 26th September at 10.00a.m. at The Swan Hotel in Southfleet to enable respective owners to discuss the above.

Yours sincerely,
Gerald Campbell

Malcolm read the letter several times before resealing it in the envelope, crossing through the address, and re-directing it to Watercolour Cottage. He sincerely hoped that this would mean an end to the beach hut. He felt certain Fran would use the remainder of her grandmother's money to secure her share of the land, but there was every chance the other beach hut owners might not be able to come up with the cash.

Minutes later, Simon was on the phone asking Malcolm rather hesitantly about Sandra.

'I know it's nothing to do with me, old chap, but Annabel saw and you know what women are like, suspicious creatures at the best of times.'

'No, it isn't anything to do with you,' said Malcolm aggressively, 'but to appease your interfering wife, tell her Sandra was picking up some papers en route to the office.'

'Knew it was something like that. I don't know what's up with Annabel, she's acting very oddly. I hope she's not going to start behaving irrationally like Fran.'

'Let's meet for lunch,' said Malcolm, 'I've got a few things I want to discuss with you. See you at twelve in Jones's.' He hung up before Simon could reply.

✿

Just before twelve Malcolm left his office and made his way down Threadneedle Street to meet Simon. He'd clinched some pretty good deals that morning and was feeling particularly ebullient. Malcolm loved everything about his job; his luxurious office, the business lunches in the boardroom, the decisions he had to make with other people's money, and the feeling of power it gave him. He also loved working in the City, but this had nothing to do with its ancient buildings or financial history, it was simply that working for a merchant bank in the City made him feel important. He felt it just wouldn't have the same credibility if he had to say, 'I work five minutes from Charing Cross Station.' To be able to say 'I work in the City,' created a picture of being at the hub of world finance and million pound decisions. He also liked the little perks that being a director gave him, the first class travel and the most expensive rooms in the best hotels. He just wished Fran would make more of an effort to slot into his world. He couldn't understand her aversion to his business colleagues, and the excuses she made for not joining him at some of the splendid dinners they laid on for the wives. He made a mental decision to be firmer with her; after all, everything she had was because of him.

Jones's was a small wine bar that had recently become the place to be seen in the City between the hours of twelve and three. It attracted the young, bright and beautiful and also a few hangers-on.

Simon glanced at his watch as he walked through the doors and congratulated himself on his impeccable time-keeping. He spotted Malcolm immediately.

'Well done for grabbing this table,' he said. 'It gets busier every time I come here. What are you drinking?'

'Just finished a G & T but get a bottle of Léoville-Las Cases wine. The news I got this morning deserves a bit of celebrating.'

'I say, old chap, if I've got to spend that sort of money I'd just as rather get a bottle of champers.'

Malcolm gave Simon a scathing look. 'I'm not expecting you to put your hand in your pocket, I've got a tab running,' he replied.

Within minutes Simon was back at the table and Malcolm poured the dark ruby liquid into two glasses and, handing one to Simon, said, 'I was at your parents' house last night and they told me they're planning to sell Watercolour Cottage.'

Simon's expression changed from one of smug contentment to shocked surprise. 'I can't think Mum and Dad would go ahead with something like that without talking to Fran and I about it first,' he said.

'Well, it is all a bit odd. Apparently an estate agent in Southfleet was approached last week by someone wanting to buy it.'

'But it's not on the market.'

'Well, these people fell in love with it and asked the agents to find out who it belonged to in case they were thinking of selling.'

'Fran would be heartbroken if it was sold, and I'm pretty cheesed off with Mum and Dad for not having the decency to talk to me about it first. Not that I care that much for the place, but it's the principle of the thing.'

'They did ask me not to mention it until they had spoken to you, but I want you to give them that little push. Fran needs weaning off Warbleton, she'll always be running back there otherwise.'

'She's still got the beach hut.'

'Now this is the real bit of luck,' said Malcolm, and he told Simon about the letter from the solicitor.

'I don't know about all of this. I don't want to do the dirty on Fran. I know she's a pain but she is my sister.'

Malcolm gave Simon a long, hard look.

'The other thing I want to talk about is the latest takeover in the pipeline. I assume you want to be in on it? This sibling love is all very touching, but it would be sad if it resulted in you losing your Porsche.'

'Quite,' said Simon.

Malcolm and Simon were already working their way through another bottle of Léoville-Las Cases wine by the time Lydia eventually surfaced from beneath her duvet. The watery sun of early morning had fulfilled its promise and now shone brilliantly from a cloudless sky. The disillusioned holidaymakers of yesterday began drifting back to the beach, hardly daring to believe in the overnight change. They settled themselves into sand dunes, or strolled aimlessly along the shore. Some decided to make the most of the reappearance of the little ferry boat and went across the estuary to explore the delights of Southfleet, a town lost in a time warp. Guest house signs were displayed discreetly in windows and the genteel ladies who owned them referred to their customers as paying guests. Their deceased husbands had been colonels, admirals or bank managers. They all treated their guests with impeccable politeness whilst somehow conveying their superiority. The houses and neat gardens had an aura of stately serenity reminiscent of the thirties and forties. Aspidistras took pride of place on hall tables, and ladies and gentlemen sat in the smart hotels sipping afternoon tea out of porcelain cups.

The promenade was lined with brightly painted beach huts, so different from their poorer cousins across the estuary. The holidaymakers in Southfleet who took the ferry to Warbleton rarely ventured further than the beach next to the jetty. Some, a little more curious, went as far as the beach huts, only to turn away disappointed by their stark simplicity.

George had decided to drive to Southfleet to buy the ingredients he needed for the evening meal he was planning for Phoebe. He felt slightly guilty for not buying what he needed from Mrs. Kennard, but he knew it was very unlikely she would have in stock such items as fresh ginger and lemongrass. Unfortunately, all the items in the shop were dreadfully overpriced too, which discouraged people from going there, although George knew it was a Catch 22 situation because everyone in the village would be horrified if the shop closed.

He was back home well before high tide, but now he prayed Lydia wouldn't turn up with Grace to look at the otters. It seemed unlikely, because there wasn't even a hint of a breeze, so Fran wouldn't be out windsurfing. He went into the kitchen with his box of groceries and shut the bottom half of the stable door to prevent Flash coming in and spreading mud everywhere; he didn't want Phoebe to think he lived in a pig-sty. He had always felt first impressions were very important and he definitely wanted to create the right one on their first date. Grabbing a beer out of the fridge, he sat down at the kitchen table to think about the timing of the meal. He needed his cookery book, but he had no idea where it might be. So many of the boxes he'd brought with him to Tamarisk Cottage remained unpacked, although most of his books were already on the shelves that lined the walls of the sitting room. Many were from his schooldays, which he still couldn't quite bring himself to part with. He heard a soft tap and looked up to see Lydia smiling at him over the top of the stable door. He thought she looked absolutely stunning in a skimpy white sun top.

'Hi,' she said, 'Grace isn't with me, but I thought I'd pop over and see you anyway.'

Oh fuck! thought George. He rarely used bad language but this was a dilemma that needed some sort of expletive, even if it was only in his head.

'Wonderful,' George replied, completely thrown and incapable of making any sensible conversation.

'I cycled over here on Fran's bike, awful old wreck, I think she must have had it for years.'

'Come in, I'm just having a beer, would you like one? Better still, wait here and I'll bring one out to you. I'm afraid the place is in a dreadful mess.' He felt it was safer to keep Lydia outside. He just couldn't see her in his kitchen amongst all the unwashed dishes and clutter. 'Sit on that old seat, I won't be a tick.'

He sat next to her on the bench and handed her a chilled beer. He found it difficult to keep his eyes off her bare midriff, and unbelievably long tanned legs.

'You must find all this a bit dull compared to London,' he said.

'I don't know about that, I think the rural idyll has a certain appeal. I'd love you to show me the inside of your pretty little cottage.'

George swiftly got her through the kitchen and into the sitting room where things were a little less chaotic. The room was full of everything dear to George; his fishing rods, portraits of dogs that had been family pets from his childhood, his gun which rarely shot at anything other than clay pigeons, and some superbly illustrated bird books. Although not a great reader, he loved Henry Williamson, and had every book the author had ever written. Some of them were first edition prints that he particularly treasured. He watched as Lydia fingered the books. She opened a bird book at a page that showed a delightful illustration of a Bittern. Unable to resist talking about his favourite subject, he told her about the rare birds of the marsh, the passage migrants that began to appear in small flocks along the shoreline in the autumn, and the efforts being made to reintroduce the once common Bittern to the reed beds of Suffolk.

Lydia sat on the settee, which was just in front of the bookcase. It was one of those old, squashy settees that most people would have put in a skip but George felt it fitted in perfectly with all the other bits and pieces he'd bought to fill the cottage.

'I'll just get us another beer,' he said, 'or would you prefer a glass of wine?'

'Actually, I adore wine. Have you got something white and dry?'

George opened the fridge door and took out the bottle of Pouilly Fume that he'd bought to complement the meal he was going to cook for Phoebe.

'So, have you always lived in London?' he asked, as he poured her a glass of wine.

'Yes, apart from when I was at boarding school. Annabel and I went to Benenden in Kent. Did you know Princess Anne was a boarder there in the sixties? That seemed pretty rural to me. Although I suppose it's only about thirty miles from London. I hated it there. Of course, Annabel, was good at everything; sport, art, music and top of her class in just about every academic subject. But, I was the one the boys climbed over the wall to seek out.'

'I bet you were,' said George to this little tirade of Lydia's.

Sitting there on his settee, George thought she looked like one of the rare exotic birds that sometimes alighted amongst the reed beds when strong winds blew them off their normal course.

'I don't think either of us wants to talk about our schooldays, I think we could have much more fun doing something like this,' said Lydia. She leant across and kissed him. Her tongue traced the outline of his lips and by the time their tongues met, George was completely lost. He took his treasured bird book from her, placed it carefully on the floor, and trailed his fingers across the tantalising bit of flesh between the top of her jeans and her t-shirt. Lydia responded immediately by unzipping her jeans. He couldn't quite believe what was happening and sat there just staring at her.

'Aren't you going to help me?' she asked, laughing provocatively at him.

He eased the jeans over her hips.

'Now it's your turn,' she said.

With as much style as he could conjure, he began to remove his clothes. Lydia was far too preoccupied with taking her pants off to notice how George was trying to undress himself. As they rolled onto the floor and she folded her long legs round him, sanity briefly returned to George and he suggested they be careful, but Lydia said all that was taken care of. He wanted to question her about this, but felt to bring up Aids and sexually transmitted diseases at such a moment would be completely insensitive.

No! This is madness, he thought, and pulled himself away from her.

'Look, if you're that worried, use this,' said Lydia. She

reached for her handbag and took out a single neatly wrapped condom and placed it in George's hand. She expertly helped him put it on, and then wrapped her legs round him again.

'Happy now?' she asked, as he sank into her.

She was quickly satisfied and George felt a moment of great relief that he hadn't embarrassed himself. He gently ran his hands through her hair; it was beautifully soft, but when he turned to bury his face in the golden strands, Lydia stood up to adjust her little white top and began to remove the numerous dog hairs that were clinging to it. She put her clothes back on as unselfconsciously as she'd removed them, easing herself back into her jeans as though dressing in front of a man she hardly knew was an everyday occurrence.

'Shall we go up to The Reed and Whistle for a bite to eat?' she suggested.

George thought a cosy lunch in the pub with Phoebe looking on was probably a seriously bad idea, and decided he'd just have to tell a white lie.

'Sorry, Lydia, I've actually got to dash. I'm due at a meeting in Norwich at two.'

Feeling he couldn't just leave it at that, he lamely added he would see her again very soon.

They walked back through the kitchen to the stable door, and found Flash had deposited a particularly gruesome dead animal in the entrance. Lydia gave a little girly shriek and stepped round it with her hand over her nose.

'Disgusting!' she exclaimed. 'I don't know how you can cope with that sort of thing. I'll never have animals, not even a cat. Our family cat's dead now, thank goodness. We were always finding dead birds and the insides of animals in the utility room. When Mum and Dad were away once, I actually had to clear it up. I was vomiting for at least an hour afterwards.'

'You poor thing,' said George, trying his best to sound sympathetic. He got the bike and wheeled it to where Lydia was standing. 'I'm very impressed that you cycled all the way over here. It must be about five miles by road.'

'I'm a very fit girl. I go to the gym every day when I'm in London, to aerobic classes at least five times a week, and yoga four.'

George thought the whole thing sounded awful. He could think of few worse ways of trying to get fit than being on one of those cycling machines that went nowhere and left people looking red and exhausted.

'Perhaps we should exercise together,' she shouted, as she cycled off up the rutted track that led to the road. 'Bye for now.'

The elation George had felt after his sexual encounter with Lydia had now turned into a feeling of mild panic. He almost felt he had been set-up. He'd only had a few one-night stands in the past, but there'd always been a touch of tenderness in them. Lydia reminded him of a copulating animal. Their encounter had been pure sex with no other emotion involved. He felt a fool to care, for it somehow undermined his masculinity, especially as he knew most men would give anything to have sex with Lydia, with or without emotion. His younger brother Josh was certainly one of them. On his last visit home, just before his new job, Josh was dating at least three different girls, and had been horrified to hear that George had been without sex for over a year.

'You're going to start seizing up if you're not careful,' he'd joked, but George hadn't found it very funny.

His attention was caught by a pair of Oyster Catchers flying low past his cottage, calling out in alarm to each other at some hidden threat. He watched them as they swept on over the reed beds and past Tom's cottage, until they alighted on the shoreline. He could see the long shingle beach with the small cluster of beach huts, and was just able to make out the holidaymakers down by the jetty looking like little figures from a Lowrie painting.

He removed the decomposing body that Flash had left, and went to clear away the evidence of his session with Lydia. The bottle of Pouilly Fume was on the kitchen table and he replaced the cork and put it back in the fridge. He couldn't face driving over to Southfleet to get another bottle. He'd just have to make do with one of the indifferent wines that Mrs. Kennard stocked.

On the other side of the reed beds things weren't going according to plan for Tom, either. His day had started not to the sound of a cockerel crowing, but to an eerie silence that sometimes smothered the marsh when the sea had no more movement than the dark water in the dykes. The reed beds stretched away like smooth, newly mown hayfields and he knew his windsurfing session with Fran was off. He felt a vast disappointment that was completely out of proportion to such a probable turn of events but he had so wanted to see her again. He remembered every detail about her, even her small, capable hands that were ring-less apart from the wedding band.

In his teens, he'd picked up a book at a girlfriend's house and glanced through the pages. It was a novel by Barbara Cartland, but after spending a few minutes leafing through the pages he'd decided that sort of romantic nonsense should be left for girls. The description of the heroine suddenly came back to him now. '*Small, heart-shaped face, with enormous blue eyes and long black curly hair*'. It had been something along those lines, and could have been a description of Fran.

When he'd first set up his business in Greece, he'd been amazed at the number of exceptionally beautiful women who came to his watersports centre, but he found he was always attracted to the ones that aroused his interest in a more indefinable way. He remembered one summer being particularly taken by a ginger-haired, freckle-faced girl who had the cheekiest smile and an allure that had nothing to do with symmetrical beauty, but was far more powerful. After he had seen Fran in The Reed and Whistle, he realised that, for the first time in his life, he hadn't analysed why he was attracted to her, he simply wanted to be with her. He stayed by the cottage all morning in case Fran called to see him. Just when he was about to give up hope, he heard a bicycle coming down the track, but to his intense disappointment it was Lydia.

'I was hoping you'd be in,' she said. 'Fran and I thought you might like to come up to Watercolour Cottage tonight and have supper with us.' She had no intention of inviting Fran, but she knew that by using her as bait, Tom would definitely accept the invitation. His interest in Fran the previous night had not gone unnoticed by Lydia and she was rather piqued by his obvious preference.

'Thank you, I'd love to, what time do you want me to come?'

'About six, and if the weather stays like this we can have drinks in the garden first. Bye for now.'

❦

The door of the beach hut was wide open, allowing the sunshine to fill the room. Minute specks of dust hung suspended in the rays, for Fran had spent the day in an orgy of cleaning, using some of the energy she had planned for her windsurfing. She was disappointed that the fickle wind had eased and by dawn had disappeared completely.

The sound of voices from the holidaymakers by the jetty drifted as far as the beach hut, but by then it had become a whisper on the still air, reminding Fran of endless days as a child when every part of Warbleton was her playground. Her early disappointment at the abortive windsurfing session had lifted. She was here for at least another ten days and decided to make the most of every minute of it.

Grace played on the wooden-slatted veranda in front of the hut. Fran had insisted on it being built as soon as Grace was born, in a rush of protective motherhood, and had been determined to take her to the beach hut as soon as spring made an appearance. It was designed so that the sides were high enough to prevent even the most adventurous small child from climbing out, but not so high they restricted the view.

Grace spent most of the morning racing about in her

baby walker and by lunchtime she was exhausted. Fran fed her chicken with vegetables out of a jar, spooning small amounts into her eager mouth. She always felt guilty whenever she gave her ready-made meals, but sometimes it just made things easier. She then mashed up a banana that was quickly devoured. 'Well, at least that's nice and healthy for you,' she said. She talked to Grace all the time, and was sure that most of her words were understood. 'And now for a little sleep.' She carried her to a cot that was tucked away at the back of the hut. A pretty blue curtain with dolphins leaping across it divided it from the rest of the room.

The day continued fair and by early afternoon was warm enough for several of the holidaymakers to take a dip in the cold sea. Even after a hot summer, the North Sea never lost its penetrating chill, and only a handful of hardened bathers spent more than a few minutes in it, shrieking either with delight or horror, it was difficult to tell which.

Fran wished that her bike up at the cottage had a baby seat on the back so she could cycle into Southfleet with Grace, something she had loved to do as a child; going across the narrow bridge over the estuary and buying butter buns in the baker's shop. The thought of butter buns, even now, made her mouth water. She wondered if the garage in the village that hired out rather ancient old bikes might have one with a seat. It was certainly worth a try.

❧

The veal casserole was just beginning to simmer nicely, so Lydia decided it was now time to think about what she was going to wear. She'd have a quick bath, apply a light application of make-up, because she had a feeling Tom would go for the outdoor type, and then nip across to the pub to get some cigarettes before he arrived.

She worked her way through the assortment of clothes that were jammed into an elegant blue case that she still hadn't bothered to unpack. Simon had asked her what on earth she'd got in it when he'd gallantly picked it up and taken it out to his waiting car. 'We're only spending two nights in Suffolk,' he'd said, 'you're not going to St. Tropez for two weeks.'

Lydia had told him to mind his own bloody business.

Lydia adored expensive underwear and clothes. Walking out of Harrods with beautiful silk lingerie and Ralph Lauren jeans made her life just that bit more enjoyable. She liked to spend hours in Karen Millen and Whistles choosing outfits to wear to drinks parties and smart restaurants, and even longer in Morgan to find sexy short skirts and stylish tops to go clubbing in.

When she'd dressed herself in a miniscule kingfisher blue silk skirt and white halter neck top, she looked in the mirror and decided the Suffolk air obviously suited her. 'And now for the ciggies,' she said to herself.

Much to her annoyance, there was no one behind the bar to serve her, and the only occupant in the room was an old black Labrador lying in front of the fire with its back legs stretched out behind like a puppy. There was no cigarette machine in sight, but she spotted an old ship's bell on the marble topped bar and rang it loudly.

Upstairs in her bedroom, Phoebe was putting a few

finishing touches to her make-up. Her full pouting lips had already been firmly outlined with lip liner, and she was just about to fill them in with some L'Oreal 'Heart's Desire' when the bell threw out its demanding peal.

Looking out of the window, she saw her father scattering grain for the geese. She swiftly filled in the lip liner with a generous amount of lipstick, and cursed whoever was creating such a din with the bell.

'I suppose it's unlikely you'd have any Moores?' said Lydia, when Phoebe appeared behind the bar.

'Moores?' repeated Phoebe. She looked uncertainly at the selection of cigarettes behind the counter.

'Oh, don't worry, I suppose I could hardly expect cigarettes like that out in the back of beyond. Twenty Silk Cut will have to do.'

'Bitch,' said Phoebe quietly under her breath. She watched Lydia stride gracefully back across the bar to the door.

Just before six Fran cycled back from Southfleet. The estuary slumbered beneath the evening sun, and cattle grazed in the flat fields that unfolded inland as far as the eye could see. Up by The Reed and Whistle, the flock of geese were all honking excitedly.

They were the pure white sort, plump enough to grace any Christmas table. Fortunately for the eight long-necked beauties, this wasn't to be their fate, for Harold, Phoebe's father, treated them as much-loved pets.

Fran got off her bike to push it up the short hill that went past Watercolour Cottage, as the gears made no pretence of working and the hill was definitely too steep to cycle up without a little bit of help. She saw Lydia and Tom as soon as she reached the brow of the hill. They were standing by the front gate of the cottage.

'Hello, you two,' she said. 'Isn't it the most perfect evening?'

'I'm so glad you've turned up,' said Lydia, 'I thought I'd have to entertain Tom on my own. I wanted you to come to supper tonight, too. You will, won't you?'

'I should really get back to the beach hut and put Grace to bed, she's already out for the count.'

'Of course you must,' Lydia said quickly. 'Well you can come another time.'

They all looked at Grace, flushed and sleepy with her thumb in her mouth.

'Why don't you let Grace sleep at the cottage whilst we all have supper?' Tom said. He put his hand gently on Grace's head and smiled at Fran.

Fran smiled back at him, missing the venomous look shot at her by Lydia. 'Why not? I feel ravenous after that bike ride.'

She went into the cottage and took Grace upstairs to a small room that was tucked under the eaves. After Grace was born it had been redecorated with pretty wallpaper with little boats on it. The cot had been there since Fran and Simon were babies and left there, Fran assumed, in anticipation of grandchildren. The cot revealed a sentimental side to their mother that had surprised her. She had always thought of her mother as being the type of woman who would view grandchildren as an unacceptable proof of ageing, and an inconvenient disruption to her organised life.

When she went back downstairs, Tom was standing by

the big bay window, looking across the fields to the harbour with a glass of champagne in his hand. He turned when he heard her and smiled.

Fran suddenly felt the sort of shyness she used to experience in her teens and, smiling back, said hastily, 'I'll just see if Lydia needs any help in the kitchen.'

Lydia was giving a convincing display of being totally absorbed in last minute preparations.

Fran looked at the venison casserole steaming on top of the hob.

'That looks wonderful,' she said, and then after a brief pause asked, 'but what exactly are you up to?'

'What do you mean, what am I up to?' said Lydia.

'Why have you invited Tom round here? I thought you had designs on George?'

'I've already had George, at lunchtime actually, but I wish his carpet had been a bit cleaner.'

'Are you serious?'

'Of course I'm serious.'

'So Tom's your next conquest?'

'If you go to bed early.'

Fran laughed ignoring the slight, unidentifiable pang that struck her. 'I promise. That casserole looks worth it.'

It was warm enough to have a few drinks outside before supper, but by the time they went in to eat there was an autumn chill in the air. It came drifting up from the marshes, and off the inky sea.

'Now, tell us all about this naughty husband of yours,' said Lydia, the moment the food had been served. 'Have you left him forever?'

Fran said she was sure Tom didn't want to hear about her marital problems. She wondered how on earth Lydia could be so tactless.

'Rumour has it he's being unfaithful to you, but I'm sure it couldn't possibly be true, you're much too sweet and pretty to have a husband go astray. I wouldn't give it another thought.'

Fran desperately wished Lydia would just shut up.

'I really think we should persuade her to return to her husband, don't you, Tom?' Lydia gave Tom the benefit of a long, intimate look, the sort she knew most men found impossible to resist. 'I know I'd return to such a handsome, wealthy man. Well, at the end of the day it's your decision. Now, shall we try and get Tom to tell us some of his dark secrets? I hear you're hot gossip in the village. You can't expect to turn up somewhere like this without exciting the natives.'

Tom was systematically interrogated by Lydia. It was like a game of ping-pong. No sooner had he answered one question than she fired another at him.

Fran was silent until he mentioned the windsurfing centre he owned in Greece, and the places around the world where he'd windsurfed.

'I thought the North Sea seemed an unlikely place to get so good at windsurfing,' she said.

As the evening progressed, Fran found it impossible to have any sort of conversation with Tom, because the moment a topic drifted out of Lydia's sphere, she brought it to an abrupt end. By ten o'clock, she regretfully decided to leave Lydia to her seduction plans.

'I'd better get to bed,' she said, 'I feel exhausted after that bike ride.'

Tom laughed. 'Do you think you're fit enough for a windsurfing session?'

'You bet,' she replied.

Tom got up from the table and kissed her on the cheek.

'Don't forget my windsurfing kit is waiting for you whenever you want to use it.'

Fran instinctively looked out of the window at a group of trees framed against the night sky. The moon touched the leaves, making them appear almost silver, but they were motionless in the night air, not even a hint of a breeze disturbing them.

'If only the wind would start blowing again,' she said.

'I don't think anyone else wants it to blow again,' said Lydia, irritably.

Upstairs, Fran opened her bedroom window wide. The gentle rhythm of the sea drifted across the marsh and up to the village and she stood motionless, letting the beauty of the night wash over her. Within a few minutes she heard the click of the side gate and saw Tom walk across the green to the path that wound down onto the marsh. She felt a rush of happiness knowing that he hadn't succumbed to Lydia's charms, and then wondered why she cared.

꧁

The coastguard cottage over at Dunsmere was full of exotic smells from the excellent meal that George had cooked for Phoebe. Even the wine from Mrs. Kennard's shop hadn't been nearly as bad as George had anticipated. Sitting on the settee, with Phoebe snuggled up next to him, he knew he should be feeling rather pleased with himself, but he wasn't. Perhaps he was just old-fashioned, he thought, but the image of Lydia lying beneath him on the floor made him feel dreadfully guilty.

'Well, I am impressed,' said Phoebe. 'If I'd known what a good cook you were, I'd have gone out with you ages ago.'

'Gone are the days when a chap could hardly boil an egg. All my mates from university can knock up a pretty decent meal.'

'Maybe, but I do think that was exceptionally good. Shall I pour us some more wine?'

'Actually, Phoebe, I'm going to have to run you back home now, I've got an early start in the morning.'

George tried not to notice the look of disbelief on Phoebe's face. If he stayed on the settee with her much longer, he knew he wouldn't be able to keep his hands off her. She was a completely different shape to Lydia but just as inviting; probably more so, he thought, looking at her generous cleavage.

'You poor baby,' she replied. 'Surely you can cope with the odd late night?'

He slipped his hand under her soft pink top and drew her closer to him. Phoebe's mouth was on his, and her tongue played with the inside of his lips. He could feel himself tipping over into a blanket of desire.

3

It was just after eight the next morning before Fran heard any sound from Grace. It had been a source of amazement and relief to find her so undemanding and happy. She and Malcolm had assumed life with a newborn baby would mean living in a house that was reverberating with crying, endless nappy changes, and sleepless nights.

During a rare intimate lunch together, Fran's mother had told her nightmare stories of buckets full of soaking nappies, and inadequate twin tub washing machines. On one particularly dreadful day, she'd filled the old twin tub with nappies and turned the temperature knob up to boiling point. It was the heat-wave summer of '76 and the plants in the garden were labouring under a cloudless sky. By the time she'd watered all the wilting plants and returned to the kitchen, it was awash with boiling water. 'I wish I'd had you and Simon in the disposable nineties,' she'd said. Fran had thought of her stock of paper nappies with relief, and had given her mother a sympathetic smile.

Fran took Grace downstairs and put her in the old wooden high chair. She thought of her mother using it for her and Simon, but try as she might, she couldn't imagine Daphne spooning scrambled egg into a baby's mouth; pearls and smart clothes just didn't fit in with such a domestic scene.

The Warbleton postman still did his round on a bicycle, and seemed determined to keep the true image of the village postman alive. He was very protective of his bike and wheeled it up paths to front doors, convinced that it was going to be stolen if he took his eye off it for one second. He knew everyone in the village, and was quite happy to pass the time of day with anyone who wanted to talk to him. He waved cheerily to Fran through the window before placing a single letter through the letterbox. She was surprised that Malcolm had forwarded the letter to her, but when she read its contents and realised he had already opened it, she understood why. He would be delighted that her ownership of the beach hut was threatened.

She sat down on a kitchen chair and tapped Malcolm's work number into her mobile phone. As soon as he answered, she said, 'I've received the letter you forwarded, but why have you started opening my mail?'

There was a brief pause before he replied, 'I'm sorry, darling, I didn't realise it was addressed to you. It looked a bit official, so I immediately assumed it was for me without looking properly at the envelope.'

'Well, you obviously know the contents, so I needn't explain why I have to stay down here for longer than I originally planned.'

'Come home and I'll help you sort this out. We can go to the meeting at Southfleet together.'

'You know I've decided to stay here for at least two weeks, so an extra few days isn't going to make any difference.' Fran had always found it difficult to stand up to Malcolm, and even though he was nearly a hundred miles away she felt her stomach pitch nervously.

'You're being stupid, Fran. If you want to sort things out with me, you'd better get back here quickly. I'm fed up with being made to look a fool.'

'I think I'm the one that's been made a fool of.'

'So I'm guilty without trial? Well, you're barking up the wrong tree if you've convinced yourself I'm having an affair with Sandra. If Brendon Richards had gone on that trip with me, you wouldn't have given it a second thought. Just because Sandra answered the telephone in my room, it doesn't mean we were in bed together.'

Fran remembered the horrible moment when she'd heard Sandra's voice at the end of the line, but to her disappointment she found herself almost apologising.

'Just be patient and let me stay here for a few weeks. I promise I'll come back immediately after the meeting. I'm sorry if my suspicions are unfounded, but you must admit it did all seem a bit odd.'

Malcolm was immediately conciliatory. 'Don't worry, darling. Perhaps a little holiday is what you need, and if you want any help with negotiations on the beach hut, I'm here. Give me a call in a few days, and give Grace a big kiss from me. I do love you both, you know.'

Fran felt she had been completely out-manoeuvred. She wiped Grace's mouth, scooped her out of the high chair and decided to go and pay Elisabeth a visit at the vicarage. She walked out of the house and drew in great breaths of the fresh Suffolk air.

The vicarage was large and imposing but the walls were softened by virginia creeper and great swathes of wisteria. In summer, roses blossomed around windows in a wonderful assortment of colours. Elisabeth adored roses and within days of arriving at the vicarage she had gone off to the local nursery to buy a selection of her favourites. The delicate creamy buff 'Gloire de Dijon' now spread across the north wall, happy in the shade, and her favourite 'Summer Wine', a delicate, soft, coral pink, covered the front porch. Elisabeth felt incredibly lucky when she thought about most of the residences that were now allocated to the clergy. Bungalows and ugly modern houses, often in the grounds of the old vicarage, were normally what came with a parish. Why this particular house hadn't been sold off was a mystery, but one Elisabeth didn't want to delve into. She just hoped they could stay in it for many years to come.

The usual tranquil atmosphere in the vicarage had been ripped apart by Ruby, with all the skill of a rebellious seventeen-year-old. When James opened the door to Fran, she noticed an uncharacteristic ruffled look about him, and no sooner had he deposited her in the kitchen, where Elisabeth was looking equally ruffled, than he disappeared, mumbling something about visits.

Fran and Elisabeth were old friends. When, on an unusually balmy summer's day eleven years ago, James and Elisabeth and their four small daughters had moved into the vicarage, Fran was the first person to call on them. Although she was only thirteen and Elisabeth twenty-seven, an instant friendship had sprung up between them. Fran was always popping in and out of the vicarage during the summer months, helping with the four girls that Elisabeth had produced, in what some people considered unseemly haste, over just five years. When the ladies of the village cooed over the latest occupant in the big old pram, and the pretty faces half buried in their mother's skirts, they expected the little angels to possess names like Catherine and Victoria, or maybe even Charlotte. Ruby, Chloe, Octavia and Pearl seemed outlandish heathen names to them.

Elisabeth had missed Fran since her marriage to Malcolm, and on the infrequent occasions when she had met him, had found her friend's choice of husband strange. Despite his good looks and charm, he lacked the warmth and down to earth qualities that she had expected to find in the man Fran loved.

'Don't even ask,' said Elisabeth to the unspoken question she saw on Fran's face. 'I don't know who I'm more annoyed with James, or Ruby.'

Elisabeth opened a big cupboard door next to the pantry and brought out a box full of toys for Grace to play with.

'She's the sweetest little thing, Fran,' she said, 'and look at all that lovely hair. It's very unusual for a ten-month-old to have such thick hair.'

'I'll tell you something, Elisabeth, it really gets to Malcolm that she's got black hair. He was convinced I was going to produce a blond-haired boy.'

'I take it Malcolm isn't exactly flavour of the month.'

'No, he certainly isn't, but tell me what's going on here. There's nothing like someone else's problems to take your mind off your own. Not that I wish any problems on you, of course,' she added hurriedly.

Elisabeth related the incidents of the past few hours, her words interspersed with a few tears. Ruby had fallen for one of the many penniless artists that found their way to Warbleton. Unfortunately, this one was twenty-six and James was already unhappy that his seventeen-year-old daughter was seeing someone that much older. When he had woken Ruby that morning, he'd seen a packet of contraceptive pills carelessly left on her bedside table. Elisabeth, a natural peacemaker, had wanted them all to sit down quietly and talk things through. James could only bellow his rage, and Ruby was threatening to leave school and live with the artist in his eyrie at the top of the lighthouse.

'So there it is. James is behaving as though the whole family has been raped and pillaged, rather than one daughter succumbing to the charms of a romantic dark-haired artist.' Elisabeth thought of Edward's high cheekbones, brown eyes and lovely dark hair, and really couldn't blame Ruby for falling for him at all.

'Time for coffee,' she said, putting the kettle on the enduringly comforting Aga, 'and a stiff brandy to go with it.'

'Brandy at this time of day?' remarked Fran, looking at the amber liquid being poured carefully into two glasses. 'I'd love all those pompous people on the church council to see us now.' They laughed quite hysterically at the thought, and decided that sipping brandy and coffee at ten thirty in the morning might not solve their immediate problems, but it was certainly a therapeutic process.

It was difficult for Fran to drag herself away from the

sanctuary of the big warm kitchen, but another hour had flown by whilst Elisabeth had persuaded her to talk about her own problems. When Fran eventually stepped out onto the imposing front porch, the billowing storm clouds, which had hung threateningly on the horizon since early morning, had completely disappeared. It was definitely brightening up and going to be another glorious day. She could almost hear the landladies breathing a collective massive sigh of relief.

Elisabeth's usual enthusiasm, that helped carry her through even the most demanding days at the vicarage, seemed to evaporate as she walked back into the kitchen. All the little jobs normally disposed of so efficiently had taken on monumental proportions. She studied her weekly organiser that hung next to a large watercolour of a bored-looking heron gazing into a pool of water. An endless list of duties littered the days of the week and, with the Harvest Supper looming ever nearer, there was barely an hour over the next fortnight that she would have to herself. *Damn the lot of them*, thought Elisabeth mutinously and, pouring another brandy, she began eagerly scanning the '*Situations Vacant*' pages of the local newspaper. The advert for a part-time secretary with an estate agent in Southfleet leapt out of the page at her. If she could persuade stuffy old Bidwell, whom she vaguely knew, to give her a job, she'd go for it.

$\mathscr{ll}$

Despite the ups and downs of the property market, Bidwell & Symmonds, who operated from a smart building on the main high street in Southfleet, were a highly successful and respected firm of estate agents. They had cleverly weathered the occasional collapses of the property market over the past thirty years and with both Bidwell, and Symmonds having sons following in their footsteps, the company looked good for many decades to come.

Rupert Bidwell put down the receiver and wondered what the world was coming to when vicars' wives started applying for jobs.

'I'm in a damned awkward spot now,' said Rupert to his son. 'I've just agreed to interview Elisabeth Green, the vicar's wife from Warbleton. Why on earth would she want to come and work here? It's probably all those silly books and films about vicars' wives doing odd things that have affected her.'

William adored his father, but despaired of his inability to move with the times.

'What's wrong with a vicar's wife working?' he said, removing his head from a filing cabinet. 'You've got to move with the times, Dad.'

Rupert shuffled through some papers on his desk, refusing to comment. He'd just make sure he offered the job to someone else.

'When is she coming for an interview?'

'In an hour, and I don't want *you* piping up,' he said, giving his son the sort of look that had terrified William when he was a child.

'Of course not, Dad, I wouldn't dream of it.'

Finding she was about five minutes early for her interview, Elisabeth looked at the neat display of properties for sale in the window of Bidwell & Symmonds. There was an interesting selection of houses, from little terraced cottages in outlying villages to an imposing manor two miles from Southfleet. One of the brightly painted beach huts next to the promenade was marked up for what seemed to Elisabeth a ridiculously high price. She couldn't begin to imagine what the vicarage would be worth if it was put on the market. She hoped the Church of England was investing its funds more wisely now and wouldn't have to sell off the few old vicarages still in its possession. Elisabeth checked the hands of her watch and, telling herself just to go for it, went in.

She sat opposite Rupert and, from his first few words, got the distinct impression that he was trying to put her off. He fiddled about with the papers on his desk and then asked William to go and make them both a coffee.

Elisabeth thought it was a delightful office. Nice and light and airy, with big sash windows looking out onto the bustling street and large enough so that everyone wasn't sitting on top of each other.

'And how's the vicar?' Rupert asked, making eye contact with Elisabeth for the first time since she'd sat at his desk.

'James is fine. Always busy, of course, especially now he's had to take on the parish of Dunsmere as well.'

'All these churches amalgamating… Such a shame, but I know you're not here to talk about church matters.' He shuffled some papers on his desk and then said, 'I don't know if you realise, my dear, but we do need someone who is computer literate for this job. It's not just a matter of filing, and typing a few letters.'

Sarcastic old sod, she thought, but she took a deep breath, smiled at him sweetly and said, 'I am computer literate. I did a course two years ago and everything connected with the parish is now done on the computer.'

'Have you got any other experience, apart from working for your husband?'

Elisabeth wondered if she could be bothered to go into any detail. She suddenly felt a great weariness pushing her down. He'd obviously made up his mind he didn't want her. Only the thought of the horrid calendar at home full of parish duties made her rally.

'Actually yes, I've had quite a considerable amount. I worked in London for three years before I married James. I ended up as Secretary/PA to the Marketing Director of Save and Prosper.'

'The unit trust company?' asked Rupert.

'Yes. I know it was some time ago now, but I'm sure my typing speed is still over sixty words a minute, and if you ever need anything taking down in shorthand, I can do that, too.'

Rupert was beginning to look impressed.

At the end of half an hour, Elisabeth felt she had answered all Rupert's questions satisfactorily, and probably given him more than he'd bargained for. Out of the corner of her eye, she could see William giving his father a thumbs-up sign.

Rupert shook her hand and said he'd be in touch. At the door, Elisabeth turned to smile at them both, and was certain William winked at her.

'You've got to give her the job Dad,' said William. 'She's smart, attractive, and I bet she's bloody efficient. She'll certainly sort you out.'

'I do wish you'd stop using the word *bloody* in every sentence, but if you feel I'll be moving with the times by employing a vicar's wife, then I'll do it. She was rather special, wasn't she?'

'We should have asked her if she knew the people who own Watercolour Cottage,' said William.

The receipt of such a substantial offer for a property that wasn't even on their books had surprised both Rupert and William. It was only when they heard the transaction was to be dealt with through a third party, that they realised the prospective purchaser wanted to remain anonymous.

'Perhaps the offer comes from a famous pop star,' said William.

'It doesn't matter who it is, so long as completion takes place.' Rupert was eager to get his hands on the two per-cent commission.

'I'll give the Pryde's a call again this afternoon, and see if they've decided to sell.'

❦

Elisabeth always enjoyed the drive round the estuary from Southfleet to Warbleton and today was no exception. She pulled over and parked in a lay-by that gave a wonderful view of the marsh. This little part of England had claimed her and she had every intention of staying sane enough to enjoy it, even if it meant disrupting life in the vicarage.

'Why have you got make-up on?' asked Chloe, shrugging her coat off and looking suspiciously at Elisabeth's smart clothes. Octavia and Pearl flew past them both, oblivious to anything other than the pony in the paddock at the back of the house.

'Why isn't Ruby with you?' asked Elisabeth, ignoring Chloe's question.

'Don't worry Mum she hasn't eloped with Edward, she'll be back in a minute. Why are you all dressed up?'

'Wait until Ruby gets back and I'll tell you both.'

'I wish I was older and beautiful like Ruby so someone would fall in love with me.'

'In two years' time, you'll have men falling at your feet,' promised Elisabeth.

When the phone rang a few minutes later, Elisabeth let it peal out several times before picking it up. Chloe saw a broad smile light her mother's face.

'Thank you, Rupert. Yes, Monday will be fine.'

She gave a little skip and smiled at Chloe. 'Don't look so worried, it's good news, I'll tell you in a minute.'

And now for the difficult part, she thought; *explaining all this to James and employing a full time cleaner...*

The despondent figure of Chloe sitting at the bottom of the stairs greeted Ruby as she entered the vicarage, along with raised voices spilling out of the kitchen into the hall.

'I suppose I'm in for it again,' said Ruby. 'Hasn't Mum calmed Dad down yet?'

'I don't think this has got anything to do with you. Mum was going to tell us something when you got back, but Dad arrived first.'

James's reaction to Elisabeth's news didn't surprise her in the least. He was horrified, and furious that she hadn't consulted him first. She hoped that after the first shock he'd become gracefully resigned to the inevitable. There was no hint of this graceful acceptance over supper, though. A stony silence seemed to chill even the warmth from the Aga.

At breakfast next morning, a good night's sleep had done nothing to improve his humour.

'Amy Cooper will think heaven comes before death if you ask her to be your secretary. Imagine how she'd love lording it over the other church wardens,' said Elisabeth.

'I don't think upsetting the church wardens would be a very constructive measure, and I don't know if I could cope with Amy in anything but small measures.' James glared at the front page of *The Telegraph*, pretending to read, but as Elisabeth and the children knew he couldn't read without his glasses, it was a rather pointless gesture.

'I'm going to place an advert in Mrs. Kennard's shop to advertise for a cleaner.'

'Are you going to advertise for a nanny as well?'

'Don't be silly, James. My hours are from ten until three so I'll have plenty of time for the children.'

'But not much for me,' he muttered under his breath.

'Don't worry, Mum, we think what you're doing is brilliant,' said Ruby.

*

Mrs. Kennard looked at Elisabeth in disbelief when she explained why she was advertising for a cleaning lady. 'But who will look after the vicar and the four little ones?' she asked.

'I'm not abandoning my family, Mrs. Kennard, and the children are hardly little ones any more.'

'Yes, dear, but they still need their mother to be at home when they get back from school, or the next thing we'll know is people will be calling them latch-key kids. You want to keep your eye on Ruby, she's at a difficult age.'

Elisabeth felt herself bristling. Despite having spent so many years being diplomatic, she still found it a struggle.

Her lack of response didn't deter Mrs. Kennard. 'Amy and I are most concerned about her relationship with that artist. Do you think it's wise, dear? He must be nearly twice her age.'

'Hardly twice, Mrs. Kennard. I'm sorry but I've got to dash.'

The old-fashioned bell on the shop door jangled harshly as Elisabeth shut the door. *Silly old bat*, she thought.

Ten minutes later, when Elisabeth came round the side of the beach hut, she saw Tom and Fran sitting on old, striped deck chairs deep in conversation.

'Hello,' she said, wondering if she should have turned and gone quietly back over the sand dunes.

'Have you two met?' asked Fran.

Tom smiled at Elisabeth, and told Fran they'd met in The Reed and Whistle.

'I'm afraid I haven't got round to attending one of your husband's services yet.'

'I wouldn't worry too much about that,' said Elisabeth. She'd seen Tom for the first time only a couple of weeks ago, and had liked him instantly. He had an easy manner and listened to what you had to say, but not in the intense, eye-locking way of so many men, who didn't fool any reasonably intelligent woman. His interest was different, although it would have been difficult to define it. He both received and gave, making conversation with him a pleasure.

'I've just come to give you a little bit of gossip before Mrs. Kennard does, and it's about me.'

'Don't tell me the vicar's wife is rebelling,' said Fran.

'Well actually, yes she is, if rebelling is getting a job.'

'That's brilliant news!' Fran leapt out of her deck chair and gave Elisabeth a hug. 'It's about time you spread your wings outside the four walls of the vicarage.'

Tom thought he'd better leave before he started joining in with the hugging. Fran looked far too pretty with the backdrop of the sea and sky behind her, smiling delightedly at Elisabeth.

'I must go,' he said. 'I promised George I'd go up to the otter sanctuary with him this afternoon. He's got to pick up two otters to release back into the wild.'

'Do you know what the forecast is for tomorrow?' asked Fran.

'It's looking promising, possibly a force four. I'll come round in the morning, and I can always stay with Grace whilst you're out on the water. You probably won't last long, anyway if you haven't been out for a while.'

'I might surprise you,' she laughed, 'but you're probably right.'

'Now, isn't he gorgeous!' said Elisabeth.

'He is rather,' agreed Fran.

'You looked as though you were having a rather a cosy conversation.'

'If you're going to accuse me of fancying Tom, who wouldn't?' said Fran, looking out to sea at the tiny boats which seemed anchored on the horizon. 'But as I'm a respectable married woman that's all it can be.'

'Bin him, and I don't mean Tom.'

'I can't believe you just said that. Malcolm's my husband and father of my child.'

'We all make mistakes and marrying Malcolm was a fairly major one on your part. Change things, Fran. Find out exactly what Malcolm is up to.'

The sea lay smooth and inviting only yards away. Sheltered from the breeze by the beach hut, it felt like a hot day in mid-summer. The long, straight line of the shore between Warbleton and Dunsmere was completely deserted, apart from a seal pup basking in the unusual warmth.

'Let's skinny dip,' said Fran, 'and if you beat me into the water, I'll start doing some detective work.'

To this comment there was no reply, because Elisabeth was already frantically pulling her clothes off, determined to reach the water first.

⸙

'Cheer up, Vicar,' said Phoebe, to the depressed-looking figure of James hunched over his beer. 'Have there been too many funerals recently?'

James nodded absently at Phoebe and stared into his pint of beer, wondering how, in so short a space of time, his cosy world could have fallen into such disarray. Even his belief seemed to be wavering amidst the politics of parish life. He had always felt that God should be served with a generous and open heart, removed from pettiness. But the church was subject to the same kind of backstabbing that went on in companies. And Amy Cooper! What a nightmare that silly, bustling little woman was, so full of her own self-importance. He'd only offered her Elisabeth's role two hours ago and she'd already reorganised the flower rota and church cleaning duties and taken it upon herself to give him a little lecture about Ruby. He felt life was never going to be the same again, and he really didn't think he could forgive Elisabeth for being the cause of it.

James was still staring despondently into his pint of beer when Lydia came in and sat on the bar stool next to him. She asked Phoebe for a glass of very chilled dry white wine.

'Where's all the local talent?' she enquired, looking hopefully round the room.

Phoebe felt herself bristle. She had a moment's thought that dogs must feel like she did now when they encountered another dog they didn't like and a ridge of hairs appeared on their back but, not wanting to appear churlish in front of James she said: 'There's not a lot of talent about at the moment apart from George and Tom who you met the other night, but quite a few tasty blokes come in during the summer. Actually, Edward's rather dishy, but he's taken, isn't he Vicar?' she said pointedly, turning to James.

'I wouldn't be so sure about that. Ruby's far too young to be going out with that man,' James returned grumpily.

'I definitely think George is dishy,' said Lydia. She turned her back to James and leaning across the bar whispered to Phoebe: 'I had a rather interesting lunchtime drink with him yesterday. I think the time he spends watching his wild animals has rubbed off on him. There was certainly an animal lust to his love-making.'

Phoebe's legs went weak and a sick feeling knotted the pit of her stomach.

'You were with George yesterday lunchtime?'

'I certainly was.'

Phoebe was not averse to intimate chats with her close friends, but she couldn't understand women who discussed the physical side of their relationships with almost complete strangers. She had met women like Lydia before, who happily revealed details of their latest amorous adventures to anyone who would listen to them. They spoke about men as if they were horses whose form needed to be marked down on a race card.

To be told that George had made love to Lydia only hours before he had to her was almost too much to bear. Phoebe looked at Lydia's perfect body, her blonde hair that was straight out of a shampoo advert, and her long, painted fingernails, and felt sick. *I don't stand a chance*, she thought, furiously wiping an already dry glass. Only the sound of Lydia's mobile phone playing a ridiculous tune stopped her leaning across the counter and slapping her face.

James and Phoebe watched as Lydia's smug expression changed to one of horror.

'Oh, no! She's dead, isn't she? Tell me the truth. You promise you're telling the truth? I'll get Fran, she's got the car here, we'll be back tonight.'

James leant across and put his hand on her arm. 'What's happened? Can I help, my dear?'

'It's Annabel.' She leapt off her stool and rushed across the room, tripping over the dog in her anxiety to get to the door.

4

Hospitals, Fran decided, were the sort of places you either just took in your stride, or were terrified by. An irrational panic swept over her as she walked through the doors of St. Thomas's and along the corridors to the private room where Annabel lay.

Annabel was being fussed over by a young nurse in an immaculate white uniform. She told Fran not to stay too long, gave a final pat to the bedclothes and left the room.

Fran took Annabel's hand and asked her how she was feeling.

'Not too bad, really, but I'm a dreadful patient, I just want to get out of here.' She looked at the flowers Fran had placed on the bedside table. 'Wild at Heart?' she asked.

Fran gave a rather sheepish smile. 'You know I love any excuse to lose myself amongst the flowers there.'

'Thank you, they're beautiful, and a nice change.'

Fran glanced round the room. It was completely devoid of any floral decorations.

'Four bouquets arrived this morning,' said Annabel, 'all lilies, bold, suffocating flowers. I've never liked them.'

Fran laughed. 'There are always lilies in your house when you have a party.'

Annabel pulled a face. 'Well, I've changed. I think they're

overpowering and extravagant. Now, why on earth did you and Lydia come tearing back from Warbleton just because I had a little accident?'

'I don't call being knocked down by a taxi a little accident. Lydia was quite hysterical all the way back. She was convinced you were dying. I hope she was calmer when she came in to see you.'

'Lydia likes being hysterical,' said Annabel dismissively, 'but you were sweet to stay with her last night. Did Malcolm mind?'

'Malcolm doesn't know I'm back, and I don't think anyone has told him about the accident yet, but I'm going to have to see him before I go back to Warbleton.'

The room had darkened whilst they'd been talking. Dusk seemed to be creeping over the day even though it was only mid-morning. Annabel turned on the bedside lamp, and Fran's flowers twinkled beneath the electric rays.

'You see,' said Annabel, 'your flowers still look beautiful even under such a harsh light.'

'Annabel,' said Fran gently, 'what's all this about?'

'I don't know, really. I just feel, well, differently about things and I want to ask a big favour of you.'

'Of course, ask away.'

'When you go back to Warbleton, I want to come with you.'

'That's hardly a big favour, but I thought you found it a bit bleak at Watercolour Cottage?'

Memories of Annabel with a fur wrap draped over her shoulders, and shivering from the cold, came flooding back to Fran. She wondered if the accident had affected her more than she realised.

'I want to get away from London for a bit. Having something like this happen just makes you take a new look at yourself, and your life. I'm afraid I've come to the conclusion that I lead a pretty shallow existence.' Annabel lay back amongst the plumped-up pillows and gave a little sigh. 'I think Simon is up to no good, and I'm pretty certain Malcolm is involved, too.'

'Involved in what?'

'Haven't you ever wondered why they're both so wealthy?'

'I suppose not,' said Fran. 'I know it sounds pretty pathetic, but I don't give our finances much thought. Malcolm deals with everything.'

'Well, there's definitely no way Simon's salary could pay for all the things we have, and he said something very odd to me when we arrived back from Warbleton.' Annabel hesitated and fiddled with the edge of the crisp white sheet. 'I just don't want to stir things up.'

'Tell all,' said Fran. 'That is if you feel well enough.'

Annabel related what had happened on arriving back in London, seeing Sandra on the doorstep, and Simon's insistence that nothing was said to Fran.

Fran stood up and walked over to the window. It looked out onto a fountain whose water cascaded down into a large pond full of lily-pads. She supposed that was one of the things you paid for in a private hospital; 'a room with a view'.

'Say something Fran?'

Fran turned away from the window and looked at Annabel, lying pale and anxious in her hospital bed. 'I thought older brothers were supposed to be all protective with their little sisters,' she said. 'Simon's never been like that, but I did think he would show me some loyalty.'

'I don't think it's that simple. I think Malcolm has got some sort of hold over Simon.'

'That's still no excuse. What did you think when you saw Sandra?'

'I suppose at the time I did think she must have stayed the night with him, but on reflection I thought there was no way Malcolm would be so stupid. It's a bit blatant doing it in the family home.'

'I might lose the beach hut,' Fran sighed. She wanted to turn her mind from the picture of Malcolm having sex with Sandra in their four-poster bed.

'Well, I'm not surprised, the sea's almost up to the veranda already. It could be swept away one wild night when you're in it.'

Fran couldn't help smiling. 'I don't mean like that…' and she told Annabel about the solicitor's letter, and that Malcolm had read it first.

Before Annabel could reply, the nurse pushed open the door and told Fran firmly that she must leave. 'Mrs. Pryde needs lots of rest,' she said.

'Don't let Malcolm bully you,' Annabel shouted after her retreating figure. 'Remember, the ball's in your court.'

Fran felt dreadfully despondent as she walked down endless corridors to find the exit. It had been a wrench leaving Warbleton so abruptly. Outside the hospital she hailed a taxi to take her back to Lydia's flat to collect Grace, and then immediately regretted not walking, as the taxi lurched away from the hospital and joined the streams of traffic jamming up the roads in every direction. She was going to have too much time to dwell on what Annabel had just told her.

When she eventually got back to Notting Hill and put the key in her front door, she tried to remember Annabel's parting words. 'The ball's in your court,' she'd said, but she didn't feel that was the case at all.

Walking into the wide, airy hall, the first thing she noticed was all the empty vases. When they were filled with flowers, the high-ceilinged entrance hall was welcoming; now, it seemed unfriendly and austere. In the sitting room, the stale odour of cigarette smoke hung in the air. Every morning, as soon as Malcolm left for work, she flung the windows open wide to try and eradicate the smell.

In the kitchen, she found some eggs and began preparing an omelette for Grace.

At least Grace was happy, crashing about the kitchen in her little baby-walker. *Do children always adapt so long as they're loved and fed?* she wondered.

She didn't go upstairs until it was time to put Grace down for her afternoon nap, and even then she hesitated before going into the bedroom at the end of the corridor. The four-poster bed, which Malcolm had bought just before their marriage, dominated the room. The cream duvet lay in a distorted heap across the bed, and most of the pillows were on the floor. It seemed as if Malcolm had experienced a restless night. She sat on the edge of the bed and looked for signs of a woman having shared it with him. Was there a hint of perfume amongst the sheets? Did the blonde hair on the pillow belong to Sandra or was it Malcolm's? Sandra had short blonde hair the same colour, so she couldn't confront

Malcolm with it as evidence. Did men who watched their wives give birth have affairs too? She supposed they did because so many men had affairs. She shied away from the thought, but pictures of Malcolm in bed with Sandra kept appearing in her mind.

It was just after seven thirty when Fran heard the Porsche pull up outside. She immediately went into the sitting room to pour herself a drink. Holding a glass somehow always made her feel braver; it wasn't the alcohol she needed, it was just having something to do. The ice-cubes stuck to her hands as she tried to tip them out of their squares into the glass, and the tonic fizzed down the sides of the bottle. *This is ridiculous*, she thought. *I can't even pour myself a gin and tonic.* She thought of Annabel and her mother; they filled cut glass tumblers with gin, tonic, ice cubes and lemon with swift dexterity, making it look like a proficient juggling act.

Malcolm's enthusiasm at seeing her again challenged her doubts before she'd even voiced them. She poured him a gin and tonic with a little more panache than she'd managed her own, and told him all about Annabel and the flight back to London.

'You should have rung, darling.'

'I know, but when we got back I was exhausted. Lydia was hysterical, and by the time I'd settled Grace it was after eleven.'

Malcolm sat down on a big carver chair at one end of the pine kitchen table and pulled Fran onto his lap.

'I'm sorry about Annabel, sweetheart, but it's great to have you home. How's Grace? I'll take a peep at her in a minute.'

'Grace is the most adaptable little thing. She didn't cry once, even though she woke up when I took her over the sand dunes to the car. She fell asleep again as soon as we started driving.'

Fran said nothing of her conversation with Annabel. Perhaps there was an innocent explanation to both the business trip and Sandra's early morning appearance at the house.

'I know you don't like business dinners but there's one tonight,' said Malcolm. 'Now, I don't want any excuses. I'll find a babysitter and you go and choose a nice, sexy little dress to wear.'

'But, Malcolm…' Fran desperately tried to think of an excuse for not going. 'Annabel might call and need me.'

'Take your mobile with you. The hospital isn't going to let you go visiting in the middle of the night, anyway. Now, be a good girl and go and get changed.' He patted her on the bottom. Fran had never thought much about this habit of his before, but now it seemed rather patronising.

'It's a bit short notice to get a babysitter.'

He lifted a magnetic organiser off the fridge door, and ran his finger down the names of babysitters and their telephone numbers.

'There seem to be a good few names to work through. Now run along we're supposed to be meeting at eight.'

Upstairs, her wardrobe was full of beautiful, expensive clothes. When Malcolm had first started dating her, she'd been flattered when he'd whisked her off to Paris for the night, bought her designer clothes, and wined and dined her in expensive restaurants.

It was only two years ago, but now, looking back at the person she had been then, she seemed no more than an impressionable teenager. She lifted out three dresses that were simpler in their design to most of the others. 'So I'm back on the old merry-go-round,' she said aloud to herself, 'and I've got a nasty feeling it's going to be pretty impossible to get off.'

'First sign, Fran,' said Malcolm, entering the bedroom noiselessly.

She hated his habit of suddenly appearing in a room without any warning. Most men made too much noise, but Malcolm's athletic frame moved silently about the house with the light step of a woman.

'Wear this one,' he said, pulling out a dress in a wonderful shade of burgundy.

Fran remembered when they'd bought it in Paris, in an exclusive little shop just off the Champs-Elysee. The price tag showed a sum exceeding most people's monthly salary. She'd suggested to Malcolm that perhaps one of the other dresses would be more suitable. The shop assistant, in almost perfect English, told her that no French lady would turn down such a wonderful present from a husband. It had been neatly folded in tissue paper and placed in a box and Fran had left the shop unsure whether she was pleased or annoyed.

'It's a bit low-cut and short for a business dinner.'

'I like showing you off, Fran. Do try not to be such a little prude.'

At eight o'clock the taxi arrived to take them to the West End.

'It's just a low key affair,' said Malcolm.

'Will Sandra be there?' asked Fran quietly.

'Yes, but for God's sake don't start all that nonsense again. Why would I have an affair with Sandra when I've got such a delectable little wife?' He put his hand under her dress and followed the line of her thigh to the point where her hold-up stockings ended. He nibbled her ear. 'Perhaps we should have stayed in,' he said.

The seating arrangements were exactly as she had feared. She was ushered by an attentive waiter to the spare seat between the Marketing Director, Brendon Fletcher, and the Managing Director, Peter Roberts. There was a marked similarity between the two men; they were both below average height, considerably overweight, and also extremely boring, as well as lecherous. The first time Fran had met them, she thought they looked like a pair of garden slugs. Malcolm hadn't shown the slightest amusement when she'd whispered her comparison to him.

Sandra sat to the left of Peter Roberts, and Fran felt a rush of apprehension when she looked at her. She was very similar in build and colouring to Lydia, although without quite the same drop-dead good looks, but she was still pretty stunning.

'Hi Fran,' she shouted across the table. 'Oh dear, I haven't got to have your husband sitting next to me, have I? I hope he's not going to talk shop all night.'

Looking at the other wives, all in their mid forties and dressed to kill, made Fran think of a cage of squawking parrots.

Brendon poured her a glass of champagne, and asked her what the attraction was of the little place in Suffolk she kept sneaking off to. Fran had no intention of discussing

Warbleton with him. He was the last person on earth who would understand her passion for the beach hut and windswept marsh.

'I don't go very often now,' she said.

'Well, I think Malcolm's damn lucky. I wish Marjorie flitted off to Suffolk rather than the Bahamas every time she was fed up; it would make the old bank balance look a lot healthier. Mind you,' he whispered in her ear, 'if you were my wife, I'd be quite happy to pay for little trips abroad. You're a sweet, sexy girl, and much too good for Malcolm.'

He pressed his leg against hers under the table and winked at her.

Peter Roberts draped his arm round the back of Fran's chair and asked what the two of them were talking about.

'A little place in Suffolk,' said Brendon.

'Ah, the place you disappeared to a week ago. Malcolm told us you'd taken off for a short holiday.'

Fran wanted to push away the florid face that was much too close to hers. With Brendon pressing her leg, and Peter stroking her shoulder, she felt like the filling in a sandwich.

Across the table, Malcolm and Sandra seemed to be sharing a particularly amusing joke. Fran remembered the first time she'd seen Sandra at an office drinks party. She had been wearing the type of high-heeled shoes that Fran, in her wildest imaginings, wouldn't have attempted walking across a floor in, and one of the most elegant dresses she'd ever seen. Malcolm had told Fran later that they had hardly recognised her as she always wore trouser suits in the office. She had a slightly icy manner, and 'I'm better than any man in the workplace,' written all over her. They'd spoken briefly with each other. Sandra hadn't been able to hide her amazement that a woman could be happy staying at home looking after a child. 'If I ever get round to having a baby I'll be back at work within days', she'd said. 'How do you manage, cooped up all day with a screaming brat?' Fran had decided that particular line of conversation wasn't worth pursuing.

Sandra was looking far from icy tonight. She was giggling into her glass of champagne like a schoolgirl, and Fran wondered what had brought about the change.

Malcolm suddenly stood up. 'I'd like to make a toast. 'Here's to Peter, congratulations on being one of the longest serving, most successful Managing Director's in the City.'

Everyone raised their glasses. They all stood up, apart from Peter. Fran felt his hand slide up the back of her dress and squeeze her bottom.

Almost before the thought was in her head, she'd done it, and a full glass of champagne landed rather neatly in Peter Roberts' lap. It looked like the purest accident, and Fran silently congratulated herself.

Malcolm's mood as they were going home in the taxi frightened Fran. She'd always been unnerved by his ability to work himself up into a fury, especially after he'd been drinking. Nothing had ever happened, but she often felt he had difficulty keeping his anger under control. 'So embarrassing!' he shouted at her. 'Why are you so damned clumsy? Of course it had to be Peter you doused in champagne.'

Fran had never mentioned the suggestive comments and subtle pawings that went on whenever she encountered the hierarchy of Malcolm's company. She felt sick of the whole pretence. Peter and Brendon weren't the golden boys Malcolm liked to think they were, and she'd damn well tell him.

'If either Peter or Brendon touches me again I'll pour a whole bottle of champagne over them. I've never been to one of your company dinners without someone fumbling under my skirt.'

It had begun raining, a heavy, depressing rain that washed over the taxi in an unremitting deluge.

'You're so bloody righteous and prim and proper,' he snarled.' Most girls would be flattered by a bit of attention, but oh no, not you, you take everything so damned personally. If a bit of flirting helps my prospects in the firm, then why not just go ahead and flirt?'

Whilst Malcolm was pouring himself a brandy and still swearing about her under his breath, Fran went upstairs. She looked in on Grace burrowed under her blanket with her thumb in her mouth. Just the sight of her daughter made her feel happy again. In the bathroom, she picked up a bottle of cleanser to take her make-up off and noticed a small, insignificant blue bottle tucked just behind it. The words *'Contact lens solution'* were printed on the label. Neither she nor Malcolm wore contact lenses.

Next day a persistent drizzle, which had settled in during the night, gave London a bleak look. The cloud cover was low and heavy. After the windswept shores of Suffolk, Fran felt particularly trapped.

Breakfast would have been a nightmare without Grace. Fran kept having images of Malcolm in bed with a woman. Had he been? She wished she knew the answer, and she wished she'd been brave enough last night to confront him with the mysterious bottle.

Just before Malcolm left for work, the phone rang. It was her mother, asking her to go round as soon as possible.

It was only a short walk to her mother's house and even with Grace in the pushchair it took barely five minutes.

'Isn't this all just frightful?' said Daphne, letting them in through the side door that led straight into the kitchen. Fran wasn't sure whether she was referring to Annabel's accident or the weather.

'Oh, the poor little lamb looks frozen.' She took Grace from Fran.

'She's not cold, Mum, look feel her hands.'

Daphne had the ability to make Fran feel a completely useless mother every time they met. She knew it was unintentional, but it irked her just the same.

They sat in the pristine kitchen whilst Daphne made coffee. Everything, as always, was in exactly the correct place. Fran could never remember any room in the house being untidy, except her own, and that had to be rectified the moment her mother saw any hint of chaos. Everything matched perfectly; there wasn't a single discordant note to jar on the senses, but neither was there anything to excite them.

'Now, dear,' said Daphne, taking a sip of the piping hot strong coffee, 'I've got something to tell you which you're not going to like.' She paused for a moment and held her hand to her forehead in a theatrical gesture. 'Daddy and I are going to sell Watercolour Cottage.'

With a jolt, Fran felt as if a lifeline had suddenly drifted from her reach. Watercolour Cottage, her childhood, all that had ever been really important to her during her adolescent years was, in one short sentence, being snatched away from her.

'But you can't sell Watercolour Cottage!' She knew she sounded like a petulant child.

'Eight hundred and fifty thousand pounds is far too good an offer to turn down.'

'You don't need the money.' Fran looked at the rings on her mother's fingers. Apart from her wedding band, Daphne was wearing two exquisite diamond rings, one sapphire, and an enormous ruby surrounded by tiny pearls. The rings alone were worth more than the cottage.

Daphne fingered them nervously. She knew Fran hated such an extravagant display of wealth.

'I don't understand…' Fran's voice was tremulous with tears and shock. 'I didn't even know the house was on the market. Have you told Simon?'

'It wasn't on the market. We had a phone call from an estate agent in Southfleet two weeks ago, asking if we were interested in selling.'

'Who wants to buy it?'

'We don't know, and that's neither here nor there. We hardly ever go to Warbleton now.'

'But you know how much I love it.'

'Well, you've got that funny little beach hut to go to.'

Fran told her mother about the possible disposal of the land the beach huts were on.

'I'm afraid that doesn't change anything. Your father has made up his mind to sell.'

Fran wished her mother could show a little bit of sadness or regret, or even simply say she was sorry it had to go, but nothing was forthcoming.

'Now, I've simply got to fly,' said Daphne. 'I've an appointment at the hairdressers in half an hour.'

Fran decided to cheer herself up by going to Wild at Heart where she could always find her favourite flowers. She spent the afternoon lost in a cloud of blooms of all shapes and hues as she mixed the most unlikely ones together to create a garden of colour throughout the house. She let Grace play on the floor amongst broken stalks and discarded flowers, sometimes removing petals from her mouth. She was sure her mother would think her quite irresponsible, but even if Grace chewed on a petal it wasn't going to do her much harm. By the time Malcolm returned, she had made up her mind to confront him about the contact lens solution. She'd bathed Grace and put her in her cot, turned on her musical mobile and quietly crept out of the room. She peeped back in a few minutes later, and saw that she was already curled up like a little kitten with her thumb firmly in her mouth.

Back in the kitchen she pulled down the blind to shut out the gloomy night, and poured herself a large glass of wine. It turned out to be just as difficult as she'd feared. He actually turned the tables on her and told her not to be such a suspicious little bitch.

'How dare you call me a bitch?' she said, in a tight controlled voice. 'How did it get there?'

'I don't know. It probably belonged to one of your friends who stayed and you've forgotten.'

'I haven't had anyone to stay for ages, and no one comes into our en suite bathroom, anyway.'

She watched as Malcolm swirled his whisky round in the glass.

'Just back off Fran', he said warningly. 'I've had a hard day, and I really don't need this.'

⚘

Although the leaden skies over London also extended to Suffolk, Elisabeth was feeling none of its depressing effects. For the first time in years she actually felt fully alive. Perhaps the novelty would wear off, she thought, but all the same, a wonderful sense of freedom came over her as she jumped into her Mini and headed off round the estuary to go to work. She adored her Mini, and wouldn't have exchanged it for any of the posh cars people buzzed about in these days.

Rupert and William were discussing Watercolour Cottage when she walked through the door in a shower of wind and rain.

'Do you know the people who own the cottage?' asked Rupert.

'Yes, but I didn't know they'd put it up for sale.'

He explained the peculiar circumstances surrounding the sale. 'We're expecting the mystery person's name to be revealed this morning. I really think all this cloak and dagger stuff is a bit unnecessary.'

The name came through just a couple of minutes after twelve o'clock. It meant nothing to Rupert and William, but it certainly meant something to Elisabeth. *What on earth was*

Malcolm up to, she wondered, *buying Watercolour Cottage in this secretive way? Could he be giving it to Fran as an extravagant gesture to woo her back?*

A few minutes later, William took his smart herringbone tweed jacket off the back of his chair and informed his father he was meeting Tom for lunch. On quizzing Rupert, Elisabeth found it was the same Tom who was the windsurfer.

'He's related to the Millers. Sir Charles died three months ago, only sixty you know, and Matthew's inherited the estate. He and Tom are great friends. Now, if you nip across the road to the delicatessen and buy us a couple of poached salmon and cucumber sandwiches, I'll put the kettle on for coffee and we'll have a little gossip. Mum's the word, though.'

The delicatessen in Southfleet was more like a traditional old grocer's shop from the early sixties, but it did stock an enormous selection of mouth-watering cheeses, and exceptionally good home-made sandwiches. Rupert moaned about the high prices, but every lunchtime he still sent Elisabeth out to buy them. She came back with a little pot of olives as well, and two slices of carrot cake. 'These are on me,' she said.

'Now, where were we, my dear?'

'Tom. You were going to tell me how you know him.'

'Ah, yes! Tom used to come to Southfleet every summer. He'd spend a few weeks with the Millers on their estate. That's how William got to know him. Super chap, set up some damn funny thing abroad, though. Jet-biking, or windsurfing, all the same thing, really, isn't it?'

Elisabeth was far too interested in what he was saying to point out that the two sports were worlds apart.

'His father's a farmer down in Kent on the Romney Marshes. If you think it's bleak here, my dear, you want to go to that god-forsaken bit of reclaimed land. You either love it or hate it.'

'So how's he related to the Millers?'

'His father and Charles were cousins. I used to think we were a bit like 'Happy Valley' up here.'

'I hope no one got shot,' said Elisabeth. 'I remember watching White Mischief. It was a series of adulterous affairs awash with alcohol.'

'It was just the party atmosphere that made me think of the similarity. We were all madly in love with our own wives, so there was never a question of adultery, although we all enjoyed a little flirt. Tom's father was married to a beautiful young girl. I only met her once just after they married. She died tragically, shortly after she'd given birth to Tom. He was devastated and I didn't see him again for about eight years. He married again but not for a long while. I think Tom must have been about twelve.'

'What a sad story,' said Elisabeth.

Rupert patted her hand.

'Anyway, that's all in the past and he's been very happily married now for many years. Sophie is a beautiful, intelligent woman, although somewhat bohemian for my taste.'

'Why doesn't Tom go back to the Romney Marshes when he's not in Greece?'

'He does, my dear, that's why you've not met him before.

He often comes back here for a week or two and stays at the Hall, but then it's back to the Romney Marshes, where he does goodness knows what all winter.'

Elisabeth's little Mini screeched into the drive of the vicarage, causing James to jump up from his chair and look out of his study window. *What on earth was she up to?* he wondered, as he watched her leap out of the car and rush around the side of the house to the back door.

Elisabeth had searched her conscience after learning about the sale of Watercolour Cottage, and come to the decision that loyalty to her friend was more important than her job. She'd be bitterly upset if she lost it, but she'd just have to take that risk.

Elisabeth rarely raised her voice, but even from his office James could clearly hear her opening sentence.

'I shouldn't be telling you this, Fran, but Malcolm is about to buy Watercolour Cottage.'

When the conversation eventually drew to a close, James confronted her.

'I have to say what you did just then was totally unethical. I'm surprised at you, Elisabeth.'

Elisabeth looked hard at the man she'd fallen in love with eighteen years before, and was disappointed with what she saw. Physically, he had hardly changed at all, but his mind, once so open, receptive, and uncondemning, had changed considerably.

'I love this place so much,' she said, 'the house, the surrounding countryside and all the diverse characters who live here and visit it, but I don't think it's done you much good. You've become a dried-up old kernel. You used to be such fun. You had such vision. I suggest you take a long, hard look at yourself, or you'll become just like all those vicars you abhorred when you were a curate.'

She left the room without waiting for a response, changed into a pair of jeans and decided to go for a quick walk before the children arrived back from school.

Down on the marshes the air was cool, and she felt a few drops of rain touch her face gently. In the far distance she could see the dark outline of the woods over at Dunsmere, spreading up and away like storm clouds. A breeze came eddying in off the sea, stirring the reeds and rippling the water. The cool touch of air reminded Elisabeth that autumn was on its way. She hoped Amy Cooper had everything under control for the Harvest Supper, but she hadn't dared broach the subject with James. The Harvest Suppers were becoming rowdier every year. Now the girls were older, a large group of their friends came along, transferring the occasion from a quiet celebration of God's bounty to something nearer a rave. Elisabeth thought it was a big improvement.

Deep in her reverie of drunken disorder and outraged parish councillors, Elisabeth didn't notice Tom coming down the path from the village.

'Hello, he said. 'Sorry to startle you, you were obviously miles away.'

'Unfortunately I wasn't, my thoughts were far too close to home for comfort, but I won't expand on that.'

'I've just been having lunch with your business colleague.'

'My goodness, that all sounds very formal, I don't think Rupert and William think of me as a business colleague.'

Elisabeth laughed. 'I'm really not much more than a glorified filing clerk, although Rupert was very adamant at my interview that I had to be a bit of a wiz with computers.'

'He's a funny old codger, but he really has got a heart of gold.'

It was cold down on the reed beds. The wind tugged at Elisabeth's scarf and blew her hair into her face. 'Shall we keep walking?' she suggested. 'It always seems a few degrees colder down here on the marsh.'

When they reached his cottage he asked her in for a cup of tea. Elisabeth looked at her watch and knew she should really get back to the vicarage before the children returned from school or, in his present state of mind, James would use it as ammunition against her. *Oh well*, she thought, *one more crime wasn't going to change things very much*. 'I'd love a cup of tea,' she said, smiling at him.

The front door opened straight into the sitting room. It was a bare room with a slightly unlived-in look about it. The furniture was very worn, having seen eight summers of holidaymakers, and the whole place needed redecorating. Elisabeth followed Tom into the little galley-like kitchen. Its contents were sparse like the rest of the cottage, but from the window there was the most glorious view right across the reed beds to Dunsmere and beyond.

'I've often passed this cottage out walking and wondered what it was like inside,' she said.

'I wish I could buy it, and then I'd spruce it up a bit, nothing too drastic because I love its rawness, but it's going to deteriorate badly if the owners don't do a few things to it soon.'

'How long are you here for?'

'I'm renting it for the whole winter, although I'll be spending some time with my family on the Romney Marshes, and then I'm back out to Greece again towards the end of March.'

'Oh yes, I've heard all about your watersports centre, although Rupert seemed a bit confused as to what exactly you do out there.'

Tom handed Elisabeth a mug of tea, and they both walked through into the main room just off the kitchen. Its simplicity made Elisabeth feel peaceful. Many of the old floorboards needed replacing and plaster was flaking off the walls, but she could understand why Tom wanted to get his hands on the cottage.

'The main thing I run is windsurfing holidays, although I've branched out into a few other things to keep the tourists happy.'

'You really should see Fran windsurfing, she's brilliant,' said Elisabeth. 'The children and I loved watching her. Whenever there was wind, she'd be out playing amongst the waves. We used to call her 'the windsurf girl'. It's such a shame she doesn't get the chance to go out now because I know she misses it dreadfully.' Elisabeth looked at Tom, sitting back in an old leather armchair which had seen better days, and thought what an attractive man he was. He was tall, with long legs and arms. His light brown hair framed a face with high cheekbones and large, serious grey eyes, but his attraction also lay in the aura about him. It was plain to see that he took life in his stride, and she had a sneaking suspicion he had a great sense of humour.

'Is Fran coming back?'

'Yes, I spoke to her last night. Annabel is on the mend and I think they're all coming back at the end of the week.'

'Hopefully she'll be able to get out windsurfing then.' He hesitated. 'I'm going to ask you a very impertinent question, and you have every right not to answer it, but is she happily married? Some comments from Lydia made me wonder.'

Now it was Elisabeth's turn to hesitate, as she questioned the wisdom of telling him what she really felt about the whole sorry saga of Fran's marriage.

'Fran married Malcolm when she was still quite young and impressionable. Her parents thought he was the 'bee's knees', but I won't mince my words, I thought he was overbearing and arrogant. He doesn't make Fran happy, and I definitely think he's a philanderer.' Elisabeth knew that James would be appalled if he could hear her discussing Fran's marriage with a man she hardly knew. Perhaps yesterday she would have been more reticent, but her conversation with Rupert had given her an insight into this man who she had an instinctive liking for.

'I'm surprised I haven't met Fran before, but I suppose I've normally been the other side of the estuary.'

'She might not be able to come to her beach hut for much longer. The land is being sold. You know the landowners, don't you?'

'Yes, Charles was my father's cousin, he sadly died three months ago. Matthew has inherited the estate, but I didn't know he was selling off any land.'

'Fran's frantic with worry, she can't bear the thought of losing her little hut, and there are more things going on, too, but I really can't tell you about those just at the moment.'

'And I've no intention of pressurising you,' said Tom with a smile.

'I promise I'll keep you posted,' responded Elisabeth. 'Now, I've got to go or I shall have a fretful husband on my hands, and they're worse than babies!'

The low cloud cover made it seem like early evening when she walked out of the door.

'Shall I walk you home? It's a bit murky out here now.'

'And get all those village spinsters' tongues wagging? I don't think I can risk it. You'd be amazed at what they see even after dark!'

5

Annabel was kept in hospital under observation for three days. At the end of them, she felt she needed to get back home for a rest. There had been an endless stream of visitors depositing grapes, flowers, and chocolates on her. It was all quite embarrassing. The lack of pleasure she got from being the centre of attention puzzled her. In the past, she would have enjoyed all the fuss, and probably sent Lydia off to Harvey Nichols to buy some attractive wraps and nighties to wear. She knew she was beginning to irritate Simon, and had stopped mentioning Warbleton to him. He obviously thought her decision to go back there was some perverse act just to annoy him.

On her return from the hospital, she saw that the answer-phone was flashing frantically. She nearly left it for Simon to pick up the messages later, and then decided to flick through them in case any were urgent. The first six were all from dinner party acquaintances hoping she was on the mend after her accident. She'd given them all a nice little topic of conversation for the dinner table. The only one to interest her was from Fran. It was somewhat garbled but obviously urgent. As soon as she'd taken her coat off and put the kettle on, she returned the call.

'What's Malcolm been up to now?' she enquired.

'I'm in a state of complete bewilderment. I need someone to pick through the pieces and try and make some sense of it. Do you feel up to it?'

'If it means giving Malcolm his just desserts, I'm up for anything. Come round, Simon's not here.'

Fran arrived fifteen minutes later, with Grace cuddled up to her like a monkey clinging to its mother.

'That's a good contraption,' said Annabel as she let Fran in. 'It looks like the thing women wear to hold their babies in when they're working in the paddy fields.'

'It's perfect to carry her around in at the moment,' said Fran. 'She's as light as a feather.' Grace gave Annabel a cheeky smile, and then burrowed her face into Fran's fleece.

'If I could guarantee having a dear little girl like that, I'd be almost tempted to have a baby myself, but I'd probably end up with a great lumping boy that howled all the time. Pop Grace on the floor, there's nothing within reach that she can harm herself on.'

Grace shot off immediately, doing a funny crab-like crawl at an amazing speed across the kitchen floor.

'What will it be coffee, or alcohol?'

'I'm drinking too much alcohol. I think it had better be a coffee.'

Fran immediately felt soothed just by being in Annabel's company. She had that effect on people, a wonderful, no-nonsense attitude but without the insensitivity which was often part of the package. It was more than six years since she had first met Annabel. After a stream of unsuccessful and rather dubious girlfriends, Simon walked through the door with her one evening and they all fell slightly in love with her.

Daphne adored her instantly, and David defrosted sufficiently to open one of his favourite wines in her honour.

Fran was seventeen, and had infuriated Simon by continually asking him when he was going to ask Annabel to marry him. 'I don't want to be shackled down by marriage,' he'd replied. All the family thought he was a fool.

When he finally walked down the aisle with her, they were all overjoyed, especially Fran, who immediately adopted Annabel as her older sister. At the wedding, Fran caught Simon kissing the chief bridesmaid behind a large horseshoe-shaped flower display. She'd given him a sound kick on the shins, and had glared at the bridesmaid. 'Some friend!' she'd shouted at her.

'Have you lost your make-up bag?' Fran asked. 'I don't think I've ever seen you without make-up on.'

Annabel glanced down at her fingernails. 'And no nail varnish. I've decided to get back to basics. All the endless dinner-parties and spending a fortune on clothes has lost its allure for me. I'm sure it's easy to say that when you've been able to go out and spend eighty pounds on one bra, but how immoral is that?'

'Is this the result of your accident?'

'I suppose it must be, but I've been feeling dissatisfied and useless for some time now.' She picked Grace up off the floor and let her play with a jade dolphin that hung on a long chain round her neck. 'I don't really want children, although you know I love Grace. I'm not sure I ever will, but sometimes I wonder if it's just that I don't want children with Simon.'

'Well, I can certainly understand that,' said Fran. 'He's so self-centred.'

'Now you know why I want to get back to Warbleton. It will give me the chance to think things through without Simon breathing down my neck. Oh, Fran,' she suddenly exclaimed, letting a restless Grace wriggle back down onto the floor, 'I feel dreadful! You've come hear to talk through your problems and I'm burdening you with mine.'

'Don't be silly, but what I've got to say could screw things up for both of us. Watercolour Cottage is going to be sold.'

Annabel looked at Fran in amazement. 'It can't be!'

'That's exactly what I said, but it is.'

'But Simon hasn't said anything to me, and when Daphne came to visit me she didn't mention a thing about it, either.'

'And guess who's buying it? Malcolm.'

'You're joking!' Annabel walked over to the Rayburn and lifted off the cafetiere of coffee, and slowly filled their cups up again.

'I'm afraid I'm not, but I haven't the faintest idea what it's all about. I'm certain Mum and Dad don't know that it's Malcolm who's made the offer.'

'How did you find out?'

'Elisabeth.'

'But how on earth did Elisabeth know?'

Fran told her about Elisabeth's new job, and the phone call she'd received from her yesterday.

Annabel had always thought Elisabeth a bit wishy-washy, but this news of her recent actions lifted her in Annabel's esteem considerably.

'Well done, Elisabeth! Now, I wonder what that rat Malcolm is up to…'

Talking of rats reminded Fran of the contact lens solution. It seemed such a silly innocent item, and she hesitated before telling Annabel.

Annabel didn't look in the least bit surprised. 'Do you still love Malcolm?' she asked.

'I don't think so. I realise now I hardly knew him when we got married, and instead of my love for him growing, it seems to diminish by the day.'

'Well, I think he's up to no good in more ways than one, and I know you don't want to hear this, but it wouldn't surprise me in the least if he was having an affair. Men like Malcolm live off their egos, they need conquests to boost them, and quite probably dodgy, lucrative business deals, too.'

Fran stood up and walked to the window and saw that the heavens had opened and great sheets of rain were cascading onto the pavements. It was a depressing sight, grey and miserable. Rain in Warbleton never looked like this whatever the time of year.

'It seems to have been raining ever since I arrived back in London,' she said.

'And you have a habit of looking out of windows whenever you're upset.' Annabel walked over to Fran and put her arm round her shoulder. 'It's not quite such a good view as the one over the estuary, is it?'

'Why do you think Malcolm's buying the cottage in this devious way?'

'Well, I don't think he's going to give it to you as an anniversary present.'

'Do you know, for the briefest moment it did cross my mind.'

'Silly girl. I think he's doing it for control. He can't bear the fact that you've got somewhere to escape to. If he whisks the cottage from under your feet, he's got just that little bit more control over you.'

'But he knows I've still got the beach hut.'

'Mmm, the beach hut.' Thinking of the beach hut still made Annabel doubt Fran's sanity. Draughty Watercolour Cottage was one thing, but a little hut on a windswept beach was quite another. 'Well, you can hardly sleep down there in the middle of winter with Grace. He'll be banking on you losing that, too. I wouldn't put it past him to offer a huge sum of money for the site and the beach huts.'

'Could he do that?'

'I don't see why not. If Sir who-ever-he-is, gets a nice big lump sum offered to him, he'll probably forget all about trying to do the right thing by the beach hut owners.'

'And what's Malcolm going to do with the cottage?'

'Probably sell it again, or let it out.'

The noise of farm animals sprang up from the corner of the room where Grace was playing with one of the toys Fran had brought along to entertain her. A realistic succession of mooing, squawking and barking filled the kitchen.

'It still doesn't make much sense,' said Fran wearily. 'I can't believe he's that obsessed about trying to stop me going there to go to these lengths.'

'Why do you think he doesn't like you windsurfing?'

'He's never actually said he doesn't.'

'What about when we went to France before you were pregnant with Grace? You said the conditions were perfect for windsurfing, and there was that centre right next to the hotel with kit for hire, but whenever you tried to go out, Malcolm dragged us all off on another sightseeing trip. Fran, just accept the fact, he's a control freak.'

They went into the sitting room and Fran sat Grace on a rocking horse that had a wistful smile playing on its mouth, and large, almond-shaped eyes. It had been in Annabel's family for three generations and she'd recently sent it down to a workshop in Kent to be repaired. It had come back with a beautiful flowing mane and tail, and she'd hardly recognised the sorry creature she'd sent away four weeks before.

Fran held onto Grace, absently rocking her backwards and forwards. Annabel had turned on the mock log fire that settled immediately into brilliant flames. It was just another reminder of the many things she missed when she was away from Warbleton. However authentic, it was a poor substitute for the smell of apple logs burning, or even the throbbing heat that her little pot-bellied stove released in the beach hut.

'You're somewhere else, Fran,' said Annabel, 'and that's not going to sort out your problems.'

'I was thinking about the massive fireplace in Watercolour Cottage, and the wonderful log fires we have there.'

'If that's still to be a part of our lives, we'd better put our thinking caps on and come up with something good pretty quickly. For a start, you'd better tell Daphne and David who's buying their house.'

'What's the point? Mum and Dad, as you well know, think Malcolm can do no wrong. They'll think he's acting with the best intentions, relieving them of a property they don't really want, and keeping it in the family.'

'Confront Malcolm, and ask him what he's playing at.'

'If I do that, or even if I tell Mum and Dad, I'll compromise Elisabeth, and put her job into jeopardy.'

The telephone sprang to life on the antique desk that Simon sat at occasionally, to justify having spent a small fortune on.

Annabel pulled a face at Fran and mouthed, 'It's Lydia.'

'I've been trying to get hold of Fran,' she heard Lydia say, in a slightly breathless voice.

'Well, you won't get hold of her because she's here.'

'Do you know when she's going back to Warbleton?'

'Why?'

'What do you mean, why?' snapped Lydia down the phone.

'If *you're* thinking of going back, it can only be for one reason, and that's men. For goodness' sake, Lydia, leave the poor local chaps alone, they don't need you destroying their country idyll.'

'Mind your own business, Annabel. I want to speak to Fran.'

Annabel reluctantly passed the telephone to Fran, pulling a face as she did so. She took over rocking Grace backwards and forwards. She imagined Grace would be quite happy rocking for eternity, with her little hands clasping the silky mane.

By the time Fran hung up, it had been arranged. Lydia was coming, too.

'So who do you think she's after?' said Annabel. 'Tom or George, or perhaps the handsome vet?'

'Probably all of them, knowing Lydia, and good luck to

her. I've got quite enough on my plate at the moment without complicating matters.'

'So you do have a soft spot for this Tom chap. Lydia hinted as much.'

'Perhaps Malcolm and I both need different types of people. It's not his fault, I'm just not right for him.'

'Don't start feeling sorry for Malcolm. For a start, he's twelve years older than you, and knew exactly what he was taking on when he married you. Your parents should never have pushed you into it.'

'I should never have been so weak as to let them.'

'Let's be positive, Fran. I've got a little plan hatching in my mind. Now I'll ring for a taxi, because you can't possibly walk back in this rain.'

The first thing Annabel did when Fran walked out of the front door was to ring directory enquiries to find out the number of Companies House. After working through the usual sequence of recorded messages and pressing different numbers in the hope of getting through to the right department, she had a bit of success. A rather impatient man at the end of the line told her she could have access to records of all company mergers and takeovers during the last twelve months. She was convinced that Malcolm was doing some insider dealing, and that Simon was his stooge. The difficult part would be proving it.

Half an hour and two gins later, she felt she'd devised a fairly foolproof plan. Unfortunately, it revolved around blackmail but, considering the recipient deserved everything he got, she didn't feel too guilty.

Simon's study was at the top of the house. It was a typical

man's den and, much to Annabel's amusement, even had a rather tasteless calendar pinned to the wall showing scantily clad girls grinning down at him when he sat at his desk. She could understand the calendar, knowing some men never really grew out of their adolescent yearnings, but she was surprised to see a small pile of porn magazines on the windowsill, partially obscured by the curtain. She couldn't remember the last time she'd been up to his study, but she was sure they hadn't been there on that occasion.

She systematically worked her way through his filing cabinet and took out all the share certificates she could find, and a nice, thick wedge of bank statements that looked as though they covered several years. They'd always had their own separate bank accounts as well as a joint household one. Whenever she'd asked Simon where all the money came from to buy expensive cars and enable them to lead their extravagant lifestyle, he'd been evasive but if she was honest, she'd always felt the sums didn't really add up. She made sure nothing looked as though it had been disturbed, and went downstairs feeling quite exhausted. They weren't going back to Warbleton until the day after tomorrow, so she had time to photocopy the share certificates and bank statements, and pay a visit to Companies House tomorrow.

Fran felt a stirring of anxiety. She'd already had a bath and got ready for bed but Malcolm still wasn't home. The clock looked accusingly at her, as the hands kept notching up the hours and still there was no phone call to let her know where he was, or why he was still out after midnight. There'd been many nights when she'd sat in the house alone and actually rather enjoyed her solitude, but that was when Malcolm had called and said he was out drinking with business colleagues. She hadn't minded at all; she expected him to wheel and deal after working hours. He was always telling her it was an unavoidable part of his job, along with the golf tours and trips abroad. Work officially finished at five thirty, although he was never home before eight. Tonight, for the first time since they'd married, there was no call, and when she tried his mobile phone it appeared to be switched off.

She rang Annabel to ask if he was over there, but Simon answered the phone and irritably told her that Malcolm wasn't there, and what the hell did she think she was doing ringing up after midnight when Annabel was convalescing.

She had just drifted off into an uneasy sleep when he came into the bedroom. She heard him fumbling for the light switch.

'Where have you been?' she asked sleepily. 'I had visions of you in a head-on collision round Piccadilly Circus.'

'Fat lot you'd care,' he muttered.

She felt such a sense of relief that he was safe, that she sank back into the time when he'd meant so much to her.

He sat on the edge of the bed looking sad, and even a little bit lost.

'I do love you, Fran,' he said, and taking off his clothes, he slipped into bed beside her.

She'd refused to have sex with him since her return, but now her sleepiness and relief made her accept his advances.

I have to try and make it work, she thought, *just one more time. I must try.*

It was still dark when Malcolm left the next morning. He had to be in Amsterdam by ten and was driving to City Airport to catch an early flight. Fran snuggled back under the duvet, and was just congratulating herself on having such a model baby when an unusual wailing came from the little room at the end of the corridor. Fran jumped out of bed and trod on something sharp and pointed. Bending down, she found it was a pearl earring. She placed it on the bedside table and went to get Grace. Her arms went up to be lifted out of the cot as soon as Fran went into the room. Her little scrunched-up face was wet with tears, but Fran had no idea why she'd been crying. Her nappy was clean and the moment Fran picked her up she seemed happy.

With Grace in her arms, Fran walked back to her bedroom. She put her down to crawl on the carpet, then looked again at the earring. *Earrings normally come in pairs*, she thought kneeling down beside the bed to see if she could find its partner. After a short search, she found it. They were pretty earrings featuring a circle of small pearls round one larger central one, but they weren't hers.

Annabel rang after lunch telling her she'd been to Companies House and proved beyond doubt that Malcolm was doing some 'insider dealing'. Fran told Annabel she had no idea what 'insider dealing' was.

'Well, I wouldn't, either, if I hadn't done that dreadful temping work in the City before I married Simon. I'll explain all when I see you.'

They made plans to drive back to Warbleton the next morning. Fran couldn't face telling Annabel about the earrings. She felt sick and couldn't settle to doing anything; even entertaining Grace was a chore.

When the sun miraculously appeared, she put Grace in a pushchair and went to her favourite café only five minutes walk away. She sat in the corner and smiled absently at the Italian waiter whilst he cooed over Grace. He flirted with Fran charmingly, and asked her why she hadn't been in for so long. Fran found it difficult to return the harmless banter. She just wanted to sit quietly on her own and decide what on earth she was going to do. She opened the little brown tube of sugar and stirred it into her coffee through the froth. An old lady walked in and sat at the table next to her. Having charge of a baby was just as bad as walking down a street with a small, cuddly puppy, it was impossible to merge into the background and remain anonymous. People homed in on you and struck up conversation when they wouldn't have dreamt of doing so if you'd been on your own. The old lady proceeded to tell Fran that she had nine grandchildren. Two were in Australia, one in South Africa, and she wasn't too sure where the other six were. Fran found herself wanting to say, 'My husband's being unfaithful to me!' but she just smiled and asked a few questions about the grandchildren and then concentrated on clearing up the mess Grace was making with a biscuit.

Malcolm rang from City Airport at five to say he'd be home before Grace went to sleep, but he had to call in at the office to sort a couple of things out. He sounded just like he used to when they were first married, warm and fun. 'Don't prepare supper,' he said, just as the signal was beginning to fail, but the rest was lost in a mixture of dislocated words.

Despite his promise, Grace had been asleep for over an hour when he walked into the hall with an Italian take-away, two bottles of Charles Heidsick champagne and an exquisite bouquet of flowers from Wild at Heart.

'Now, you sort this little lot out,' he said, walking through into the kitchen and placing everything on the table, 'and I'll have a quick shower. Let's eat in the dining room,' he shouted, as he took the stairs two at a time.

As soon as he disappeared, she uncorked the champagne and poured herself a glass. She gulped it down as though it was a glass of lemonade and quickly poured herself another one. She wouldn't think about the stupid pearl earrings again until after the meal, she decided.

She felt as though she were acting out a scene from a play as she sat at the table with Malcolm, eating the Italian meal as though she hadn't a care in the world. She sipped champagne, smiling in response to his light-hearted teasing. She was sure there had to be another reason for the earrings, other than her worst fears, but what? Was she being incredibly naïve? All the obvious signs of infidelity over the past few weeks could not be a coincidence.

Malcolm uncorked the second bottle of champagne and topped up their glasses.

'I've been thinking,' he said, 'about buying a place in France. Nothing too fancy, but with Eurostar operating a little more efficiently now, we could be across the channel and tucking into some rather nice French cuisine in less time than it takes to get to Warbleton on a Friday night. Brendon's just bought a place about half an hour's drive from Calais, and a property's come up for sale in the same village. He's going to put some feelers out this weekend when he goes over there. How about that, Fran? A place in France!'

'Next door to Brendon and Marjorie!'

As soon as the comment had left her lips, she regretted making it, as Malcom's expression immediately changed, making him look like a different person.

'You just have to do it, don't you?' he said furiously. 'At least they're more entertaining than those country yokels you mix with in Warbleton.'

She knew it was the wrong time to bring it up; she told herself not to say anything even as the words were coming out of her mouth. One moment she was about to say how selfish she was and how wonderful a house in France would be, with or without the Fletcher's as neighbours, but instead she found herself saying: 'Pearl earrings. I don't wear pearl earrings, but I found a pair in our bedroom on the floor, they were next to my side of the bed.'

For a full minute he stared at her, and then just said he was sorry.

'What do you mean, *sorry*?'

'These things happen, Fran. It meant absolutely nothing. I swear I won't do it again.'

'So you're not going to say the earrings are mine, and that I'm just going mad, or they belong to a friend of mine who decided to wander into our bedroom and throw them on the floor?'

'You've just summed it up, the evidence is too damning.'

'Damn you, then!' she shouted at him, jumping to her feet.

He leaned back in his chair, clasped his hands behind his head and cooly said, 'You're so bloody naïve, Fran. Loads of men have affairs. Let's just forget all about it and make a fresh start.'

'Until the next time.' She was so tense and angry, she was finding it difficult to breathe.

'There won't be a next time, I promise.'

'But in our bed!'

'It wasn't meant to happen like that.'

'How was it supposed to happen? In a hotel room? In the back of a car?'

She wished she could be calm but she couldn't. Too much champagne was making her head swim, and she had the dreadful feeling that she was going to break down and cry, which would be the ultimate humiliation.

She choked out the words, 'Was it Sandra?' not knowing if she wanted to hear the truth.

'Does it matter?'

'Yes, it does matter, it matters a lot, because if it was Sandra, then it obviously happened out in Moscow as well.'

'I'm not saying who it was.'

'You don't bloody well need to, it's too obvious, you bloody bastard!'

Malcolm was looking at her as if she had suddenly turned into something rather nasty, and she felt she had. She wanted to pick up her plate and throw it in his smug face, and keep shouting, 'Bloody bastard'. A little mewing cry came out of the baby monitor. The sound transfixed Fran. What on earth was she doing, shrieking like a fishwife?

'I'm going to bed,' she said, in as dignified a way as she could manage, 'and it won't be in our bedroom.'

'It's so annoying that Lydia's coming,' said Annabel down the phone early the next morning. Fran was in the kitchen drinking glassfuls of water; a sleepless night and too much alcohol had taken their toll. 'I'm just dying to tell you what I've found out. You're not going to believe it, sweetie. Malcolm and Simon are in it up to their necks.'

'I hope they both get strangled,' Fran muttered down the phone.

'I didn't quite catch that.'

'I said, I hope they're both bloody strangled,' she shouted. 'What's he done?'

'Had sex in our four poster bed with some tart, who I'm pretty certain goes by the name of Sandra.'

Fran knew she was going to cry again. She despised herself, it was just too pathetic for words. There was a brief silence at the other end of the line.

'Well, I can't say I'm surprised. Let's just get to Warbleton and unload Lydia, and we'll talk about everything there,' said Annabel calmly. 'And don't you dare cry, no man's worth it.'

Fran tried to be positive on the drive back to Warbleton. She knew her love for Malcolm had died long before she was prepared to admit it to herself. It was the blatant betrayal that hurt. The A12 seemed to wind on interminably. She just wanted to get there and hide herself away in the beach hut.

Lydia asked her what she'd been crying about.

'Nothing,' she replied, staring at the road ahead and willing the miles to fly by.

'Don't be silly, you don't cry about nothing, and your

eyes are all red and puffy so you've obviously had a good crying session.'

Annabel told Lydia to shut up and show a little more sensitivity.

'Don't tell me to shut up, I'm only asking.'

Grace was being unusually fretful in her car seat next to Lydia, and grizzled and kicked her legs.

'Can't you make her stop that horrid noise?' grumbled Lydia.

'Sometimes,' said Annabel, 'you're quite unbelievable.'

The beach hut had been invaded by mice during the six days Fran was in London. It was impossible to discover where the little vermin had entered, but it happened every year. Their telltale droppings were everywhere; in the small larder, behind the bread bin, even on top of the pot-bellied stove, although what they hoped to find there she had no idea. She was going to have to lay mousetraps in strategic places well out of Grace's reach. She hated doing it and felt evil when she found the little limp bodies, but it had to be done.

She turned the calor gas on and fired up the stove to make a cup of tea, and felt the usual peace spread through her. It never changed. The moment she touched down in Warbleton, the world seemed to tilt on its axis and resume its correct planetary position.

Lydia knew something was up. Both Annabel and Fran were acting oddly and they obviously didn't want her in on their little secret. She felt irritated and resentful, and now Annabel was fobbing her off with some ridiculous notion that she wanted to go for a walk on the marsh to clear her head. Annabel didn't walk anywhere, she either went in a taxi or drove Simon's Porsche. During the drive back up to Warbleton, she had begun to wonder about the sanity of her decision. It really wasn't her sort of place at all, but she did want another session with George, and she certainly wasn't going to let Tom escape so easily.

'That sister of mine,' said Annabel, 'is a complete pain.' She slotted herself onto the little bench that doubled up as a bed and took off her fur jacket. 'Darling, is Grace all right crawling about on this floor?'

'Probably not. I've got to exterminate all the mice in here. I can't have mouse droppings everywhere.'

Annabel gave a little grimace, and checked the bench she was sitting on for any trace of vermin.

'If you want to reject London and the dinner party set and spend more time down here, you're going to have to throw away your fur coat and control your passion for wanting to disinfect everything,' pointed out Fran with a smile.

'Give it time,' laughed Annabel, 'I'm working on it. Now, where shall we start?'

'You go first.'

'Okay, but you've got to concentrate. No wandering off thinking about adultery, because if you want revenge, I've got bucket-loads of it.'

Annabel had diligently photocopied all the share certificates and bank statements that she'd taken out of Simon's file, and then replaced them carefully in what she hoped were exactly the right places. The trip to Companies House had proved her suspicions were correct. Eight out of the ten companies Simon had bought shares in over the past six months had been the subject of take-overs or mergers within a few days of the purchase. The share prices had immediately rocketed and Simon had sold, making an enormous profit. Looking at his bank statements, Annabel saw that a large sum was always paid out soon after the funds were credited to his account. It didn't take a genius to guess who received the money.

'They're living dangerously, Fran. A tip-off from us could lead to a jail sentence.'

'I'd no idea it was that serious.'

'And I'd no idea Simon and Malcolm could be quite so stupid, but now we must decide how we want to use the information. We've definitely got Malcolm nailed. One little phone-call from me, and hopefully I'll have him grovelling.'

'But won't he think you'll back off if it means incriminating Simon?'

'I'll bluff. I'll say I don't give a damn if Simon is taken down with him, although I wouldn't really want to see Simon in jail.'

'I'd be quite happy if Malcolm rotted in jail!'

'Well, sweetie, I don't blame you, but let's keep clear heads and hopefully we'll save Watercolour Cottage.'

Fran thought of her mother's clinical attitude towards the sale. She had always had the ability to emotionally detach herself from anything that hinted of sentiment.

'Mum and Dad will sell the house now, anyway, I'm certain of that.'

'Blocking Malcolm's offer will give us time. As long as the house doesn't fall into his hands, I'm sure that between the two of us we'll come up with something.'

6

George had experienced a nightmare week with Phoebe and could only come to the conclusion that Lydia had unwittingly landed him in it. Nothing else could account for the way she blanked him when he went into the pub. She was barely civil, and slammed his pint down so hard on the marble-topped bar that he feared for its safety. This lunchtime, however, he was optimistic that he'd see her seductive smile again, and those wonderful nut-brown eyes light up with enthusiasm. He was going to ask her to accompany him to the Harvest Supper. He'd heard it was quite a wicked do, unlike the sorry little affairs he'd been to throughout his early teenage years, where you'd been lucky to get a tepid glass of Liebfraumilch.

The geese were in a peaceful group, lying on the green in front of the pub, but when they spotted George, they swayed their necks in unison and greeted him with a tumult of noise. All the locals were used to the geese but they deterred many a casual visitor. Sometimes they wandered onto the road and had a querulous conversation with each other until some brave motorist moved them on.

George had enthusiastically adopted the pub as his local when he'd walked through the doors on a cold spring morning six months before. What he loved most about The Reed and Whistle was that, in a changing world, it seemed to be treading water. It had old floorboards instead of carpets, no fruit machines or piped music and, best of all, beer and cider were drawn from a cask. It didn't get much better than that, he thought.

The geese, in a sudden flurry of excitement, surrounded George and followed him to the door. One vicious old gander spread its swings, stretched out its neck and gave him a vicious peck on the leg. 'Shoo!' shouted George and fell into the pub in an embarrassed heap.

'Damn geese,' he grumbled to James and Jack, who were sitting in their usual lunchtime places up at the bar, 'I've never had one of them peck me before. It had quite a murderous glint in its eye.'

There was no sign of Phoebe so he asked James if the Harvest Supper tickets were for sale yet.

'Amy Cooper's in charge of things this year. I think she's decided to sell the tickets through Mrs. Kennard in the village shop.'

Phoebe swept back into the bar in a haze of smoke, holding her cigarette with the awkwardness of an occasional smoker.

'We were just talking about the Harvest Supper,' said George casually. 'Would you like to come to it with me, Phoebe?'

'I'm not too sure I want to go with an animal.'

George was completely lost. What on earth was she on about?

'Sex with Lydia,' Phoebe announced loudly.

George glanced at James and Jack, and saw them exchange a quick grin.

'I know you did it with Lydia, and apparently with great animal passion.'

George wished he could just disappear beneath the floorboards.

'I can explain all that, Phoebe.'

'I really wouldn't bother. Now, if you'll excuse me, I've some barrels to change.'

'Never mind,' said Jack, giving George an affectionate pat on the back, 'the course of true love never did run smooth.'

George watched Phoebe's retreating figure. 'You can say that again!'

Phoebe stood in the back garden willing herself not to cry. Waterproof mascara completely failed to live up to its name after a crying session, and the result was enough to make you want to cry again.

*

Tom had been dreadfully tempted to call round to the beach hut to see Fran, but decided to leave her for a few days to settle in again. He didn't want her to think he was pestering her. If she was having marital problems, then the last thing she needed was him hanging around like a lovesick teenager. A good, long walk would sort him out. He had a twinge of guilt when he looked at his laptop firmly closed on a makeshift desk, but cash-flow forecasts for next season were going to have to wait. He'd head off across the reed beds and pay George an early morning call.

The vast stretch of marsh between Warbleton and

Dunsmere was utterly deserted. The enthusiastic 'twitchers' with their binoculars and tripods tended to drift onto the reed beds later in the morning. Most of them stayed in bed and breakfasts and wanted to get their money's worth by devouring everything on offer at the breakfast table.

The air was full of the cry of seabirds. Pairs of striking black and white Avocets circled above him, agitated and panicked by his intrusion into their peaceful morning's fishing. Amongst the reeds, insignificant little brown birds flitted and danced from one bending stalk to the next in a game of hide and seek. It all seemed a world away from Greece, rather than a short three to four hour flight.

There, at the height of the holiday season, he treasured the moments he could get away on his own, hiking up into the mountains and staying in remote villages. The old women still dressed in black, and men with wrinkled, leathery faces sat on dusty steps, smoking pipes and occasionally talking to each other beneath the hot sun. He'd come across vast stretches of sandy beaches that could only be reached by scrambling down almost sheer slopes of olive groves. The windswept shores of Suffolk could not have been a greater contrast. The grey hues of sea and sky were so different to the brilliant shades of blue and aqua that circled the Greek islands and held the warm, golden sun that rarely hid behind any clouds, but he loved the wildness of the marsh with the same passion he felt for Greece; it would have been difficult to trade one for the other.

George was devouring a substantial breakfast when Tom popped his head over the stable door.

'I wish you hadn't done that. For a split second I thought it might be Lydia again.'

'I was wondering if you'd flushed out any exotic birds recently.'

'It's not funny, Tom. I've really fouled things up this time.'

'And all for the lovely Lydia. Girls like that are bad news, I did warn you. I see your disastrous love life hasn't affected your appetite, though!'

George took breakfast seriously; he usually devoured an enormous bowl of porridge, and at least five rashers of bacon with two or three fried eggs, washing it all down with cups of strong coffee. He tried to talk through a mouthful of fried bread.

'She couldn't keep her hands off me. I've never had anything like that happen to me before. It was the sort of thing I fantasised about in my teens, a beautiful, blonde girl desperate to have sex with me. I mean, what was a chap to do? But now Phoebe knows, and only Lydia could have told her.'

'I hope you didn't... '

'Yes, I did,' groaned George, not wanting to hear Tom put it into words. 'A matter of hours later.'

Tom couldn't help grinning. 'You're a bit of a dark horse. I wouldn't have thought you were the type.'

'I'm not, it's all so horribly unfair. I've never done anything remotely like that before, ever.'

George stood up and added his greasy plate to a pile of unwashed dishes in the sink.

'What do you want, anyway?' he said grumpily. 'You must have been up at the crack of dawn.'

'Do you know William Bidwell? His family are part of the Bidwell & Symmonds estate agents in Southfleet.'

'I haven't really got to know anyone outside Warbleton yet, but James was lamenting in the pub the other night about some wretched firm of estate agents in Southfleet who had seduced his wife away from his side.'

'That's the one. I've known William since we were both little chaps messing about in boats. Come up to the pub tonight, we're meeting at eight.'

'Well, I suppose another evening watching Phoebe glowering at me will make a change!'

George arrived at The Reed and Whistle at half past eight. He'd almost decided to give it a miss, but felt it might look a bit churlish. Phoebe's demeanour had completely changed since lunchtime. She seemed to be positively bubbling over with excitement as she leant over the bar, in what George felt was a very provocative way, talking to Tom's friend William.

'William, I want to introduce you to a friend of mine,' said Tom.

William reluctantly tore his attention away from Phoebe and shook hands with George.

'So you're the new game warden,' said William.

'Hardly a game warden,' said George. 'It makes me sound as though I roam across the plains of Africa keeping an eye on giraffes and elephants.'

'Are we all drinking Adnams?' asked Tom.

Phoebe served Tom, and then continued her conversation with William, completely ignoring George's presence.

'So, you really think there might be a bit of part-time work for me?' she asked him.

'I'll check with Dad, but I'm certain we need someone else just two mornings a week to do some filing and typing. Elisabeth has turned out to be a bit of a whiz on the computer, so Dad can't fob her off with all the little jobs he was planning to. I'm afraid it won't be very exciting, but it could do the trick until you find something better.'

'What it is doesn't really matter. I just want to get away from Warbleton sometimes, even if it is only to the other side of the estuary.'

'Well, that's sorted then. I'll give you a call tomorrow after I've spoken with Dad.'

'I thought you'd just taken on the vicar's wife. Are you trying to lure all the women away from Warbleton?' said George.

'If they're all like Elisabeth and Phoebe, I'd be quite happy to,' he replied. 'I mean, just look at her,' he added, watching Phoebe have a little flirt with Jack Henshaw whilst serving him. 'She seems much more fun than the horsey types with too many teeth that I seem to get tied up with. I'm fed up with girls who can't outgrow their childhood love affair with horses.'

'I suppose you ride and hunt?' asked George.

'Well, yes I do, but I don't necessarily want my girlfriends to.'

'Hunting's barbaric. Whenever I think of hunting, I just see a load of pompous snobs dressed up to the nines intent on chasing a little creature to its death. You even dig the poor bastard out when it's won the race.'

'We don't,' said William indignantly, 'and I'm amazed, considering your job, that you have that attitude. What about preservation of the countryside, and controlling the fox population? You know full well, if hunting were to be banned there would be thousands of people out of work. It extends much further than seeing a few pompous snobs on horseback.'

'Come on, chaps,' said Tom. 'Two topics definitely not up for discussion over a quiet pint in the local are fox hunting and religion. You don't see James waving the banner in here at night.'

George knew he was embarrassing himself, but he wished the curly-haired, foppish William would stop feasting his eyes on Phoebe's cleavage. He felt a tap on his shoulder and turned round to see Lydia looking at him with what he could only describe as hungry eyes.

'Hello,' she whispered in his ear, 'I thought it was time you and I had a bit more fun.'

⋆

They met half way along the A12 in the car park of a motorway café seething with people. Annabel usually avoided these faceless places that made her feel like an insignificant ant on a mad planet, but it seemed an appropriate place to confront Malcolm. She got stuck behind an agonisingly slow lorry on a stretch of road she couldn't overtake on, the minutes ticked away and she was certain she'd be late. Fran's car hadn't helped matters. She hated driving a car she wasn't used to; all the switches seemed the wrong way round and she spent the first part of the journey watching the windscreen wipers flashing across the windscreen every time she went to indicate. When, to her relief, the road swung into a dual carriageway, she signalled and pulled out to overtake. An irate motorist blasted his horn as he screamed past and squashed her back behind the lorry. The stupid windscreen wipers were going crazy again. She felt herself shaking. It had been a near miss.

Amazingly, she drove into the car park at exactly two thirty. She saw his unmistakeable red Porsche immediately, parked by some bushes on the far side of the car park. She pulled up next to him, wound down her window and told him to get in. Her words made her want to laugh. She felt a film crew was going to appear at any moment, and she was playing the leading role. He wrenched open the door and threw himself aggressively into the seat next to her.

'What the hell's all this about?' he demanded. 'I've cancelled meetings and left a hundred and one things that need doing, so this had better be worth it.'

A couple in a Ford Fiesta parked up next to them seemed delighted by the diversion and watched with interest whilst they sipped coffee out of plastic cups. Annabel wanted to shout at them to mind their own business. She was sure they thought they were watching an illicit rendezvous. It certainly couldn't have been much further from the truth.

She undid the folder jammed full with photocopied share certificates, bank statements and all the evidence of the mergers and take-overs, and placed them on his lap.

Malcolm glanced down at them. He looked flustered and edgy. Annabel noticed small pouches under his eyes that could have been the result of sleepless nights, or too much alcohol, or quite probably both. He picked several of the sheets of paper up and then screwed them into tiny balls and threw them on the floor at his feet.

'Well?' he said.

Annabel decided to go straight for the jugular.

'I've got conclusive evidence you've been doing some insider dealing, and that Simon's involved too.'

Malcolm laughed. She expected several reactions to her statement but not laughter.

'Why are you laughing? I don't see what is so amusing about committing a criminal act that could land you in jail.' She felt a sudden urge to slap him round his grinning face.

'You girls are so silly and naïve. So long as no one finds out, and they won't, it really doesn't matter. It's all part of the game, to make money whilst you can.'

She could tell by the way he sat back in his seat and pushed the rest of the papers casually off his lap that he thought he was back in control of the situation.

'If you don't rescind your offer on Watercolour Cottage your company will receive all the evidence necessary to land you in jail.'

He looked at her in surprise.

'How the hell do you know about Watercolour Cottage?'

'Where I've got my information is none of your business. What I want to know is just what your little game is?'

Malcolm shifted uncomfortably in his seat.

'Prices are going to escalate in Warbleton and I just felt it was going to be a good investment.'

'So you were going to tell Fran, and give it to her as a present?' Annabel said with derision.

'Not exactly. I'll probably sell it on in six months.'

'No doubt at a profit.'

'If you read the national newspapers, you'd realise Warbleton and several places up in Suffolk and Norfolk have become the new 'in places' for second homes. The house prices are going to rocket.'

'So you were going to dupe Daphne and David into selling for your own gain.'

'They're loaded, they don't need the house or more money.'

'But you do?'

Malcolm suddenly flipped. She knew it was coming; the telltale fist-clenching and tiny beads of sweat on his forehead became more obvious. He thrust his face close to hers. She could smell his garlic breath and felt quite sick.

'Your husband's a fool!' he bellowed at her. 'I should have known better than to involve him in my little scam. You're going to regret this, too, you stupid bitch. What do you think Simon's going to say when he finds out?'

Annabel did her best not to flinch away from him. She had no intention of letting him think he'd managed to frighten her. She said in a calm, controlled voice: 'He won't, because you're not going to tell him, and if I hear the sale of Watercolour Cottage is proceeding, there'll be some interesting documents landing on your managing director's desk.'

'So, I'm being blackmailed.'

'No, if I was going to blackmail you, I'd tell you to go

ahead and buy the house and put it in Fran's name, but I know she wouldn't want that. You're a hard, crooked, adulterous bastard and the sooner she's rid of you, the better.'

'And what about your stupid husband? You're quite happy to land him in jail too are you?'

'I don't agree with breaking the law and as his wife, with the knowledge I now possess, I would be an accessory to the crime.'

Malcolm glared at her, his face horribly close again.

'I think you're bluffing.'

'I don't think you can afford to take that risk, do you?'

He wrenched the door-handle down and flung open the door.

'Don't think for a moment you've won, or that this is the end of it. It's just the first round.' He slammed the door viciously behind him.

Within seconds, he'd revved up his engine and screamed out of the car park.

Annabel bent over the steering wheel and took deep breaths. Her hand trembled as she went to turn the key in the ignition. The lady drinking coffee in the next car leant out of the window and asked her if she was feeling all right. Annabel didn't know whether to be grateful for her solicitude or to tell her to mind her own business, but she looked genuinely anxious and had a kind face, so she thanked her and said she was fine.

It took her an hour to get back to Walberton. She hoped she'd accomplished what she had set out to do, but for some reason she didn't feel the taste of victory.

After parking Fran's car in a small field that served as a

car park for the occupants of the huts, she went straight down to the beach hut. Up until the last few days, she had rarely walked down the path that led from the village to Fran's hut. If she wanted to sunbathe, she went to the beach next to the jetty. It was easier to reach from the car park, and she didn't have to flounder over sand dunes and trip up over great tussocks of marram grass to get to it. Whenever she ventured to the hut, the wind always seemed to be shrieking off the sea, which made sitting on the veranda impossible. Inside the hut, although she had to admit it had a quaint charm, she felt like a rabbit trapped in a cage.

Annabel's appearance shocked Fran. The wind had tugged out pieces of hair from the velvet hair-band she wore, and she looked incredibly pale.

'Goodness, you look all in,' she said 'I don't think you should have gone chasing off to meet Malcolm so soon after your accident.'

'Stop fussing, I'm absolutely fine.'

Annabel sat down on one of the chairs and tipped sand out of her shoes.

'Is our game plan up and running?'

'You bet it is. I think I've well and truly nailed the bastard. He definitely won't be buying Watercolour Cottage. Now you've just got to think of a way of persuading your parents to keep it.'

'I wish I had enough money to buy it.'

'Fran, sweetie, you're being very naïve. If you divorce Malcolm, you will.'

'I don't want a penny of his dodgy money.'

'You're not talking rationally. You've got a baby to look after, you can't survive without money.'

'I'll rent a shop in Southfleet and have the florist's shop I always wanted. I've still got some of my inheritance money left.'

Annabel decided this was not the right time to give Fran a lecture on the realities of life.

'Are you going to fire up your funny little stove and make us a cup of tea?'

They went inside and the kettle soon filled the hut with steam, and Fran had to open the top part of the stable door because Annabel said she felt she was going to suffocate.

'So Malcolm just agreed to withdraw his offer without a fight?'

'I think he very quickly realised he'd no choice, all the documents tied up. Within days of Simon buying shares in a company, there would be a takeover or merger and the share prices would rocket. He would then sell his shares at an enormous profit, and every time a large sum of money was deposited into his account, half was transferred to another bank account. Well, it doesn't take a genius to know whose account that was.'

Fran picked Grace up and took a large pebble out of her mouth that had somehow found its way into the beach hut. Annabel watched as large tears welled up in Fran's eyes and she started crying. It began with quiet sobs but swiftly turned into great big gulps.

'I still can't quite believe he slept with Sandra,' she said, between sobs. 'It's the sort of thing that happens to other people, like illness and other bad things. You never quite believe such disasters could actually happen to you. Do you suppose it's a safety barrier that's put into everyone's minds at birth so the human race can function properly?'

Annabel sat on the narrow bench next to her and swept them both into her arms.

'So stupid, crying,' Fran gasped between sobs. 'I know I don't love Malcolm any more. I loved the person I thought he was, but it's all so sordid. I feel what he did was a betrayal of Grace, too.'

She gave Annabel a swift kiss on the cheek. 'Thanks you're an angel to have gone off and confronted Malcolm, but now I'm wondering why you bothered.'

'It's escalated beyond saving the house,' confessed Annabel. 'The moment I realised the extent of their fraud, I knew I had to put a stop to it. In a way, we're doing them a favour. They'd only have got caught in the end. Now, calm down or you're going to upset that precious bundle.' She took Grace out of Fran's arms, and stroked the cap of dark hair that made her think of the smooth coat of a mole.

'When does a baby's hair start to grow?' she asked.

'Soon, I can just see some little curls beginning to appear. Oh, how could he, Annabel? How could he risk losing Grace?'

'You've just got to be strong and face up to it. You're going to have to divorce him, and it's all going to be beastly, but I'll help you through it.'

'You're such a special person, Annabel. Why are you doing all this for me?'

Annabel looked at her and knew exactly why she was doing it. It wasn't that she felt Fran was incapable of standing up for herself, or that she was too weak to fight her own battles. She quite simply loved her just as if she really was her little sister. Fran was funny and kind, and she'd shown Annabel that not everyone in life was out to gain at the expense of others. It was a unique quality. She thought about Lydia and all the nasty things she'd done since she was quite a small child. She had tried to love her from the moment she realised she didn't; it had been an uncomfortable companion all these years, but it was difficult to love someone who lived in a cocoon of gratuitous self-centredness all the time. She didn't feel it was an appropriate moment to start pouring all this out to Fran, though, so she simply told her that girls had to stick together.

'Now, no more crying, we've got to keep cool heads for the next part of our strategy.'

They were both delighted when Elisabeth appeared a few minutes later.

'Here comes the heroine of the story,' laughed Annabel.

Elisabeth had changed in the week Fran had been away. Her hair had been stylishly cut, and there was a hint of nail varnish colouring her nails, but the most noticeable thing was her new air of confidence.

'I know it's stupid,' she said, sitting in the space they'd made between them, 'but I feel like a new woman, and all because of an ordinary job in an estate agents.'

'It's not stupid, it's being your own person again, feeling you're in control. I wish I felt like that,' said Fran.

They updated her on everything that had happened over the past week, leaving nothing out. None of it surprised Elisabeth.

'So what happens next?' she asked.

'We're working on it,' replied Annabel.

The faintest pitter-patter of rain on the roof of the beach hut suddenly became a hammering.

'It looks as though we're going to be holed up here for a while, so you can now give us the latest on Ruby and Edward,' said Fran.

'It's definitely love, and James is beginning to accept the inevitable. Ruby's told me she wants to get engaged on her eighteenth birthday, and why not, I say. Marriages seem just as likely to fail when people are older. Oh, I'm sorry.' She put her arm round Fran and gave her a squeeze. 'That was dreadfully tactless.'

'Don't be silly,' said Fran. 'I'm not some delicate little blossom that needs gentle handling.'

⁓

It was five o'clock before the rain eased and Annabel and Elisabeth were able to walk back up to the village. Elisabeth popped into Mrs. Kennard's to buy a few things she'd forgotten when she'd done her weekly shop in the supermarket. The sweets, tightly packed in large jars behind the counter, always reminded Elisabeth of her childhood. In fact, the whole shop did. It had captured the time warp of Southfleet, and was a jumble of miscellaneous items, from skeins of wool and pattern books, to rolls of chicken wire. Even Mrs. Kennard was from a different era, with her twin-set and tweed skirt.

Elisabeth had forgiven her for taking her to task about

going out to work. She could hardly expect that indomitable lady to move with the times when she was obviously locked back in the fifties.

She pounced on Elisabeth as soon as she walked through the door, raising her voice above the jangling bell.

'I'm all of a fluster, dear. I've just had Amy in here and she thinks that dreadful girl Lydia is having a relationship with your Ruby's Edward.'

The items Elisabeth had come into the shop for completely flew out of her mind.

'Why on earth does she think that?'

'This morning they were deep in conversation down by the harbour where Edward had set up his easel.'

'And that means they're having an affair? Really, Mrs. Kennard, this sort of gossiping has got to stop, it can do so much harm.'

Mrs. Kennard gave Elisabeth one of her most disapproving looks. She had an uncanny ability to look down her nose when challenged; she'd perfected it over the years, and newspaper boys who were late for deliveries, and customers who returned stale goods were given the benefit of it.

'I really can't remember what I came in for,' said Elisabeth, and made a hasty exit before she challenged Mrs. Kennard and told her what a silly old bat she thought she was.

෴

The house stood at the end of a sweeping, tree-lined drive, its turreted roof giving it the appearance of a small Scottish castle. It was as ancient as the lineage of the family, and Tom always felt privileged to be able to walk up the wide steps to the massive front door and be welcomed like the proverbial prodigal son. Charles and Josephine had always made him feel like the younger brother they'd so longed to give Matthew but, as Josephine had told him on his last visit, it hadn't been through lack of trying!

He touched on the subject of the beach huts as soon as he and Matthew had exchanged the usual boyish comments that they still couldn't quite grow out of.

'Why sell the land,' he asked, 'when it's been in the family for so many generations?'

'Some things have had their day,' replied Matthew. 'It's a useless scrap of land, and I'm always being hassled by the council about campers pitching their tents behind the beach huts in the summer. I can't be down there every day pulling up tent pegs and reading the riot act to a few holidaymakers. A small injection of cash into the estate wouldn't go amiss, either.'

Tom saw his point; of course he didn't want to be bothered with 'a scrap of land', as he put it. He looked across the terrace to the parkland beyond, all immaculately manicured; it was a far cry from the windswept dunes and marshland that surrounded the beach huts.

'Why the sudden interest in Walland Marsh?'

'Cupid's struck, but I've had a rather nasty trick played on me. The girl I've fallen for is married with a young daughter.'

'And the beach hut?'

'That's where I first saw her. She owns one of the huts.'

'I never took you as the sort to go after married women.'

'It's not all that it seems, Matt.'

'It had better not be. Now, let's go and have a sharpener before supper, and I hope you've got a good reason for going after this girl.'

They left the cosy study and walked across the pillared hall. Its lofty dimensions and historic atmosphere deserved a few suits of armour, but the only concession to ancient ancestry were the portraits of previous generations of Millers hanging on the walls.

'Mother's in the drawing room, we'll go and join her there.'

The drawing room was every bit as imposing as the hall, but well-worn chairs and a blazing log fire relieved it of any austerity.

'Tom darling, how wonderful to see you! It's been rather gloomy here since Charles died. We need cheering up, and you're just the person to do it.'

Tom gave her a hug. Josephine was the true aristocrat that she appeared to be. She could trace her family tree back through a long succession of nobles to William the Conqueror. Tom loved her no-nonsense approach to life and warm humour. The affection she'd shown him when he was a small child had grown into a strong friendship since he'd become an adult.

She linked arms with him and walked over to the large sash windows. A peacock was strutting magnificently across the lawn towards his mate, showing the full glory of his tail feathers.

'Now, Matthew and I have decided to have a little dinner party here next week. Charles would have hated the house to be so silent. Your chum William is coming, and he's asked if he can bring a young lady with him. I think her name is Phoebe.'

'George is going to love me for this,' Tom muttered.

'What was that, darling?' enquired Josephine.

'I was just thinking out loud.'

'We've got quite a few young men coming, so can you supply the ladies?'

'I think so, but two of them are married.'

'I'm not planning on the entertainment going further than the dinner table,' said Josephine, with a twinkle in her eye. 'Now, how many, and what are their names?'

'Lydia, she's the unmarried one, her sister Annabel, and Fran. Be careful who you sit Lydia next to though; she's a man-eater!'

'And are you partial to any of these young ladies?'

Tom gave Josephine a disarming smile. 'If you could sit me next to Fran I'd be forever in your debt.'

'I'll just have to see what I can manage, as long as you promise you won't behave like that peacock!'

'It's a deal.'

'What's a deal?' said Matthew, walking in and handing Tom a whisky.

'We're talking about our little dinner party next week. Tom is bringing three young women with him.'

'That's an impressive tally.'

'I'm sure he'll share them with you, dear, he was always good at sharing his toys when you were little boys!'

'Mother, that could be taken the wrong way.'

'Don't be so silly, I'm only having a little joke. Now, go and ask Mrs. Parkin how long supper will be. I'm absolutely ravenous.'

7

It was her hair that had first attracted Edward to Ruby, one Sunday morning almost six months before. As she knelt three pews in front of him in her father's church, he was quite transfixed by its glory. When for the briefest moment she turned to whisper something to one of her sisters, he saw, with a sigh of relief, that her beauty wasn't just in her hair. She had the type of profile artists dream of. He knelt next to her at the altar rail to take communion, causing the churchwarden to frown at the queue-jumping. Edward was far too intent on getting a closer look at the girl, who looked as though she'd just stepped out of a Titian painting, to care about the disapproval of a fusty old man.

Edward was twelve when he had seen his first painting by Titian of a woman with flowing red locks. Since that day, he had always wanted to find a model he could paint who possessed the flaming hair that was Titian's trademark. Ironically, it had taken Ruby six months to persuade him to paint her in the nude. He had never mixed work and pleasure, and from the moment he had his first conversation with her, on the steps of her father's church, he was in no doubt that he wanted her as a girlfriend far more than a model.

Ruby reclined on a green velvet settee with nothing on

but a straw hat. In her tummy button there was a gold stud, and round her neck a string of yellow beads. Her long curly hair contrasted wonderfully with the rich green velvet material, heightened by the sun slanting in through the large studio windows. The little straw hat perched on her head had once belonged to her grandmother, a charming old lady who in her youth had been the image of Ruby. The artificial flowers entwined round the brim had been replaced with new ones several times over the intervening years, and now were a mixture of bright yellow and violet.

'Ruby, you're going to have to keep still,' Edward said in exasperation. 'You keep wriggling about, it's quite impossible for me to paint you.'

'I *am* keeping still,' she grumbled, shrugging her shoulders in irritation. 'I'd no idea it was going to be so boring. Will you include the painting in your exhibition?'

'And what will your parents say if there's a nude portrait of their daughter hanging on the wall?'

'Mum will be cool about it, and if Dad doesn't like it, that's tough.'

'Don't you think there's enough hostility from your father without aggravating the situation?'

'If he's not prepared to recognise and appreciate good art when he sees it, that's his problem.'

'That's not really what we're talking about. If you're not careful, I'm going to think you're only going out with me to annoy your father.'

'Don't be silly, Edward, you know I'm madly in love with you.'

'Put some clothes on, we'll have a break.'

Instead of watching her dress, as Ruby thought he would, Edward was concentrating on cleaning his brushes.

'I thought artists made passionate love to their models after they had sat for them,' said Ruby, tilting her body provocatively towards him.

'For goodness' sake get dressed, Ruby, they're different things.'

'You mean because you're going out with me, there's no need to make love to me after I've posed for you?'

'I didn't mean that. It's just that when I'm working I have to concentrate on what I'm doing. I can't have sex and then start painting away again, it doesn't work that way for me. If you want to be painted and have sex during the coffee breaks, there's a chap over at Snark who has a good reputation for it.'

'Don't be disgusting,' said Ruby, and put her clothes on.

'Shall we go and have a pint? Your father isn't usually in the pub Saturday lunch time is he?'

'Does it matter if he is?'

'No, but it's nice to have a quiet pint every now and again.'

'Pretend you haven't seen her,' said Ruby, spotting Amy Cooper strolling past the pub. 'She's got her horrid little terrier with her.'

'Hello you two,' hailed Amy. 'Have you just been for a nice walk? It's turned into a beautiful day, hasn't it?'

'We haven't been walking. I've actually been sitting… '

'She's been, or rather, we've been sitting down by the estuary,' said Edward hurriedly.

Amy gave Ruby a piercing look. 'How are you all coping now your mother is a working lady?'

'She's always been a working lady.'

'Yes, I know, dear, I didn't mean it in that sense.'

'Actually, nothing has changed except for the fact that Mother no longer has to organise all those boring parish functions, and be at everyone's beck and call. I understand you've taken on that role.'

'I'm helping your father at what is, I feel, a very difficult time for him. I don't think he needs you to add to his worries.' She stalked off, pulling the dog after her.

'You were going to tell her you'd been posing nude for me, weren't you?' said Edward accusingly.

'Yes, and so what?'

'You're behaving in a very childish way at the moment. Didn't you know children like to shock, and that's just what you're trying to do.'

'I'm only having a laugh at a pompous old biddy. Just chill out, you're beginning to sound like my father.'

The pub was empty apart from a few locals propping up the bar and drinking their pints of Adnams. Phoebe was standing behind the bar looking particularly dejected.

'Gosh, it's dead in here, and what's up with you? You look pretty miserable,' said Ruby.

'I've been having an argument with Dad. I'm going to work at the estate agents and Dad doesn't want me to.'

'So you've been lured away to the bright lights of Southfleet as well! Why are men so difficult? Dad is still sulking about Mum working over there. I'd do what she's done and just go for it.'

'The way Dad's behaving, you'd think I was off to Australia.'

'A pint would be nice, Phoebe,' said Edward.

'Sorry, Edward, not much of a barmaid, am I? Have this on me. A pint for you too, Ruby?'

'Lovely,' said Ruby.

'Shit,' said Phoebe under her breath, 'that awful Lydia has just come in with Fran.'

'Fran!' Ruby turned and flung her arms round Fran. 'How long are you staying in Warbleton this time?'

Edward gave them both a smile and asked what they wanted to drink.

'You want to watch that man-eater,' Phoebe whispered to him.

'She seems a really nice girl to me. You never struck me as the bitchy type, Phoebe,' said Edward.

Ruby was far too intent on her conversation with Fran to notice Lydia flirting quite outrageously with Edward. Ruby was definitely the love of his life, but to have a woman as devastatingly attractive as Lydia hang on his every word and beg to be allowed to see his work, was enormously flattering.

'I spend as much time as possible when I'm in London going to art exhibitions,' lied Lydia. 'And if you need a model, I'll happily pose for you. I used to sit for a life-drawing class.'

Edward didn't know quite what to say. An abrupt refusal would seem rude, but he could hardly have Ruby going out from one sitting, and Lydia coming in for the next.

'I'm working on a portrait at the moment, but thanks, I'll bear it in mind.'

'I'm planning on staying down here for a few weeks so there's plenty of time for the portrait, but I'd still love to see your paintings. Can we arrange that now?'

'Monday morning,' said Edward. 'I live at the top of the lighthhouse.'

'How fascinating, I can't wait.'

'Why's Lydia here?' Ruby whispered to Fran.

'I don't know, but Annabel is convinced it has to be something to do with men.'

'Well, she'd better keep her hands off Edward, or I'll kill her,' said Ruby.

Amy Cooper was seething with rage as she left Ruby and Edward. She really felt it was time she had another word with James about the child. She was quite obviously being led astray by that awful artist who painted goodness knows what in his lighthouse.

James was coming out of the vicarage gates just as her dog Jason stopped to have a pee against the high brick wall.

'James,' called Amy, after his retreating figure. She caught him up with quick, tottering steps, dragging the poor dog after her. 'James, I'm not going to beat about the bush, and I'm sure you'll think it's no concern of mine, but I am worried about young Ruby.'

'I think it's for Elisabeth and I to be concerned about Ruby.'

'Quite, but sometimes things can be seen more clearly from a distance, and I do think you and Elisabeth are blinding yourselves to the potentially disastrous consequences of Ruby's relationship with that debauched artist.'

'You're going to be had up for defamation of character if you're not careful, Amy. Now, don't you worry about Ruby.

If Elisabeth thought the relationship was harmful, she'd definitely put a stop to it.'

'Well, I've a nasty premonition about this. I hope you don't have to eat your words.' With that, she strode off, determined to pursue the topic with Mrs. Kennard.

Half an hour later, Jason was still tied up outside the village shop. Inside, the formidable tongues of Amy and Mrs. Kennard were working ten to the dozen with no sign of let-up.

'They often come in here together,' said Mrs. Kennard, 'arms draped round each other and all lovey-dovey, but at twenty-six he's going to want more than a few kisses.'

'Artists are all odd, anyway,' said Amy. 'I'm sure they ply their trade as an excuse to paint women in the nude. Think of all those disgusting portraits of women with folding flesh and great pendulous breasts. How can that be described as art? Now Monet, he was different with his poppy fields and prettily attired women. Edward should take a leaf out of his book.'

'And what about the comings and goings in Watercolour Cottage?' said Mrs. Kennard. 'They're all back there again. Fran, her sister-in-law, and that stuck-up blonde girl who obviously thinks she's God's gift to men, and of course, Fran's adorable little girl. It's odd the husband never comes, too.'

Jason's persistent barking eventually attracted Amy's attention. 'I must go,' she said, 'but keep your eyes open, we don't want the village turning into a den of iniquity.'

❦

Lydia stood staring at her naked reflection in the mirror. She admired her narrow hips, flat stomach and long, slender legs. The only part she wasn't one hundred per cent happy about was her breasts, but at least, she thought, they were nice and firm with prominent, rosy nipples. Size wasn't everything, and she was sure artists didn't always want to paint buxom women.

Annabel was surprised to see Lydia up and about so early in the morning; her rising time was normally well after ten.

'Where are you off to this morning?' she asked suspiciously.

'I'm modelling for Edward.'

'What sort of modelling?'

'Nude, of course.'

'And does Ruby know about this?'

'What's it got to do with Ruby? He's an artist and can paint anyone he wants to.'

'Did he ask you to sit for him?'

'Oh, for goodness' sake Annabel, you're just a jealous old cow.'

'And you're a bitch. Why don't you go back to London, and stop causing trouble here?'

*

Amy Cooper had been on patrol since eight o'clock. She had spent at least forty-five minutes down by the estuary, determined to keep a careful eye on the lighthouse to make sure Ruby didn't go there instead of school. Even when a slight drizzle set in she stuck to her post, until she knew the school bus was well on its way. The appearance of Lydia took her quite by surprise. It was not what she'd been expecting but it certainly made the long wait rewarding.

Edward was in a world of his own when a knock on the door reverberated up to his eyrie. At the beginning of the summer he'd treated himself to a telescope and now spent many an hour scanning the horizon. Sometimes it was so clear, it looked as though a straight line had been drawn separating the sky from the sea. On other days, the two merged together in one grey mass, making the horizon disappear completely.

Today, the mist and drizzle obscured a rather interesting boat, but just as it became clearly visible, Lydia's persistent hammering on the door registered with Edward. He cursed the intrusion. He had few visitors and couldn't imagine who it might be at this hour of the morning.

'Lydia!' he exclaimed in surprise, as he threw open the door. He'd completely forgotten about her visit.

'I hope I'm not too early, but I can't wait to get started.'

'Get started?'

'Yes, I'm posing for you, remember?'

Edward was absolutely certain he hadn't agreed to paint her. This was all most embarrassing.

'I thought you were just coming to look at my paintings.'

'That as well. Now, are you going to ask me in or shall I just stand here getting drenched?'

She followed him up the steep, winding steps and wondered why men sometimes played so hard to get. It was ridiculous when they always succumbed to her charms in the end.

'Coffee?' asked Edward.

'Why not have a break in a minute.' She walked over to the settee and began taking her clothes off. 'Do you want me sitting or lying down?'

Edward felt quite panicky. 'Look, Lydia, I'm sorry, but I've got too much work on at the moment to paint you.'

Lydia was already down to her bra and pants. She stood up and walked across to him.

'Are you sure you're too busy? It could be fun.'

Ruby's flaming hair shouted at Edward from the canvas across the room. He knew he loved her totally. He also knew he stood every chance of losing her because she was still so young. But he was prepared to take that gamble. He had absolutely no desire to have sex with Lydia, and felt an enormous happiness that love could have such power over a man.

'Please get dressed,' he said, 'I don't paint just anyone in the nude.'

As soon as he'd said the words, Edward knew he had chosen them unwisely. Lydia's eyes suddenly turned to liquid pools of ice.

'And what will Ruby say if I tell her you tried to persuade me to take my clothes off?'

'She wouldn't believe you.'

'We'll have to see about that, won't we?'

Outside, Amy Cooper was getting wetter by the minute, but it was worth it when she saw Lydia emerge from the lighthouse apparently in a complete rage. She wondered what that dreadful artist had done to make Lydia shout something up the stairs, before she furiously slammed the door. She followed Lydia up through the village with aching legs, and watched her disappear into Watercolour Cottage. Within minutes, the door opened again and Fran appeared without her little girl. Amy thought she'd have a quick bite to eat, and then check on the beach hut to see what Fran might be up to.

After lunch, the rain had disappeared completely, but in its place was a brisk south-east wind. Amy pushed herself across the bridge to the field behind the beach hut, dragging a reluctant Jason behind her.

The full onslaught of the wind hit her as she came over the sand dunes by the beach huts. To her disappointment there appeared to be no one in sight. Then she saw the sail, giving all the appearance of flying across the water on its own. The wind caused tears to stream down Amy's face and at first she failed to notice Fran standing by the water's edge, dressed in what she could only assume was some sort of rubber outfit.

'Who's your chaperone?' asked Tom, as he lifted his board and rig clear of the shore-break.

Fran turned round and saw Amy huddled next to one of the beach huts.

'That's Amy Cooper, the village busybody. By tonight, most of the village will know I've been windsurfing with you.'

Tom lowered the boom to suit Fran's height and adjusted the foot-straps.

'If you haven't been out for a couple of years, you might find the conditions a bit tough out there.'

Fran looked at the waves as they pounded the shoreline and knew without any doubt that she could cope with the wind strength and the size of the waves. She only hoped she was fit enough to stay out and enjoy the conditions for more than a few minutes. Even three years ago, she could play amongst waves bigger than today's for hours at a time, but that had been when windsurfing was the most important thing in her life. She watched the spin-drift flying off the tops of the waves and felt a tight little knot in her stomach that was part excitement and part fear.

'Don't you worry about me,' she said and timing her entrance through the shore break to perfection, went out to play amongst the waves.

Tom was seriously impressed with her skills and grinned with admiration. He heard the shingle crunch behind him and Amy appeared at his side.

'What on earth does that girl think she's doing out there?'

'It looks to me as though she's having an enormous amount of fun.'

Amy for once was speechless, and when Tom looked again she had gone back over the shingle ridge from whence she came.

Half an hour later, Fran was back on the beach absolutely exhausted. She could barely lift the board and rig out of the water.

'I'm so unfit,' she groaned as Tom helped her.

'I suppose you think I was impressed with that little display,' said Tom, throwing himself down next to her just out of reach of the waves.

'Well, were you?' she laughed.

'Just a bit!' and he leant over and kissed her. It happened so naturally and so quickly that for a split second Fran thought she must have imagined it.

He told her to go back to the beach hut and get out of her wetsuit before she got cold, while he sorted out the kit. Back in the hut, she took off her wetsuit and changed into jeans and a jumper and then put the kettle on to boil. She felt the happiest she'd been since the day Grace was born.

They sat next to each other on the veranda sipping tea and talking like old friends. Fran felt she could be completely natural and at ease with him.

'So where did you get that good?' Tom asked curiously. 'As you pointed out the other day, the wind isn't consistent enough in England.'

She told him all about her time in Cape Verde and lots more, but she didn't touch on the subject of Malcolm. When she said she had to go back to Watercolour Cottage to pick up Grace, he took her hand.

'I don't want to invade your privacy, and I've no idea what is happening in your life at the moment, but the kiss wasn't an accident or a spur of the moment thing. I'm sure the last thing you need right now is a man chasing you, but what I feel for you is so strong it has to be said.'

She didn't know what to reply, so she just smiled at him.

When Fran arrived back at the cottage, Annabel told her Daphne had been on the phone. She wanted Fran to ring her immediately. 'She's all in a tizz about the house. I tried to fob her off but she insisted you call her.'

'How's Grace been?'

'I put her down for a sleep at two as you told me to and I haven't heard a peep out of her since. You're looking very flushed and pretty. Is that just from the windsurfing?'

'I've had a brilliant windsurfing session, but I've also

spent one of the happiest moments of my life talking to Tom. Is that just escapism?'

'I don't think being happy is escapism,' said Annabel. 'Happiness can be so intangible that it's gone before you knew you had it. To sit as you did, and let happiness wash over you, is wonderful.'

Fran went into the sitting room, and reluctantly picked up the phone to call her mother. As soon as she heard her mother's voice at the end of the line she knew Daphne was in one of her panics.

'Hello Mother, what's up?'

'You might well ask what's up. I hope this hasn't got anything to do with you, because something very odd is going on. Within minutes of your arrival back in Warbleton, the buyer for the cottage withdrew his offer.'

'Don't be ridiculous, Mother, how could it have anything to do with me?' Fran crossed her fingers, and looked guiltily at Annabel. Fran could visualise her mother anxiously fingering the pearls she always wore round her neck.

'It just all seems so odd. The contracts had been drawn up for signing, and he, or she, wanted completion to take place as soon as possible.'

Fran heard the clink of ice and she guessed her mother was already downing a gin and tonic.

'You don't need to sell it now. I don't believe you really wanted to anyway.'

'Well, I don't think your father will agree with that, I think he'll put it straight back on the market. Oh dear… '

Fran could hear her sighing loudly down the phone.

'I don't know whether I'm coming or going,' Daphne

continued. 'Annabel said you were out windsurfing. I hope you're being careful, you've got a child to look after now.'

'It was perfectly safe, and the chap whose kit I borrowed was watching, so I'm sure he'd have raised the alarm if I'd suddenly been eaten by a shark or something.'

'I do wish you wouldn't be so flippant, Fran. Who was this chap, anyway?'

Fran felt her mother was cross-examining her like she used to when she first started going out with boys.

'He's just a friend, Mum, and perfectly respectable. He's related to the Millers from Starston Hall.'

'What's his name?'

'Why on earth do you want to know his name?'

'Could you please just answer a simple question.'

'I'll tell you all about him when I next see you.'

'I don't know why you have to be so mysterious. I certainly don't think it's appropriate for you to be gadding about with other men when you're a married woman. It seems to be one thing after another, I don't know why you don't just come back home.'

'Mum, I've got to go, Grace is crying. Bye.'

'Phew,' Fran said as she replaced the receiver. 'I think Mum must be going through some sort of mid-life crisis, she's acting very oddly.'

Annabel walked back into the room carrying Grace. Her sleepy face smiled the second she caught sight of Fran, and she clutched her tightly round her neck the moment Annabel put her in her arms.

'Don't worry about Daphne. We both know, with the greatest respect to your Mum, that she's a drama queen.

What I want to know is what happened on the beach. I don't believe that glow is just from windsurfing.

'He kissed me, and it wasn't a question of 'should I let him,' it just happened, but it was the merest contact, nothing invasive.'

'I should hope not,' said Annabel, with a smile.

'It's all too silly for words. I don't know what I think I'm up to, but he made me feel peaceful. Amongst all the tumult of the wind and waves, and the thunderous shore break that was practically washing over both of us, I felt at peace.'

'I must say I've never found a man who has had that effect on me.'

'But it was more than that. I wanted to sit there forever and listen to him talk, and in the beach hut when he held my hand I didn't want him to let go. Does that all sound horribly corny?'

'Actually, yes it does.'

They both laughed, but Annabel became serious and told Fran to remember the old rebound thing.

'It's the easiest thing in the world to fall for someone who's being kind to you, especially after what you've been through,' she warned. 'I hope you're going to behave yourself at this dinner we've all been invited to. Things are looking up. I'm very impressed that you've managed to get us invited to a stately home.'

Fran suddenly remembered that she had brought nothing with her apart from jeans, tee shirts and jumpers.

'What on earth am I going to wear?'

'I'm sure Lydia will lend you something.'

Fran thought about all the different clothes she could remember seeing Lydia in, and really didn't think anything would be suitable for her.

'She's got some really cute things, but little skimpy tops and short skirts aren't me.'

'Let's take a trip to Southfleet tomorrow. I think I might need a nice new outfit, too.'

They made an early start the next morning, and shot off round the estuary like a couple of schoolgirls. The sun was out and they were going to a dinner-party, and all the pain that had engulfed Fran over the past few weeks completely disappeared.

'Let's have a coffee first,' suggested Fran.

They parked in a car park just off the large green that rolled away into a golf course. Fran remembered Simon raving about it when he'd first become keen on golf. It was warm enough to sit in the small walled courtyard of the tearoom. Annabel went in to order. Within minutes, a plateful of scones was placed on the table along with a big bowl of thick cream and some yummy-looking jam that, by its appearance, had to be home-made.

The courtyard was awash with late summer flowers, all neatly planted out in tubs and hanging containers. The waitress was pretty and friendly, and asked if Fran would like a high chair to be brought out for the baby.

'Thanks for asking, but she'll be fine in her pushchair,' said Fran.

'That makes a change,' she said, pouring the coffee into large, bowl-shaped cups.

'Most places I go to have signs saying 'no pushchairs

allowed'. Or you walk in with a child in your arms and the reception you get is, to say the least, frosty.'

'Some children are the most dreadful brats, though,' whispered Annabel, as she watched two small children on the next table behaving appallingly.

When they'd finished their coffee, they went out into the high street, and then made their way down a narrow side street that eventually linked up with the promenade.

Because it appeared to be an insignificant little street that wound off to nowhere, it was overlooked by the casual holidaymaker. Despite this, the dress shop at the end was always busy. Mary Rose's reputation for stocking designer label dresses at affordable prices reached as far as London.

'Do you think she'll mind the pushchair?' asked Fran, as Annabel held the door open for her.

'It's tough if she does. If she wants our custom, she'll have to put up with it.'

'I can't wait for you to have kids,' laughed Fran, 'you'll definitely blaze a trail for mums.'

Mary Rose not only didn't mind the pushchair, she seemed to adore babies, and cooed over Grace whilst Annabel and Fran were left to try on dresses. They emerged from the shop almost an hour later, thrilled with their purchases.

'That was even more fun than Harvey Nichols,' said Annabel, 'and the dresses were half the price.'

Fran looked at Annabel and smiled. 'The way our lives are going at the moment, it could be one of our last purchases for some while.'

'If that's true, then perhaps I should have bought the green dress as well!'

They laughed together and for one brief moment Fran felt as though she hadn't got a care in the world.

'Do you really think it's appropriate to show your underwear tonight?' said Annabel.

Lydia glared at her, then took another look at her reflection in the mirror.

'I'd rather show my underwear than look a frump.'

'Oh! come on Lydia, you can hardly accuse your sister of looking a frump; she looks absolutely stunning,' said Fran.

She had just got back from taking Grace over to the Vicarage as Elisabeth had insisted on looking after her for the night. Fran had been quite happy to take Grace along with her, she was still small and adaptable enough to tuck down in a travel cot almost anywhere, but Elisabeth had insisted.

'It will do you the world of good to just go off for the evening and forget about everything apart from having some fun,' she'd said.

Fran had admitted that she was in two minds whether to go or not, and pointed out that it was Matthew Miller whose land the beach huts were on.

'Yes, of course it is,' said Elisabeth. 'I'd somehow forgotten about that connection. Perhaps fraternising with the enemy might help your case.'

'Perhaps, but I can hardly bring up the subject at the dinner table, can I? I'd much rather stay here for the evening.

I've always found dinner parties an ordeal at the best of times.'

'You've experienced too many ghastly business dinners with Malcolm and his colleagues. Tonight could surprise you.'

Phoebe changed her outfit four times before she felt she was wearing the right dress, and even then she wasn't completely happy with her appearance. She wondered why the little black number always came out in times of crisis, but what else did you wear to a dinner party at an ancestral home? It was the first time she'd been to one and the way she was feeling it would probably be the last. She was sure she'd make a fool of herself, use the wrong cutlery, and say the wrong thing; in fact, she wished she wasn't going at all.

Sitting in William's Morgan as they drove around the estuary to Southfleet only added to her agitation. She felt she was playing in a game that was out of her league. The thought of George and his little cottage over at Dunster suddenly made her want to cry.

William, not one to be at a loss for things to say, rattled on about this and that until he realised he was getting no response from Phoebe.

'I can't wait for Josephine and Matthew to meet you, they'll adore you,' he said.

'They won't adore me when they learn I'm just a barmaid.'

'What's wrong with being a barmaid?'

'Don't be patronising,' said Phoebe, 'you know exactly what I mean.'

'Anyway, you're not just a barmaid, your father owns the pub.'

William briefly took his eyes off the road in front of him and glanced at Phoebe. He thought she was the most stunning girl he'd seen in years. He adored brunettes, and she had that sultry look about her that he found quite irresistible. The sweet fragrance of roses filled the car, causing William to feel slightly drunk. Phoebe, never one to stint on anything, had sprayed herself liberally with her favourite perfume.

Driving up the tree-lined drive that led to the house did nothing to quell Phoebe's nerves, and when the magnificent house stood before them in all its glory she felt sure it must be one of those country estates that were open to the public. She just couldn't imagine anyone actually living anywhere so grand unless they were a member of the Royal Family. Fortunately, the Miller's finances were in good health and they hadn't yet had to resort to supplementing their income from the general public.

'They're the most unpretentious people you could meet,' said William, as they walked up the massive flagged steps that led to the front door. 'It's people who are on the periphery that are the problem, always feeling they've got to prove something.'

Phoebe took a deep breath and hoped he was right.

&

Everyone was gathered in the drawing room sipping

champagne cocktails. The music coming from the sound system was a mixture of jazz and blues which drifted unobtrusively into the room, and had none of the destructive effect on conversation that some loud pop music had. Fran remembered her first dinner party at Brendon and Marjorie Fletcher's. She'd been subjected to a constant stream of loud music that she felt would have been more appropriate blaring out of the bedroom of one of the couple's teenage sons.

The music tonight had an almost soporific effect on her. She felt calm, and far away from the abrasive nightmare of the last few days.

Josephine stood by a table with an elaborate urn on it.

'I want to make a little speech,' she said. She placed her hand on the urn. 'Charles would love to have seen the place alive again. Sorry for the pun, darling.'

She stroked the urn and smiled.

Lydia whispered in Fran's ear. 'What on earth's she on about.'

'I think the dead Charles's ashes must be in the urn.'

'I don't think I can handle an evening with someone's ashes in the same room.'

'Now,' said Josephine, 'I feel the time for mourning is over. Life has to go on. Next week, Charles' ashes are going to be scattered out to sea. It is what he wanted, and he would also have wanted everyone to enjoy themselves here tonight. So let's raise our glasses to Charles.'

Fran found she had been placed at the table with Tom to her left and Josephine, at the head of the table, on her right.

'Charles would have adored you,' she said to Fran.

'I'm only sorry I never met him,' she replied.

'I'm sure Tom will tell you all about him one day.'

Fran watched as tears briefly showed in Josephine's delicately made-up eyes.

'It's sometimes difficult to accept that my beloved Charles is now reduced to ashes in an urn. I'm just thankful he died in the way he did.'

Fran tentatively asked how that was.

'He died at the breakfast table just as he began reading the front page of *The Times*, with a cigar in one hand and his early morning tot of whisky in the other. He suddenly looked at me like a startled rabbit, and then he was dead. Anyway, my dear, as I was saying, he would have adored you. He was a bit of a rogue, but quite harmless.' She topped up Fran's glass with chilled Sancerre. 'I understand you're a windsurfer too, so I'm sure you and Tom will want to have a good old natter about your mad sport, and I must pay attention to my other guests.'

Fran saw her give Tom a knowing look.

'Do you want to talk about windsurfing?' Tom asked, smiling at her.

'We could talk about other things. Like why we're on earth, or how the universe began, or perhaps books. We could discuss our favourite authors,' Fran said, smiling back at him. They had all finished their first course and her left hand was in her lap. He placed his hand over it. His touch was light and warm.

'It's always easier to talk after a couple of glasses of wine,' he said. 'I don't mean talk nonsense, but it just gives you that edge to say things it can be difficult to say in cold blood. I want you to tell me immediately if you think I'm being out of order.'

Fran took a small gulp of wine and said she promised she'd tell him.

'I don't think everything is right with your marriage. I'm not asking for details, I'm not prying, but I just want to know if your marriage has a future.'

Fran barely hesitated. 'No, it definitely doesn't have any future whatsoever.'

He squeezed her hand gently.

'That's all I needed to know,' he said.

After supper, they all went back into the drawing room and Matthew played the piano. He was a superb pianist, and Tom told Fran that at one time he had considered taking it up professionally, but the long hours of dedicated practice over four years had burnt him out.

'I feel like a fish out of water here,' Phoebe said, sitting next to Fran on the old leather settee.

'William seems completely smitten with you. I overheard Josephine telling him to snap you up. She said how lovely you were compared to the horsey girls he normally dated, with too much of their daddy's money in their pockets.'

Phoebe looked gratefully at Fran, and smiled.

'You're gorgeous, Phoebe, don't sell yourself short.'

'The problem is, I don't want William, I want George.'

'Sort things out then, you don't have to go out with William.'

'If I told you what George had done, you certainly wouldn't tell me to go out with him.'

'You can't leave it at that! What did he do?'

Whilst Matthew worked his way through a beautiful piano piece by Debussy, Phoebe told Fran that George had indulged in sex with two women on the same day.

'Unfortunately,' she said, 'I was one of the two women.'

'And Lydia was the other?'

'Yes, the bitch. If I'd known she was going to be here tonight I would never have come.

They both looked across at Lydia who was flirting outrageously with two of Matthew's friends.

The music had reached a pitch of magical intensity, and for a few minutes Fran just listened.

'What do you think?' Phoebe persisted.

'Did he have sex with her before or after you?'

'Is that significant?'

'I think so, yes.'

'It was before me. He had sex with her at lunch-time, and with me in the evening.'

'So he hasn't actually been unfaithful to you, because you weren't going out with him at that point.'

Phoebe seemed to concentrate hard for a few minutes.

'I suppose not,' she said thoughtfully.

'Lydia isn't like any normal woman I know. She just wants to do it all the time with anyone who takes her fancy, and she loves making trouble. If only a third of what I've just said about her was true, I wouldn't say it, but she's not a nice person. I don't know what insecurities, or perhaps unhappiness, has made her like she is, but don't give her the satisfaction of wrecking what you and George might have together.'

Phoebe looked a little happier.

'Thank you so much, Fran, I'll take on board what you've said.'

They both sank back into the settee and let the music wash over them.

At midnight, Josephine announced that she thought everyone should stay the night.

'I don't know why we didn't organise this from the start,' she said. She turned to Tom and filled his empty glass up with a newly opened bottle of champagne. 'Now the drive home is cancelled, you can start drinking.'

'You're a wicked woman, Josephine,' Tom replied, grinning at her.

Fran said she couldn't possibly stay the night because of Grace, but Annabel persuaded her to ring Elisabeth and arrange to pick up Grace the next morning.

'You know she's a late night bird,' Annabel said, 'she never goes to bed until well after twelve.'

Fran went out into the hall and dialled Elisabeth's number. Elisabeth answered almost immediately.

'Just let your hair down and enjoy yourself,' she said. 'Grace is fast asleep, the baby monitor hasn't left my side, and I haven't heard a peep out of her. I've popped up to have a look at her several times. She's got her thumb in her mouth and her blanket clutched in her little hand. So just forget about being a mum tonight and relax.'

'Thank you, Elisabeth,' said Fran, 'thank you so much.'

Just as she was about to replace the receiver she heard her say, 'You deserve it.'

Phoebe announced that she really had to get back to the pub or her father would go mad. Josephine said she would phone for a taxi because she felt William really had drunk far too much to drive her back.

It was well after two before Josephine escorted her guests upstairs to show them to their allotted rooms. The bedroom Josephine took Fran into was like a honeymoon suite. A massive four-poster bed dominated the room, but it was completely different to the mock Jacobean four-poster in Notting Hill. Fran didn't need to look at it twice to see it was the genuine article. The en suite bathroom had been a dressing room in the days when the master of the house was looked after by a valet. The large enamel bath was big enough for at least two people to share without it being crowded, and the wonderful old taps gurgled and spluttered when she turned them on.

He came into her bedroom when she'd almost given up hope that he would. He knocked quietly on the door and when she said, 'Come in,' he walked over to the bed and sat on the edge, almost as though she was an invalid who shouldn't be disturbed.

He put his hands gently behind her head. She could feel him threading his fingers through her hair. He pulled her slowly towards him and kissed her.

'You know,' he said, taking his mouth away from hers, 'that this is the wrong time to go any further.'

She told him it wasn't the wrong time. How could he possibly think that time played any part in what was happening?'

She woke in the night and he made love to her again. It was so completely different to what she had experienced with Malcolm that it horrified her to imagine a life where she might have lived and died without any knowledge of it.

They lay together afterwards, talking quietly beneath the crumpled sheets. He told her about Greece, about the island he loved so much. He conjured up such an evocative picture that she could smell the warmth from the earth and see the olive groves sloping down to the sea in the dark night. He described his house surrounded by orange groves, tucked into the valley that spread inland between the mountains. He told her that in spring his garden was full of very English flowers. Hollyhocks leant their long stalks against the rough whitewashed walls, and chickens scratched between large rose bushes.

He fell asleep before she did, and she lay curled up in his arms. She kissed his mouth gently, not wanting to wake him. It seemed miraculous to her that after such overwhelming passion, there could be such peace. She fell asleep and dreamt she was a small girl again playing in an English orchard, but instead of apples on the trees there were oranges.

Mrs. Parkin, the resident housekeeper, had prepared a breakfast to vie with any of the top country house hotels in the area. The evening meal almost paled into insignificance against the amazing selection of breakfast delights. There was a choice of kipper fillets, smoked trout or haddock, porridge, scrambled eggs with slithers of smoked salmon running through it, or just straightforward poached eggs.

Fran devoured a large plate of scrambled eggs under the indulgent eye of Josephine.

'You two are early risers,' she said.

'I promised Fran I'd drop her back to Warbleton to pick up Grace,' said Tom, giving his smoked trout undue attention.

'I trust you both slept well,' said Josephine, a little smile playing on her lips.

Tom still appeared to be struggling with his trout. When he eventually looked up and met her eyes, he gave her a beaming smile. 'I think it was the best night's sleep I've ever had,' he said.

When they left, at just after eight thirty, Josephine assured Fran that Matthew would drop Annabel back. She kissed Fran on both cheeks and said how much she'd enjoyed getting to know her. When she kissed and hugged Tom, she said quietly, 'Take care, she's so lovely, but I don't want her to break your heart.'

Tom grinned at her and, whilst Fran got in the car, told Josephine that if only Fran would take it, he'd be prepared to risk the consequences.

⁂

Simon had felt rather pleased with himself the night before, as he cruised out of London in his Porsche with an enormous and expensive bouquet of flowers he'd bought from Wild at Heart lying on the car seat beside him. He had taken quite some time to choose the flowers, and managed to involve all three girls working on the stall to help him make a decision. *Damned attractive trio they were, too,* he thought, *rather like flowers themselves, delicate and quite deliciously pretty.*

The A12 was a nightmare, one long stream of traffic and no one seemingly capable of doing more than forty miles an hour. By the time he eventually reached Watercolour Cottage, he'd already regretted his impulsive decision to visit Annabel.

The cottage looked as though a bomb had hit it, with clothes strewn everywhere and a strong scent of perfume still lingering in the air. He assumed Annabel and Lydia had only just left to go over to The Reed and Whistle, but he couldn't find them in the pub. He wasn't even going to have the pleasure of a flirtation with the buxom, dark-haired bar maid, because she was conspicuously absent from behind the bar. He thought it all seemed very gloomy after the noise and bustle of London.

By ten-thirty, he'd finished his second bottle of champagne and decided to head back to the cottage. There was a slight drizzle in the air that made him feel damp and uncomfortable. Half way across the green, he noticed his shoes were covered in some sort of nasty mess which looked horribly like goose droppings. Wretched geese! He couldn't for the life of him understand why the landlord let them roam about terrorising his customers. He'd often wondered why his parents had ever bought Watercolour Cottage in the first place. As a child, he'd resented being dumped off there for the summer holidays. He'd felt obliged to swim in the freezing cold sea, and when he went out with Fran in the tiny boat, it made him feel sick and scared. It had never been his sort of place. The sooner his parents sold up, the better, especially as Annabel seemed to have developed a strange fetish for salt air and bleak landscapes. Simon's mobile phone suddenly blared out into the uncomfortable silence.

'What the hell's going on?' Malcolm roared down the phone as Simon fumbled with the front door key.

'Calm down, old chap, I haven't seen Fran yet. How did you know I was in Warbleton?'

'I didn't, you stupid arse!' bellowed Malcolm.

Simon held the phone away from his ear.

'This has nothing to do with Fran,' Malcolm continued. It's to do with you and that treacherous wife of yours. I see you've been very conveniently out of London for the past two days with your phone switched off.'

Simon wondered if Malcolm had had one too many; he sounded quite mad.

'You're barking up the wrong tree, Malc old chap. I'd forgotten to charge my phone up that's all. Now, what's all this about?'

Whilst Malcolm hurled a barrage of abuse down the telephone, with intermittent facts thrown in, Simon managed to unlock the front door and turn on the hall light.

He even managed to pour himself a stiff whisky before the tirade came to an end. What he heard made no sense at all. Now he was even more convinced that Malcolm had finally flipped.

'So you're telling me my wife is a traitor?'

The phone had gone dead. Simon found the sudden silence almost as alarming as the first onslaught of words.

Well, this was a fine to-do, he thought. Here he was in Warbleton with a seriously expensive bouquet of flowers to present to his wife who, if he was to believe Malcolm, was quite prepared to see him in jail.

By twelve o'clock, with nothing of interest to watch on television, and still no sign of Annabel or Lydia, he decided to have one last whisky and call it a day.

When he awoke late the next morning, for a brief moment he thought he was in London, but the peace, interspersed by the raucous cry of seagulls, quickly broke the illusion. He immediately remembered the horrible phone call from Malcolm. When he attempted to raise his head off the pillow, it ached and spun so much that he quickly laid it back down again. He groaned loudly, and felt it was a damned shame he couldn't down a couple of bottles of champers and have a few whiskies without feeling like death the next morning. Perhaps he'd better steer clear of the whiskies and just stick to champagne in future.

The morning dragged on interminably whilst he mooched about the cottage with nothing to do. The view of the estuary failed to excite or please him in any way. He glowered out of the window and briefly watched the boats coming and going in the estuary. He wondered what on earth possessed people to want to bob about on the ocean.

It was late morning before he heard a car pull up outside. He looked out of the window and could just make out what appeared to be a rather smart MG parked up by the gate. Minutes later, he saw Annabel walking breezily up the garden path and the car accelerate away.

When she came into the room, he noticed her changed appearance immediately.

Her cheeks were flushed, and she was wearing very little make-up. He could only remember seeing her without make-up at bedtime and first thing in the morning, and that wasn't for long. She didn't seem exactly overjoyed to see him, but she did walk over after taking her coat off and give him a hug.

'Darling,' she said, 'what are you doing up here?'

'Where the hell have you been in that dress, and whose car were you in?' he demanded.

'We all went out to supper last night at Starston Hall. The people who live there own the land Fran's hut is on. You know, the Millers.'

'Why on earth were you invited over there?'

'Lots of people were invited. We do know them vaguely.'

'Well, I certainly don't,' said Simon, 'so I can't for the life of me know how you can.' She was looking particularly pretty. If he hadn't got this damn headache, he'd be tempted to take her straight to bed.

She looked at him intently, and asked again why he'd come to Suffolk.

'I came originally,' he said, picking up the bouquet of flowers he'd forgotten to put in water, 'to give you these.' The flowers had begun to wilt and their beautiful heads drooped forlornly. He placed them in her hands and she smiled at him.

'I know where you got these,' she said. 'At Fran's favourite florist.'

He sat down in the armchair feeling a wave of nausea pass through him. He thought he might be sick.

Annabel studied Simon's flushed face and thickening body. Within a few years his lifestyle would add even more generous pounds to his weight. The boyish charm, which had first attracted Annabel to him, had already lost its veneer. Too many boozy lunches and rich food were taking their toll.

'Too much alcohol last night?' she said.

'That, and a bit of a shock, too. Malcolm called me last

night. I want you to know I don't believe a word of what he said, but he claims you're blackmailing him, and you're going to land us both in jail. Silly ass.'

Annabel turned away from him and walked into the kitchen. He followed her.

'I must put these flowers in water immediately, and I think we both need a coffee,' she said.

'Damn the coffee, Annabel, what's going on?'

He watched as she filled first a vase and then the kettle with water. She had her back to him as she carefully arranged the flowers in the vase.

'I'm not standing by while that bastard screws everyone's lives up. You'll both get caught in the end.'

She turned to face him with an expression that made him feel like a naughty schoolboy.

'How dare you interfere in my affairs, and what exactly do you think you know, anyway?' he raged, aware that raising his voice was making his head throb even more painfully.

'Simon, I know it all, the take-overs and mergers, the tip-offs from Malcolm. Do I need to say anymore?'

Simon glared at her. 'You scheming little witch,' he said.

'You didn't know that it was Malcolm who put the offer in for Watercolour Cottage, did you?'

'For God's sake, Annabel, don't be stupid.'

'He did. I put a stop to that. He said prices were going to rocket in Warbleton. He was banking on making a nice profit and getting rid of your family's holiday home at the same time.'

Lydia came crashing through the front door, slamming it so loudly behind her that Simon put his hand to his head and moaned.

'What's up with you two?' she said. She looked at Simon. 'And why are you up here?'

'What do you mean, why am I up here? It does happen to be my family's house.'

'Goodness, you're touchy. Will you jump down my throat if I ask you when you're going back to London?'

'As it so happens, immediately.'

'Wait ten minutes and you can give me a lift.'

Annabel stared at Lydia. 'Where did you disappear to last night?'

'What's it to do with you?'

'I assume your conquest didn't come up to expectations?'

'No, he didn't. He lives in a grotty little flat in Southfleet. I thought he'd live in a mansion like Matthew. I wasted a whole night on him. Warbleton sucks,' she said, and stormed out of the room.

'Don't you think we need to talk?' Annabel said, putting her hand on Simon's arm.

He ignored her, and shouted after Lydia, 'If you're not in the car in five minutes, I'll go without you.'

'I didn't do this to spite you, you know.'

'I want to know what the hell you thought you were doing, chasing around the countryside with other men. It's one thing for a chap to have the odd fling, but quite another for a woman. Especially if she's my wife.'

'So it's all right for *you* to have the odd fling, is it?' she said coldly.

'Come on, Annabel, we're all human, I've only done it once or twice.'

'Done what exactly once or twice?'

Simon looked like a rabbit suddenly caught in the headlights of a car.

'Well, you know, these things just happen sometimes.'

Annabel was genuinely shocked. She had watched Simon flirting quite outrageously with other women, but had never dreamt it had gone any further.

He watched her face, and realised he'd made the biggest blunder of his life.

'Thought you knew, old girl,' he said.

Early morning was usually a peaceful affair up at The Reed and Whistle, but this morning the geese were in a terrible state. Ruby sat on an old bench outside the pub, berating the geese as though each and every one was Mr. Nicholls, the ancient bus driver, who always ignored the entreaties of Ruby's sisters to wait just a few more minutes for her.

'The sodding bus has gone without me,' she said to Phoebe, who had come out of the pub convinced by the noise that the geese were being attacked by a fox.

'Stupid bus driver, you'd think he could hang on for a few minutes. And you can all shut up,' she said, glaring at the geese from beneath her wild tangle of red curls.

'Don't take it out on the geese,' laughed Phoebe. 'Why don't you just get up a few minutes earlier and save yourself all this anguish?'

'Every night I vow I'll leap out of bed as soon as the alarm goes off, or at least as soon as Mum calls up that breakfast's ready, but I'm just not an early riser, I hate getting out of bed in the morning. I could go home and ask Mum to take me, but it's her day off, and when I left she was already upside down in one of her beloved herbaceous borders.'

'I've got to pop into Southfleet this morning to pick up a few bits and pieces, so if you can hang on for a few minutes I'll run you to school.'

'Thanks Phoebe, you're a gem.'

They sped off in Phoebe's Peugeot 205, which was her most valued and loved possession apart from her big brown and white rabbit called Oscar. She never confessed to ownership of Oscar, it was almost as if he'd moved into the massive hutch and run at the bottom of the garden of his own accord. But the truth was she'd bought him from a pet shop, furious at the sign on his cage that said: *'Reduced for quick sale'.* She had always wanted a rabbit as a child but had never been allowed one. She'd scooped the terrified rabbit out of its tiny hutch and paid a quite ridiculously large sum of money for him, despite the deceptive reduction sale tag on his cage.

'Damn that bitch Lydia,' said Ruby, as she struggled to fasten her safety belt.

'Has she been after Edward?' asked Phoebe.

Ruby flashed her green eyes at Phoebe.

'Have the old village harridans been out gossiping?'

'No, but Lydia wrecked any chance that George and I might have had to make a go of things. Not that I can totally blame her, despite what Fran told me. I always believe it takes two to tango, he didn't have to go for it.'

'Don't be too sure about that.' Ruby held onto the door as they lurched round a particularly tight bend. 'Slow down, we're not doing a grand prix circuit! I think,' she continued, 'that it takes a pretty strong will for a man to hold back when a woman starts stripping, and let's face it, although we hate her, Lydia is stunning. Edward told me he resisted, and I believe him. Apparently she went to the lighthouse, took most of her clothes off and told Edward to paint her, and more.'

'George didn't paint her, but I wish he'd done that instead of what he did.'

'But, Phoebe, you weren't going out with him. In fact you were leading him a right old dance. Edward and I have watched you over the past couple of months flirting quite outrageously with him, and then at other times barely acknowledging his presence in the bar. The poor guy didn't know whether he was coming or going.'

Phoebe pulled up outside the school gates.

'It looks like a blooming prison, doesn't it?' said Ruby as she climbed out of the car.

'Do you think I should give him another chance?'

'Yes,' said Ruby, 'of course you should.'

Jack Henshaw tooted the horn of his slightly beaten-up old Citroen when he saw Fran, with Grace in her arms, emerge through the gates of the Vicarage. He would have liked to stop for a chat, but there seemed to be an inordinate number of home visits to ailing pets this morning. Unfortunately, there were too many old ladies with too much money. He knew they preferred to pay his high fees than risk their pets rubbing noses with animals from the council estate on the edge of the village. Of course, Mrs. Bradshaw, whose dog Gilbert he was about to visit, seemed blissfully unaware that every time Gilbert went missing, he was after a little mongrel called Molly from that very same council estate.

It had been a long, drawn-out morning with difficult pets and equally difficult women to deal with. The last call had been to Amy Cooper. Jason was beginning to show all the signs of severe arthritis.

'I do think,' said Jack, 'that you should stop walking him when the weather's wet. It's not helping the poor old chap.'

She looked at him indignantly. 'He does need exercise, you know. I don't want him getting fat.'

Jack fondled the dog's ears.

'Amy, he's old. You wouldn't drag your eighty-seven year old father out for walks when it's cold, wet, and windy, now would you?'

He left Amy and found himself feeling in desperate need of a lunchtime pint. He drove up past the green to where the pub nestled just above the estuary. He'd lived in the village for over twenty years and had seen the The Reed and Whistle change hands several times. Each time, he had been worried that he'd go in and find a hideous patterned carpet covering the floorboards, and the old pub games hidden away forever. When Wally, the current landlord, had first arrived, he promised Jack he was going to keep everything exactly as it was. He wasn't even going to remove the two sad-looking stuffed birds in glass boxes. Phoebe had demurred and wanted cigarette machines and a few modern conveniences, but Wally wouldn't hear of it.

The only unfortunate thing about The Reed and Whistle these days, he thought, *was George.* He was always hunched up at the bar like an old crow gazing gloomily into his pint.

He pushed open the door and walked into the warmth with a sigh of relief. For over an hour he could sip his pint quietly and forget about temperamental women and their spoilt pets.

'Things haven't improved then,' said Jack, sitting next to George up at the bar.

'She won't even come to the Harvest Supper with me. Fast cars, lots of money and being wined and dined have gone to her head, and who can blame her? Not a difficult choice between that, and a gamekeeper who couldn't keep his trousers up.'

'I don't think there's a lot I can say to that comment,' said Jack. He patted George consolingly on his back and asked if he could buy him a pint.

9

The thought came into Fran's head as suddenly and ominously as the dark clouds that sometimes appeared like omens on the faraway hills at the end of a particularly bright, sunny day. One moment she was happily watering the plants on her windowsills, and the next, she was staring dizzily into a black abyss. For a moment, the feeling of panic was so great that she had to go outside and sit on the veranda steps and take deep breaths. It took her over five minutes before she could pluck up the courage to go back into the hut and lift down her bag from one of the shelves to take out her diary. It was only a small diary, more like a child's notebook, but the flowered lilac cover had taken her fancy. She hated the Filofaxes everyone used these days, irrespective of need. She leafed back to the previous month; the small cross was where she feared it would be, and it meant her period was seven days late. Seven whole days late and she'd only just realised. Clutching the diary, she went out onto the wooden veranda and worked through the weeks again. The indelible cross left no room for doubt. She was either pregnant, or very late.

She quickly dressed Grace in thick dungarees and a jumper, and then worked her arms into a little Paddington Bear-type duffle coat with a hood. If she could get out for a long walk, the panic that was threatening to overwhelm her might subside.

It took just over an hour to walk along the shingle path to Dunsmere, and it could have been one of the loveliest walks she had been on for a long while. The white fluffy clouds played round the sun, creating sharp contrasts of colours and patterns on the sea.

Although the wind blew in little eddies off the sea, it wasn't persistent, and had none of the chill that made ears ache and eyes stream with tears.

They were over half way to Dunsmere when she caught sight of something large moving in the sea, going in the same direction as themselves. A massive bull seal swam fifteen yards out from the beach with all the concentrated power of a long-distance swimmer. She stopped and sat on the shingle so they could watch him. He was so close that they could see him clearly, the outline of his powerful body, the long whiskers and enormous, eloquent eyes. It had been several years since she'd seen a bull seal so close. She hoped it was a portent of good news.

She was exhausted, with the weight of Grace on her back, by the time she reached the Britannia Inn. The Inn stood a few hundred yards back from the beach behind a row of fishing boats. It was a pretty building painted in gentle Suffolk pink. On a wall inside the old front porch, that made her feel as though she was going into someone's house rather than a pub, there were some framed words about the village lost under the sea. She'd first heard the tale from the old ferryman who rowed her across the estuary to Southfleet. To a nine-year old child it had been the most haunting story. A whole village submerged beneath the waves, with fish swimming into bedrooms and sitting rooms where log fires once blazed. She'd pictured crustaceans covering the pews in the church and porpoises playing in the old school playground. He'd told her that on wild, stormy nights the villagers in Dunsmere could hear the church bell tolling out to sea, and the wailing of lost souls.

She had never liked going into pubs on her own, although she felt more comfortable walking into a village pub than a London bar. She ordered half a pint of Adnams, a bowl of soup for Grace, and a toasted cheese and tomato sandwich. The conservatory at the back of the pub overlooked the garden. It was empty apart from a massive fluffy ginger cat. In the corner of the room was an old wooden high chair that Fran gratefully placed Grace in. The fluffy ginger cat came and sat himself next to them; he let Grace put her eager fingers into his fur without flinching. When her life returned to any semblance of normality, she was going to go straight out and get a cat, and quite probably a dog too. She had no intention of letting Grace grow up without the comforting presence of animals around. No amount of pleading had ever been able to change her mother's attitude towards pets. She hadn't even been allowed to go through the guinea pig and rabbit phase. At one time, she seemed to be the only child who wasn't rushing home from school to clean out a cage with some type of rodent in it. When she'd asked for a budgie, not really wanting one but feeling it would be better then nothing, her mother had shrieked in horror, and told her she wasn't having creatures in the house that spread disease.

Grace was far too interested in the cat to pay much attention to the soup that Fran was unsuccessfully trying to spoon into her mouth. She made little bubbles with it on her lips instead, and smiled happily at the cat. The sun had disappeared behind a big cloud when she walked out of the pub and into the back garden, where an old brick stone path led to a gate with direct access to the beach. The garden was laid out with borders full of old-fashioned shrub roses, whose long, weeping stems were covered in a late summer flush of blooms. She thought of the roses in Greece that Tom had spoken of so eloquently, and wondered if she'd ever see them with him now.

The walk back through the woods and up onto the hills gave a wonderful, panoramic view of the countryside. She could see Dunsmere forest, where deer still roamed freely, sweeping down to the ancient fishing village of Dunsmere. She sat on a bench that some bereaved person had dedicated to their loved one. The small brass plaque read: *Joseph Brignall 1890-1979. He loved this coastline from east to west and the peace it gave him.* Fran thought of the two world wars Joseph must have lived through, and could understand how this landscape had brought him peace.

She could see Tom's cottage smudged into the landscape looking as though it was almost floating in the reed beds, and then the beach huts on the edge of the water. From this distance, the huts seemed more part of the sea than the land.

It was another hour before she wound back down onto the marsh below Warbleton. Instead of going back to the beach hut, she walked up to Watercolour Cottage.

'I was just coming down to see you,' said Annabel. 'He knows.'

'Who knows what?' said Fran.

'Sweetie, I know you obviously had an amazing time last night, but it can't have knocked everything out of your head! Simon was here when I got back this morning. That rat Malcolm has told him.'

'So, he guessed you were bluffing.'

Fran collapsed into a chair, and closed her eyes.

'Yes, but at least he's not buying the house. What's the matter with you? You look all-in.'

Fran kept her eyes tightly shut and said, 'I think the most dreadful thing has happened. I think I might be pregnant with Malcolm's child.' She paused and took a deep breath. 'I did it with him just once when I was back down there. I've suddenly realised my period's seven days late. Isn't that stupid? It suddenly hit me this morning when I was back in the beach hut, after I'd picked Grace up from the Vicarage.'

'Darling, don't panic,' Annabel said. 'It will be because of all the trauma you've been through over the past few weeks.'

'It's never happened before, apart from when I became pregnant with Grace.'

Annabel looked at Fran anxiously, and took Grace from her.

'Go into Southfleet right now and get one of those pregnancy testing kits. By the looks of you, you'll be having a nervous breakdown if you don't find out immediately.'

Fran closed her eyes again. 'What on earth shall I do if I am?'

'Don't even think about it. Now go, and for goodness' sake drive carefully.'

'But what about Simon? Where is he? And where's Lydia?'

'We'll talk about all that later,' said Annabel. 'Just go.'

Although it was late afternoon, Southfleet was surprisingly busy. The parking spaces in the high street were all taken, so she parked on a double yellow line, praying that at this time of day the traffic warden would be off duty. There was a queue in the chemist's. A large lady was kicking up a fuss because her photographs had been mislaid. Fran stood there for over five minutes whilst the harassed assistant conferred with her superior who was busy in the dispensary, and then checked through the drawers of the cabinet again. She eventually found the photos and spent another five minutes apologising to the huffy lady. When Fran's turn finally came, she thrust the small, innocent-looking box into the assistant's hand accompanied by a ten pound note. As soon as the box was handed back to her in a small white bag, she rushed out of the shop, too anxious to get back to care about waiting for her change. The pregnancy tester lay accusingly in her half-opened bag as she drove back to the cottage. She kept glancing at it, willing it to tell her only what she wanted to know.

Back at Watercolour Cottage, she found Annabel and Grace in the kitchen, with Annabel coaxing Grace to eat the yolk of a boiled egg.

'Have you got it?' asked Annabel.

'Yes,' said Fran. 'Yes, I've got it, but I don't want to know.'

'It's going to be all right. I thought you were on the pill, anyway.'

'I am, but with coming up here and then shooting back down again after your accident I missed taking a couple, but I can't believe just missing a few pills means I'd get pregnant straight away.'

'Of course it wouldn't.' She placed another spoonful of egg into Grace's mouth and said, 'For goodness' sake Fran, go and put yourself out of your misery.'

The instructions told her it would take five minutes. She hadn't bothered to do this with Grace, she'd just known she was pregnant and waited for her stomach to swell. She didn't feel she needed a bright circle to prove what she already knew. She closed her eyes and prayed that when she opened them there would be nothing; nothing shouting at her to say she had Malcolm's baby in her womb.

It was blue. It was so blue she felt the test tube was telling her not to hope for the briefest moment that it was wrong. She sat in the bathroom and cried. She cried because she didn't want this baby, and she cried from the guilt of not rejoicing at the creation of a new life.

In the kitchen nothing had changed. Grace was still in her high chair chewing her way through a rusk, and Annabel was sitting next to her smiling encouragement.

'I can't go through with this,' she sobbed, 'I can't have Malcolm's baby, not now.'

She completely broke down and cried in Annabel's arms. Annabel knew there was nothing at this moment she could say to comfort her, she just held her and let her cry.

That night she stayed up at the cottage. The weather had taken a turn for the worse, and the mellow late summer that had briefly settled on Warbleton had been swept away again by a penetrating north-east wind. She slept in the bedroom that had always been hers ever since she first remembered coming to Warbleton. It had the same view as the living room, looking down over the estuary. She knelt by the window and rested her arms on the wide oak windowsill. Some of the boats in the harbour had tiny pinpricks of light shining out of them. They looked in the night like old-fashioned wooden toy boats. On the hill over towards Southfleet, the lighthouse was beaming its warning to unwary ocean-goers. Would everything seem different in the morning, she wondered? Would she wake up and find that she accepted this baby growing inside her with some sort of joy, rather than dread. She touched her flat stomach with her hand. It was impossible to imagine a life was forming there.

She lay curled up on her side, the way she always slept. Normally, she was asleep within minutes but tonight sleep eluded her completely. She lay on her back and stretched out her feet until the tips of her toes touched the bottom of the bed. She tried to sink into the mattress and let the soft-pillowed night smother her, but she couldn't sleep. She got up and went to look at Grace. The new baby would be like Grace, she told herself. Of course she wanted it. She would love the little thing just as completely as she loved Grace. She went back to bed and eventually fell asleep.

The next morning, Annabel was full of brisk, no nonsense advice.

'The worst thing about any situation,' she said to Fran, 'is not knowing what you're going to do and where you stand. It's decision time and we're going to talk everything through. Could you have an abortion?'

Fran just stared at her.

'I'm not saying I think you should, I'm simply working through all the options.'

'No,' Fran said quietly. 'Even at my lowest point, even if I didn't want the baby, I could never contemplate abortion.'

'Fine,' said Annabel briskly, 'that's one option we don't have to investigate then. Do you feel you could get back together with Malcolm?'

This time Fran didn't hesitate. 'Absolutely, definitely not.'

'Well,' said Annabel, 'I'm pleased to hear that.'

'I want to stay here to have the baby.'

'If Daphne and David don't sell the house, and I'll work on that one, I'm sure they'll let you.'

Fran gave a little groan. 'How on earth am I going to explain all this to Mum and Dad?' She could picture her mother wringing her hands in despair, or fiddling anxiously with the pearls round her neck, and then probably there would be tears. Daphne always cried if she didn't like something. 'Can you imagine the pressure I'll be under to go back to Malcolm?'

Annabel looked at Fran in despair.

'For God's sake, Fran, you're not a child anymore. Why do you feel your parents have still got such an influence over you? You're a married woman with a child, you're twenty-four. What you do has got absolutely nothing to do with them.'

'I can't suddenly shake off twenty-four years of being controlled by them. You don't understand.' She looked at Annabel. Annabel was always in control, not of others but herself. Friends leant on her for support. She had an amazing ability to whittle out the inessentials of life to reach the truth.

'You can start trying,' Annabel said, 'and probably now is as good a time as any.'

'I can't face telling Tom. I'll pretend the whole thing with him was a big mistake, and I've changed my mind.'

'Now you're disappointing me. I never took you for a coward. Don't you think he deserves more than that?'

Fran looked crushed. 'Yes, yes, of course I do,' she said, 'but how can I possibly explain this to him when it doesn't make sense to me? Shall I just come straight out with it and say, 'Oh, by the way, Tom, when you made love to me I was expecting Malcolm's baby.'

'It's not your fault you're pregnant.'

'I didn't have to have sex with him, he didn't force himself on me.'

'Don't let this hang over you. You must tell him.'

'Today?'

'Yes. Do it, Fran. I know it's going to be incredibly difficult, but there's no point in putting it off.'

'Okay, I'll do it,' Fran said quietly.

'I was up at the crack of dawn,' Annabel said. 'I went to Mrs. Kennard's funny little shop. I can't believe the odd things she stocks in there.'

Fran did her best to smile. She appreciated the way Annabel was trying to distract her from thoughts of her imminent encounter with Tom.

'It's always been odd. That's why everyone loves it,' she said, 'although Mrs. Kennard can be a frosty old thing. She used to terrify me when I was little and went in to buy sweets. I'm sure she looked exactly the same then.'

Before she left to see Tom, they had cups of coffee made

from ground beans that Annabel had bought that morning from Mrs. Kennard's shop. The coffee grinder in the shop looked more like an ancient piece of woodworking machinery, but it always glowed because Mrs. Kennard was very proud of it and polished it daily.

'When did Simon turn up?' asked Fran.

'Talk about bad timing. He must have arrived here not long after we all went off to Starston Hall. He was fuming following a call he had from Malcolm. I'm not sure he's going to forgive me for this.'

'Oh, Annabel, I feel dreadful.'

'For goodness' sake, don't start worrying about me. I'm sure I can sort Simon out, although right now I'm not too bothered whether I do or not.'

Fran asked her why that was, and Annabel told her about Simon's careless disclosure that he'd been unfaithful to her.

'It's this dreadful age of throwaway marriages,' she said. 'We don't have the same need to stay together that our parents had. When they went through a rough patch, they battened down the hatches and got on with it, whereas we call it a day and head straight for the divorce courts. Couples don't talk to each other any more. We're all too busy leading manic lives.'

'But I know lots of couples who are really happy,' said Fran.

'And so do I, and if I did divorce Simon I'm certainly not saying I'd never marry again, but I'd choose far more wisely. Perhaps Lydia is the one with the right idea, trying out lots of men first!'

'Why did Lydia go rushing back to London? I thought she'd planned on quite a long stay.'

'Lydia can't stand being rejected, and I think the men up here aren't quite so taken in by her as the yuppies in London, apart from that poor chap George.'

Fran smiled gratefully at Annabel.

'Thank you for trying to distract me, but now I must do it. Wish me luck!'

When she was on the final stretch of the flat path that led to Tom's cottage, she heard his Springer Spaniel barking. She wondered where he'd got it from if he lived in Greece for half the year. It was always at his heels, so it must be an old friend; perhaps it lived with his father on the Romney Marshes when he was away.

His pleasure at seeing her was so transparent that it made her want to turn round and go straight back along the path she'd just walked down.

'I'm glad you've come. I was going to hunt you down this afternoon.' He took her hand and led her into the cottage. As soon as they were inside, he pulled her into his arms and kissed her. 'I wanted to tell you,' he said, smiling down at her, 'in the cold light of day, that I love you.'

When she didn't respond, he said: 'I know things are very complicated for you and I'm not putting any pressure on you, but everything I said last night was true, it wasn't pillow talk.' He laughed. 'Do I sound like a lovesick schoolboy?' He felt her body tense in his arms and he was suddenly aware that something was dreadfully wrong. He gently held her away from him.

'What's the matter?' he asked.

She took a few paces away from him and looked out of the window; it created a perfect frame for the muted shades of marsh and sky. She fiddled with the broken catch and said, 'I don't know how to tell you this. It's probably the most hurtful thing I could ever say to you.'

She paused and wrapped her arms round her body and lowered her head.

'I'm pregnant with Malcolm's baby. I've just found out,' she whispered. 'I know it sounds ridiculous but last night I had absolutely no idea.'

The silence was punctuated by the cry of seabirds. Fran could hear the haunting call of the curlew; it sounded sad and alone even though she knew it flew with others of its kind. She couldn't look at him. She felt she didn't have the courage to meet his eyes.

He walked over to where she was standing and gazed out of the window too.

'Isn't it the most wonderful view,' he said.

'Yes,' she replied, taking in the beauty of the wild marshland, and the distant forest and hills over at Dunsmere.

He placed his hand on her waist. 'I think you're too upset to talk about this now. I'll make you a cup of tea.' He gave her a gentle smile. 'Isn't that supposed to solve all known problems?'

Having something to do with her hands made it easier to talk. She held the mug full of piping hot tea and tried to tell him about Malcolm. She wanted to be fair. They were two such different people wanting completely opposite things out of life that the union had been doomed from the start. She had breathed the London air and felt stifled. The business dinners and fast living that Malcolm thrived on had oppressed her. She spent her days in London desperate to get out of it, as she had when she'd been a child. What madness had made her tie herself to a man who saw the countryside as merely something to be tolerated occasionally? But he'd swept her off her feet. He'd made her feel beautiful and clever. She realised now that she'd fallen in love with the idea of being loved.

Tom hadn't moved during her ramblings, he just watched her silently and let her talk.

She tried to explain how their sexual union had been a disaster, too. After each encounter she felt almost abused, although in the brief few months between meeting each other and marriage he had been more gentle and restrained.

She stood up, clenching her hands together.

'And then the last time I was in London, I felt I had to make one more effort. The next day I found out conclusively that he was being unfaithful to me.'

'You don't need to say anymore,' said Tom. 'Let's walk.'

They went down to the shore and walked along the small strip of sand that divided the sea from the shingle beach at low tide. He held her hand tightly and told her that nothing had changed. He still wanted to be with her.

'And the baby?' she said.

He smiled. 'With women now having babies in their forties, you've still got a few years to have a couple of mine!'

'But you hardly know me,' said Fran.

'I'm thirty-two, I haven't slept with lots of women, or had numerous girlfriends, but I know enough about life and women to know it's you I want to be with. How's that for the perfect cliché?' he said, grimacing. 'But there's no other way to say it.'

Fran found his attitude almost impossible to take on board. How could this handsome, kind man with whom she had so much in common with still want her?

'I can't imagine,' she said hesitantly, 'that your father will be very impressed with your choice of long-term partner.'

Tom grinned. 'You don't know Dad, he's the most understanding person I've ever met in my whole life, and my stepmother is a lovely kind lady, too. I'll take you and Grace down to the Romney Marshes and show you my home territory whenever you want to go.'

Fran felt a pang of envy. If only she could have such confidence in her family's support and love. Her parents' love had always been conditional, she'd had to earn it and work hard to keep it.

'There's so much to sort out, though,' she said. 'I don't want to go back to London to face Malcolm and my parents just yet.'

'Don't then,' he said. 'You don't have to go back yet, do you?'

'They all think I'm staying until after the meeting about the beach huts, and that's not for another ten days.'

Tom swung her into his arms and laughed. 'I think this will cheer you up. I've been browbeating Matthew and he's agreed not to sell the land. That's another reason why I was going to come and find you.'

'So my beach hut's safe?'

'Absolutely. He doesn't need to sell the land. Josephine

came in when we were talking about it, and she was furious with him. She wanted to know why he hadn't told her he was planning to sell it.'

'So we've got Matthew into trouble.'

'He would have been in far deeper trouble if he'd gone ahead and sold it. Josephine said it had been part of the estate for centuries and some of the beach hut owners had owned their huts for over forty years. She called him an insensitive young thug!'

Fran laughed. 'Did she really call him a thug?'

'Yes. Though he did point out to her that he thought her use of words was incorrect. She just gave him one of her 'lady of the manor' looks and told him to get their solicitor to write to all the beach hut owners immediately.'

'I shall never be out of your debt.'

'I quite like having a little hold over you from the word go,' he said, with a laugh.

'Can you tell him to send my letter to Watercolour Cottage? I don't want Malcolm knowing about this.'

'He's going to, anyway; he knows you're still in Warbleton. So, you've still got your beach hut. Things aren't that bad, are they?'

⁓

'The incredible thing,' said Fran to Elisabeth later that day, 'is that I really think he does love me.'

'And what's so incredible about that?'

'Have you listened to anything I've said to you over the past hour?'

'Goodness, is that really the time?' said Elisabeth looking up at the clock. 'I'd no idea we'd been talking for so long. The children will be home soon and we won't have the chance to finish this conversation.' She stood up and went over to the larder and took out a large plate full of scones. 'They're always ravenous when they get home. Help yourself,' she said, and placed a jar of home-made jam and some butter next to the scones on the table.

'I want to do this,' said Fran. 'I want to make home-made jam, and have a vegetable garden, and chickens pecking in an orchard.'

'You're an incurable romantic. It's not all roses. The chickens go broody and won't lay, the vegetables get attacked by horrid things like cabbage root fly and wilt and die, and if I could tell you the number of times my jam hasn't set, you'd wonder why I still bother to make it!' She paused and saw Fran's unconvinced expression. 'I do know what you mean, though. All those things seem to put life in its right perspective. It creates peace in a chaotic world.'

'I don't want to have to go back to London and face Malcolm and Mum and Dad. I feel the most dreadful coward, but I need time to absorb everything that's happened.'

'Of course you do. Anyway, you don't need to go and see Malcolm yet, and there's no need to involve your parents at the moment, either, or later, for that matter. You can have the baby here. That's if you and Tom aren't out in Pellini. I'd love to have a baby in the Vicarage again. Promise me you'll consider it?'

'What about James? I don't think he'd relish having a crying baby in the house again. I should think four times is quite enough for him.'

'You leave James to me, he's becoming much more manageable!'

'Is he all right about Ruby now?'

'Edward came to supper last night and he and James chatted happily together all evening. I think it's the turning point, thank heavens. Now, to change the subject completely, are you coming to the Harvest Supper?'

'I'd love to, but I don't want to palm Grace off on Annabel again. I know she doesn't mind, but I seem to have been doing it a lot recently.'

'If you want me to hunt down a babysitter so you can both come, let me know. I'm sure I'll be able to find someone.'

Amy Cooper's parting gesture was to make the Harvest Supper a complete shambles; unintentionally, of course, but it was one that would always be remembered, although not for its abundance of food. Amy had totally miscalculated the number of quiches and optional cold chicken pies needed to feed eighty people, and the puddings, even allowing for ladies on strict diets, had no chance of stretching round the tables. The parable of the fishes and loaves was uppermost in most people's minds when they saw the meagre spread, but it certainly didn't appear as though a miracle was going to produce another dozen banoffi pies or even a few extra crème caramels. It was an unmitigated disaster and even Elisabeth felt sorry for Amy. She kept muttering, to anyone who would listen to her, that her dog was dying and she hadn't been able to give the Harvest Supper her undivided attention, but everyone had seen her marching around Warbleton over the past few weeks with Jason very much alive and kicking, even though he had looked a bit stiff-jointed and thoroughly miserable. By the time the puddings were served, however, no one really cared about the lack of food. The wine was flowing freely and that was all that mattered.

James usually found himself stuck on a table with some particularly boring parishioners, but a last minute reshuffle of place names by Elisabeth had spared him this annual ordeal.

Amy, dressed in an intimidating black suit with an immaculate starched white collar framing her neck, stared at the man next to her. 'I think,' she said in her irritating high-pitched voice, 'that you're in the wrong place. I'm sitting next to the vicar.'

Robert Jarvis, who owned the garage at the end of the village, placed his hand on her shoulder and pointed to the card clearly showing his name. 'Sorry, love,' he said, 'you've been landed with me instead.'

With a full glass before him, and ten more assorted bottles of red and white littered across the table, James was feeling at peace with the world.

'Great do,' said Jack, raising his glass to James. 'Don't worry about the food, people won't need to drink so much now before feeling the delightful effects of the alcohol making their heads spin!'

James smiled sheepishly. 'I don't think that's quite what the Harvest Supper's supposed to be about,' he said.

'And for once it doesn't look as though you're practising what you preach,' laughed Jack.

George had taken a particular dislike to the loud-voiced

man sitting on Phoebe's left, who kept engaging her in conversation and laughing loudly at everything she said. He couldn't imagine why she was even bothering to talk to a lout with stupid-looking gold earrings dangling from both his ears. He seemed to be trying to create a seventies' image, but George thought he looked ridiculous.

'Don't encourage him,' he whispered to Phoebe.

'Mind your own business,' she said. 'I'm not going out with you, so don't start telling me who I can and can't share a joke with. If I want to talk to Neville, I will.'

'Neville?' said George. 'Well, that's a pretty stupid name for a start!'

Over the next half hour, Phoebe completely ignored him and he was left to make polite conversation with a charming but rather boring lady who insisted on telling him her life story. He worked his way through a bottle of wine whilst she told him about her daughter who was having a nervous breakdown because her husband was having an affair with the babysitter, and her son who she suspected was smoking illegal substances. She had just started on her worst fears about her husband when he saw Neville place his hand on Phoebe's upper thigh. George leapt to his feet, dragged him off his chair and punched him on the nose. There was blood everywhere. Phoebe screamed, but she was delighted by what was going on. In the novels she read, men were always fighting over the woman they loved, so she appreciated the significance of Neville's bloodied nose.

Jack leapt to his feet and hauled George off before he could do the cowering chap any more harm. A few people, in true British fashion, had pretended nothing untoward was happening. Elisabeth told George that if he didn't behave himself he'd have to leave. Neville removed himself to another table, terrified that George would start on him again. He'd never been in a fight in his life and any form of physical violence appalled him. He decided Phoebe wasn't worth getting a broken nose for.

It was well after two by the time the last revellers left the village hall. George walked out clasping Phoebe firmly round the waist. 'You'll come back to my house, Phoebe, won't you?' he said.

'I've certainly no intention of walking to Dunsmere at two in the morning, and there's no way you're driving your car back.'

'I thought I'd call for a taxi.' He looked up and down the road as though he thought one might appear at any minute.

'Don't be silly, you're not going to get a taxi at this time of night.'

'Phoebe,' he said, 'you do know I really regret what happened with Lydia, don't you?'

'You don't regret what happened,' said Phoebe, 'you regret the fact that I found out.'

'I say, Phoebe, that's not true at all.' He had started slurring his words. 'Please come home with me. I did sort that chap out.'

'I might not have wanted you to,' she said sharply.

'Please come home with me,' he muttered again.

'You can come back to the pub and stay in the spare room,' she said, somewhat ungraciously.

'That doesn't sound much fun.'

'That's as much fun as you're going to get. If you think

after what's happened that I'm going to leap into bed with you, you're wrong.'

'I don't think that, but I'd love to cuddle up with you, it's ever so chilly tonight.'

'It's not cold in the pub. The heat from the log fire in the bar penetrates through to the whole house.'

'Don't be a spoil-sport, Phoebe. You've been teasing me all night.'

She managed to get him as far as the pub and pushed him onto the bench outside. 'George, you're drunk and incapable of doing anything, so just be grateful of a bed for the night, and be quiet or Dad will hear us.'

She got him up the stairs and into the spare room without any mishap. He pulled her onto the bed with him, but before she had time to object he was fast asleep. She looked at him and smiled. Perhaps she would give him a second chance, but she was determined he'd have to go through a little pain first.

Elisabeth sighed deeply as she sank into bed. It was nights like these that made her wonder why on earth she had ever become a vicar's wife. James was already snoring heavily at her side, oblivious to the tightrope he'd been walking all night. There was such a fine line between allowing his parishioners to have a fun, rowdy and extremely alcoholic Harvest Supper, and keeping the churchwardens and members of the parish council happy. She had seen the look of horror on the faces of Amy Cooper and Mrs. Kennard when George had flattened poor Neville. It was just the sort of thing one of those witches would report to the Bishop and then, with a little bit more stirring, James might be called to account for the events.

It had happened once before when he was a curate. She remembered the incident as though it were yesterday. She'd been pregnant at the time with Chloe and they were living in a nasty little modern house on the edge of an estate. The vicar in the parish where James was curate was a grumpy, pedantic old misery. One day, he pushed James too far and the horrified minister of God found himself on the floor. James was taken to task by the Bishop and swiftly moved on to another parish. Elisabeth still felt it had been a miracle that he wasn't sacked from the cloth. She knew she'd have to swallow her pride and go and see Amy and Mrs. Kennard in the morning, and make some sort of peace with them. Perhaps a little bribery wouldn't go amiss. She'd have to try and remember their weaknesses.

10

Fran spent an unbelievably happy four weeks in Warbleton, despite being oppressed at times by the knowledge of her pregnancy, but it was difficult to stay down for long with Tom as her constant companion.

One day, they drove up to a village in North Norfolk and had lunch in a small restaurant that specialised in seafood and overlooked the sea. She watched his hands as they negotiated their way through a lobster. They were strong, sun-browned hands with long, tapered fingers. Artist's hands, she thought, although the texture of the skin showed he wasn't afraid of manual work. His nails were clean and trimmed, but with none of the manicured neatness of an office worker.

Grace was fascinated by the seagulls that stalked the balcony, puzzled by the empty tables and lack of tit-bits. During the summer months, the tables were jammed together to accommodate as many people as possible, but by the end of September only a few were placed outside for the intrepid holidaymaker. That day, the only occupants were the large, grey and white gulls, fluffed out and tilting in the face of the strong north-east wind.

They went off on long walks round the estuary and over the marsh. They cycled into Southfleet for coffee and ate fish and chips in the pub next to the harbour. Grace went everywhere with them, and Fran tasted real happiness for the first time since she'd been a child.

In the middle of the second week, Tom asked her to his cottage for a meal and tentatively suggested she stay the night. They were sitting behind the beach hut out of the wind, and the late afternoon sun gave a gentle warmth to the final part of the day. They'd set up the barbecue to cook two glistening sea bass that Tom had caught off the point of the estuary. He'd turned up at the hut grinning with delight at his catch, and handed her the neatly gutted fish with a bottle of wine.

She turned the foil-wrapped fish over and said she'd think about staying the night but she couldn't promise. She'd have to ask Annabel to have Grace because she didn't feel it would be right for her to stay in the cottage, too. Even in her own mind she couldn't quite understand why she felt it would be wrong to have Grace there, so how could she possibly explain it to Tom.

She smiled to soften her words, and wondered at the fear created in her by the thought of being apart from Grace, even for a night. It was a primitive, irrational fear of retribution. The word 'adultery' frequently played in her mind, however hard she might try and justify her relationship with Tom. If she stayed at his cottage, they'd make love again. The first time had been a spontaneous acceptance of something too overwhelming to deny, but a calculated foreknowledge seemed more difficult to accept. So many complex emotions were fighting inside her. She felt what almost amounted to gratitude to Malcolm, for if he hadn't allowed lust to come between him and his marriage, she wouldn't now be in a position to escape from it. She wished she didn't feel this need to justify her relationship with Tom. If she wanted to go to bed with him again, then why not? Why did she feel so annoyingly guilty about having sex with a man she loved? Surely that was better in anyone's eyes than the cold dread of sex with a man who made you almost hate your own body.

After turning everything over in her mind, she felt that to deny herself this night with Tom would be a half-hearted attempt to try and prove to herself that she was still the innocent party in a marriage break-up.

That night, he talked about his childhood on the Romney Marshes. He told her about the reclaimed land intersected with dykes where, as a child, he'd caught stickleback and minnows. He told her of the nightingales that pierced the night with their melody, and the weird chorus of croaking frogs that reverberated across the marsh in spring.

Later, when they'd finished talking, he took her to bed and made love to her as sweetly and passionately as he'd done that night at Starston Hall, and she loved him back in an intensity of joyful giving that she'd never imagined possible.

She woke up the next morning in his arms with none of the guilt or confused emotions that she'd imagined might be the aftermath of a planned night with him. She just felt quite ridiculously happy and completely at peace.

She left the cottage after a leisurely breakfast that Tom cooked, and walked up to the village shop to buy a few items she needed for Grace. Mrs. Kennard was out the front, watering a mixture of forlorn-looking flowers. Every spring she made a brave attempt to create a beautiful floral display in tubs and hanging baskets, but each year as spring merged into summer, the flowers struggled to fulfil their initial promise and then failed miserably. It was a catastrophe Mrs. Kennard could never understand, and no one liked to point out that the cause was due to her haphazard watering programme. She either doused the plants night and day for a week, or completely forgot to water them at all. Today, she was on one of her frantic watering sprees.

'I'll be with you in a minute, dear,' she said, and clambered down from a chair she'd placed on the pavement to reach the flowers.

'Do you really think you should be doing that, Mrs. Kennard? Can't one of the paper boys water the plants for you?'

'Paper boys!' she scoffed. 'They're hardly to be trusted to put a paper through a letter-box, so I certainly wouldn't let them near my plants.' She went back into the shop carrying the chair, and Fran followed her.

Fran loved the little shop. The moment she stepped into it, she was transported back to her childhood. She remembered the first time she'd been allowed to walk to the shop on her own; she must have been about six or seven. She was given fifty pence to spend on sweets and she'd stood there forever, gazing at the jars, unable to make up her mind which of the colourful selection to buy.

'Now,' said Mrs. Kennard looking intently at Fran from behind the counter. 'You have the ear of Elisabeth, dear, don't you?'

'Elisabeth's my friend, if that's what you mean.' She watched as Mrs. Kennard rearranged a small display of cakes.

'Someone has got to speak to her about Ruby and the artist. Goodness only knows what carnal acts of lust have been performed in that painter's house, and how the vicar can stand by and allow his daughter to become engaged to such a debauched creature, I've no idea.'

Fran wanted to giggle at the words Mrs. Kennard was using.

'Why do you think he's debauched?' she asked.

She leant forward over the counter and whispered to Fran. 'We all know about artists, don't we?'

'Do we?'

Mrs. Kennard somehow somehow managed to lean even further over the counter, her funny little body almost bending in half. 'Nude paintings,' she hissed.

Fran found herself repeating the words. 'Nude paintings?'

'Yes, so you do understand that you must speak to Elisabeth and stop this.'

Fran began to laugh. It bubbled up and became impossible to control. One moment she was looking into Mrs. Kennard's piercing eyes and the next, she was laughing so much that she had to walk out of the shop. She sat on the bench outside and wondered if she'd ever dare walk into Mrs. Kennard's shop again.

She drove back to London on a gloomy afternoon in October four weeks to the day from when she'd found out she was pregnant with Malcolm's baby. She hadn't forewarned Malcolm or her parents. This time, she was determined to be in control of the situation. She had no intention of allowing them time to get together and plan the best way to bring her to heel. Daphne's treatment of the situation would be to try and make her feel guilty. She'd tell her no one in the family had ever been divorced before and how could Fran do this to her. Malcolm would have a subtler approach, but it would be far more deadly.

On the morning of her departure she knew, even before she opened her eyes, that a heavy mass of grey clouds would be pressing down over the marsh and that they'd follow her all the way back to London. She packed the barest essentials, for she had no intention of staying for a single moment longer than was absolutely necessary.

She had received two letters from Malcolm over the past week, begging her to return to him and promising a fresh start. He'd put a completely different interpretation on the sale of Watercolour Cottage. Annabel, he'd written, had misjudged him dreadfully on all the subjects she had decided to involve herself in. He felt the least he deserved was that she should listen to his side of things.

She'd also received a brief, curt note from Daphne telling her to come back to London immediately, or she'd lose a very fine husband.

⁂

The A12 linked up onto the M25 far too soon; she didn't want the journey to come to an end. Memories of sitting in the back of her parent's car when the holidays were over, came flooding back. She'd always been desperately unhappy then, and the adult she'd become didn't feel any better. When the signs led her off the A12 to join the mad rush of traffic on the M25, she began to feel sick. Malcolm and her parents would somehow contrive to wreck her happiness, she was certain of that.

The first thing she noticed as she pulled up outside the house was a dim light shining from the drawn curtains of their bedroom window. It was unlike Malcolm to have an early night, but perhaps he'd been caning it recently with too many drinks parties and office dinners.

Grace stayed firmly asleep as she lifted her out of the car seat and carried her up the front steps. She even stayed asleep when Fran slipped her key quietly in the front door and opened it. Grace's bedroom, adorned with mobiles of every farm animal imaginable, was the first bedroom off the upstairs corridor. She placed her gently into her cot. Malcolm must be watching television. She could hear the noise blaring out before she was half-way down the corridor to their room.

Afterwards, when she relived the scene for Annabel, she couldn't remember who received the greatest shock, herself, Malcolm or Lydia. The odd thing about the bedroom scene was that Lydia and Malcolm could have been an ordinary married couple.

Lydia was the first to recover.

'What on earth are *you* doing here?' she gasped. 'I thought you were safely tucked away in Warbleton.'

'Obviously,' said Fran. She saw the whole scene like a freeze-frame; Lydia brazenly making no attempt to cover her body, and Malcolm clutching the sheet to him as though she were a stranger he was hiding his nakedness from.

'How long has this been going on for?' Fran demanded.

Lydia looked at her without any show of emotion.

'Absolutely ages,' she said. 'In fact, it probably kicked off the week after you got back from your honeymoon. Isn't that right?' She turned and looked at Malcolm.

Malcolm, for once in his life, was quite speechless, and muttered something about it definitely not being so short a time as a week.

'Well,' said Fran, 'it's comforting to know it might have been just over a week.'

Lydia got out of bed, and started to put her clothes on.

'I really wouldn't bother dressing, you're very welcome to spend the rest of the night here, and the rest of your life if you want to.'

Lydia stared at Fran and continued to dress.

'Actually, I don't want to, ours is a totally gratuitous relationship, isn't it?' she said, turning to look at Malcolm again.

Fran stared at her husband lying half propped up by pillows. She found it impossible to imagine that she had once loved this man.

Ignoring Lydia, she walked nearer the bed and said, 'I came to tell you that I want a divorce. I won't be unreasonable about you having access to Grace, but I'll be getting a solicitor onto it. I had planned to stay a couple of days so we could sort things out amicably, but now…' She hesitated, still finding it difficult to take on board all that had happened, '… now I know you could never really have cared about me, I think I'd rather have some distance between us.'

She went and got Grace out of her cot, carried her carefully down the stairs, and out of the front door that she never had any intention of opening again.

As she put on her seat belt she found her hands were shaking. Perhaps she'd been naïve to believe Lydia wasn't capable of such immoral behaviour, but despite everything she knew about her, she was still shocked. The immediate problem was where on earth she was going to sleep tonight. She certainly didn't feel up to facing anyone. There was only one thing for it, she would go straight back to Warbleton. She turned her lights on and they lit up the wet street. It was only two hours away, after all. Daphne was going to have to be told what was going on over the telephone. She would definitely have hysterics but that was preferable to an inquisition right now.

Feeling somewhat foolish, she edged her way through the lamp-lit streets and out into the country. 'That's the last of London!' she exclaimed out loud and, turning on the radio, began singing along to an old Abba song.

Half an hour later, the car suddenly lost momentum and came to a grinding halt. *Why did it always have to happen at the worst possible moment,* she thought, fumbling in her wallet for her RAC card. It was over half an hour before the RAC van reached her and the news was bad. She had no choice but to ring Daphne and say she was on her way.

Daphne put on her best mother/granny act as she opened the door to Fran and swept them into the sitting room as though they'd just experienced an earthquake, famine, or some equally dreadful catastrophe. Uncharacteristically, she didn't ask too many questions, although Fran knew from experience they'd definitely be fired at her the next day.

With Grace tucked up in bed, and a mug of hot chocolate in her hands, Fran felt something akin to warmth towards her mother.

'Now darling, don't tell me anything if you don't want to. We'll have a good, long chat over breakfast. You look all in. I think you should go straight to bed.

Fran relaxed in the warmth of Daphne's concern. 'Thanks, Mum,' she said gratefully and gave her mother a hug. Daphne returned it with a certain amount of affection and then detached herself, and brushed the front of her dress with her hand saying, 'I think you've deposited half of Warbleton beach on me.'

Some of the tiny grains of sand that had been clinging to her sweater had been transferred onto Daphne.

Next morning's breakfast was the inquisition she knew it would be, with both Daphne and David asking particularly invasive questions. She placed her coffee cup back in its perfect porcelain saucer, and then placed her hands on the arms of the chair as if she were about to be pushed down a slope and had to hang onto the top for dear life.

'I found Lydia in bed with Malcolm last night. They've been having a relationship for almost as long as we've been married. He's also slept with a girl called Sandra, who's his PA. I've decided to leave him, and it's absolutely no use trying to persuade me to do otherwise.'

'Oh, this is all too dreadful,' said Daphne. 'I can't believe everyone is so promiscuous.'

'And I've fallen in love with a man in Warbleton.'

'Well, I hope you're not going to live in that awful beach hut with him. I suppose he's a penniless artist. That would be just like you, Fran. You'd go off with him just to spite us.'

Fran looked at her mother in amazement. 'Why should I want to spite you, Mother? That's a horrid thing to say. I've simply fallen in love, something I never really did with Malcolm. That's one of the reasons it probably didn't work between us.'

'What about money? I'm quite sure Malcolm will see you get as little as possible in a divorce settlement.'

Fran shrugged. 'I don't care about money, I just want to be happy.'

'Well, we all want that, but it's not quite so simple, and money is important. It gave you a lot of nice things when you were a child. It's easy to be dismissive when you've got it.'

Fran felt this was a small pearl of wisdom from her mother, but it didn't alter the fact that she really wasn't interested in Malcolm's money. Most of it had been gained through dishonest means, anyway.

'Why is Annabel still in Warbleton?' asked Daphne. 'I never remember her being particularly partial to it. She used to think it was a cold, windswept place.'

'I think she's nearly as fed up with Simon as I am with Malcolm.'

'Simon and Annabel were made for each other, there is absolutely no way their marriage is going to break up.' Daphne paused briefly and looked at David. 'I think your father and I should know who this man is that you're involved with. We have to think about Grace.'

'Do you really think I'd be with anyone that I thought would be unsuitable for Grace?'

'What does he do,' asked Daphne. 'Has he any money?'

'He's got a watersports centre in Greece. I haven't actually asked him how much money he's got,' she said sarcastically. 'I suppose I could ask him to show me his bank statements.'

'I don't think it's necessary to be rude to your mother,' snapped David.

'What's his name?' asked Daphne.

'Tom Reeves.'

Fran was looking straight at Daphne when she said it and the look of horror on her mother's face was so real that it frightened her.

'What's the matter? Do you know him?' asked Fran in surprise.

'I feel ill,' Daphne said, 'I can't cope with all of this,' and she fled from the room.

'Now you've done it,' said David. 'Your mother will probably take to her bed for a week.'

The pain filtered into her dreams first. She dreamt that the bull seal she and Grace had seen was chasing her along the beach and the pain in her stomach prevented her from running. He was hauling himself across the beach, his huge tusks inches from her when she woke. As she drifted back into wakefulness, the pain was still piercing her abdomen and then she felt the wet, sticky blood between her thighs. She knew instantly what was happening. She lay for a moment and let the pain wash over her. It was just light, her bedside clock showed her it was five to six. She wondered what people did when they knew they were miscarrying. Did they just lie still and hope the traumatic expulsion of human life would subside? Should she dial 999 and get an ambulance to rush her to hospital? She went to the bathroom and wound a towel round her and walked calmly down the corridor to her parent's room.

She looked at her parents, lying side by side fast asleep in apparent harmony. They both lay on their backs with their mouths partially open; it wasn't a very pretty sight. She wondered why sleep could make some people look so ugly and others beautiful. She hesitated even though the pain had become more severe. 'Mother,' she said, shaking Daphne awake.

Her mother sat bolt upright as though she'd never really been asleep at all. 'What on earth's the matter?' she said.

'I'm pregnant and I think I'm having a miscarriage.'

Daphne just stared at her. She seemed incapable of movement. 'Who's the father?' she demanded.

Fran stared at her in amazement. 'Does that really matter right now?'

Daphne threw the duvet cover off her and sat up. 'Who's the father?' she repeated.

'Malcolm,' whispered Fran.

'Thank God for that.'

'Mother, what shall I do? Do you think I should go to hospital?'

'No, I'll call our doctor. Your father and I have got to know him really well, he's part of our dinner party set, so I'm sure he'll come out before he starts his surgery.'

She put her arm round Fran and led her out of the bedroom and back to her own room. She told her to have a bath whilst she rang for the doctor and changed the sheets.

Fran lay in the bath watching the blood seep out of her. If the baby survived, it would be a miracle. At this moment of loss, she wanted it desperately. She remembered Grace as a newborn baby, and the moment when she had been placed in her arms, when all the pain she had suffered during the long hours of labour vanished in the joy of her love for the tiny infant. She was never going to hold this baby. It had been deprived of life before it had taken one breath. She felt as guilty as if she'd walked into a clinic and demanded an abortion.

The doctor marched into the room barely half an hour later, impatient and unsympathetic. He took her blood pressure and told her he'd arrange for her to have a scan at the hospital before the end of the day. There were no words of comfort. In the small veterinary practice in Warbleton, Fran had seen Jack show more concern and care for a hedgehog.

When the doctor left, she heard the front door slam hard behind him. Daphne thought he had been positively rude. She tucked the bedclothes round Fran.

'I simply don't understand, darling. He's always been so charming and chatty when I've sat next to him at the dinner table.'

'He probably resented you using your friendship to drag him out to see me.'

'Well, if he's not careful I'll strike him off my dinner party list.'

Fran almost felt like smiling. She could see her mother was perfectly serious. She said tiredly, 'I think if a person is kind, they'd make a kind doctor.'

'Perhaps he was just exhausted, darling,' said Daphne consolingly. 'Doctors have to deal with so many patients. For all we know he could have been up half the night.'

Fran sipped water out of a glass that Daphne had put on her bedside table, and then lay her head back down on the pillow.

'Could you get my mobile out of my bag please, Mum?' she asked weakly. 'I want to ring Annabel.'

Daphne looked across the room to where Fran's bag was lying. 'I think, dear, that it would be much better if you just rested now. Call Annabel tomorrow.'

Fran said firmly, 'No Mum, I need to speak to her now.'

Annabel answered after just a couple of rings and Fran blurted everything out immediately, barely pausing between the news of Lydia in bed with Malcolm, and the miscarriage. It was such a relief to talk to Annabel that she started crying.

Annabel's immediate concern was for Fran and the miscarriage. 'Everything will be fine,' she said. 'I know you, Fran, you're feeling guilty about what's happened but Nature just does what she feels is best. Your state of mind had absolutely nothing to do with it. For goodness' sake don't start putting yourself on the rack, it will serve no useful purpose.'

Before they finished talking, she asked Annabel if she'd tell Tom about the miscarriage. She promised she would go down to his cottage immediately.

Later that morning there was a telephone call from Elisabeth. When they'd finished their conversation, her mother came in and said, 'I do like the vicar's wife. I've always approved of your friendship with her.'

Fran remembered how her mother had always interfered in her friendships with girls at school. When she was about thirteen she'd chummed up with Natasha, a brilliant beanpole of a girl who her mother thought was absolutely dreadful. She wore red nail varnish when she wasn't at school, and lots of make-up. Her parents were just as wealthy as Daphne and David, but seemed as determined as their daughter to shock society. Fran loved going round to their wacky house. Nothing matched in the wild mishmash of colours. Natasha had even been allowed to design her own bedroom. It was painted black, with abstract shapes in gold splashed across the black walls. Within weeks of the friendship blossoming, Daphne had banned Natasha from the house and refused all Fran's entreaties that she be allowed to visit her friend. The promising friendship had died, and Fran hated her mother for being the cause of its demise.

'Why,' asked Fran, 'do you so approve of Elisabeth?'

'Well, darling, she's sensible, isn't she? She's a vicar's wife.'

'She doesn't want to be sensible. She positively hates being sensible. If you knew what went on in her mind, you wouldn't think she was boring and sensible.'

'I didn't say she was boring.'

'Sensible is the same thing, isn't it?'

'I shall make allowances for you as you've just been through a very emotional experience. I want you to lie down quietly now and I'll bring you up a cup of tea.'

She knew she would be told she'd lost the baby before the scan had even been completed. She looked into the eyes of the radiologist; they were so brown they could almost have been black, and they were full of compassion.

'I'm afraid you've lost your baby,' she said, and held Fran's hand.

It was early evening when she was taken along to the operating theatre to have a D-&-C. It was the first time she'd ever been in for an operation; that's if removing the last traces of the baby from her womb could be called an operation. The thought of being put under an anaesthetic made her experience the sort of blind, unmanageable panic that even mountainous ocean waves had never managed to create in her. It was caused by the knowledge that she was going to be sent down into a dark well of emptiness where she had no control over what was done to her. She knew it was an irrational fear, but so was arachnophobia. Nothing could be more harmless than an English house spider.

She concentrated on the face of the nurse walking next to the trolley. She was plump and pretty, with short dark hair. She gave Fran a lovely smile and said, 'Don't worry, you'll be fine.' Fran tried to smile back at her but found she was too tired to even move her lips.

The next morning, she woke in the small, white, clinical room that she'd been returned to after the operation the previous night. She tried to imagine what the baby she had lost would have been like. She wondered what she would have called it, and if the small embryo that had been the promise of a new life had been a girl or a boy. She played with different names. Joseph for a boy, and Evie for a girl. But there was no baby. It was almost as though there never had been. It would be several hours before Daphne came to collect her, but then tomorrow she'd be back in Warbleton. She just had to hang on to that.

11

Tom lay in his bed wide-awake before dawn had made any attempt to rouse a new day into life. He turned onto his side and wondered if it was worth trying to get back to sleep, but his mind was as active as if he'd been awake for several hours. He pressed the button on his bedside clock to illuminate the face and saw it was only ten past five.

He pulled the bedclothes round him. He found it wonderful and disconcerting that love could have such a powerful influence over his life. He'd certainly never had it disturb his sleep before, but he also knew that he'd never really been in love until now. He wondered at the definition of love, and knew achingly that this was it. It had nothing to do with self-absorbed gratification. Love had shown him that it was made up totally of a desire to give.

When Annabel had told him about the miscarriage, the only emotion he had felt was one of intense sadness. He wondered why the loss of another man's child affected him so profoundly, but it was Fran's loss, and because he loved her it became his loss, too. The strength of this love terrified him. He found it impossible now to imagine a life without her. Birdsong drifted through the lifting darkness and he knew dawn was already touching the marsh. He wasn't a religious man, but nevertheless he prayed to some unknown

God that she'd come back to him. The miscarriage would definitely have traumatised her. He could feel her guilt from a hundred miles away. He just hoped her common sense would prevail and make her realise that losing the baby had nothing to do with her initial despair at finding out she was pregnant.

He had wanted to drive down to London immediately to be at her side, but Annabel had foreseen this reaction and wisely told him to stay put and give Fran space. But it was so difficult. He wasn't worried that she would return to Malcolm; he knew perfectly well that that relationship was doomed before he'd come on the scene, but she'd be desperately miserable stuck down there in London.

He got out of bed and went to the window to see what the day had to offer. Wisps of clouds made streaks across the pale blue sky, but there wasn't a breath of wind to give movement to the dormant landscape. Only the wheeling, calling birds brought life to the new day. The cottage now had a winter chill to it in the mornings. The owners had never installed any semblance of central heating, but as soon as he lit a fire in the old stove the room began to heat up to a perfectly acceptable temperature. He knew he spent far too much time thinking about Fran. Within the space of a few weeks she had completely taken over his life. Her physical absence made no difference, she was still there beside him throughout his waking hours.

If he knew when she was coming back he could get down to the Romney Marshes to see his father before her return. He had spoken briefly to him shortly after he realised Fran was going to be a permanent part of his life, but to ask what he wanted over the phone seemed insensitive after so many years. He decided that he would see how things worked out today and, if Fran wasn't going to return for a few days, he would drive down to Ivychurch tomorrow.

He pulled on some old jeans and a thick jumper and when he'd lit a fire in the stove, he went into the kitchen and put on the kettle. When Fran had stayed, they'd drunk tea in bed and snuggled under the bedclothes. They'd giggled foolishly when the hot liquid had spilt over the sides of the mugs onto the white sheets. Later, she'd tucked into a cooked breakfast he'd prepared for them both with a heartiness that delighted him. He had always found women with picky appetites irritating. He hoped last night's weather forecast was going to prove correct, but there was still no hint of the predicted force six. A session out amongst the waves would do him the world of good, although he knew pictures of Fran pulling off manoeuvres with ridiculous ease would be with him the whole time. It was incredible, he thought, how quickly she had got under his skin. He just hoped she wanted to stay there.

While dawn was breaking over the reed beds and the haunting cry of the curlew was carried on the wind up to the sleepy village of Warbleton, Daphne was listening to the sounds of London awakening. She had spent a restless night knowing she had to tell Fran the truth. David lay on his back snoring at her side. If only he would stop sleeping on his back, the nightly annoyance of his snoring might cease. She pushed him angrily and he turned on to his side, the harsh sound stopping instantly.

She had never questioned the judgement of her decision not to tell Fran. Why did anyone need to know? It had been pushed so firmly to the back of her mind that when at odd moments it had surfaced, she couldn't quite believe it herself. The bed shuddered as David flopped onto his back again, the snoring immediately building up to an impressive crescendo. The only good thing about it at this early hour, she thought, was that it completely obscured the sound of the Underground heaving into life, and the tap-tap of feet on the pavement as the endless daily cycle began once more.

David lingered over breakfast. He sat reading his paper and drinking numerous cups of coffee until Daphne wanted to scream at him to go. He went through his usual routine before leaving the house, which consisted of wiping his shoes several times with a soft cloth, and giving his coat a meticulous going-over with a clothes brush. Even the fastidious Daphne thought the whole performance completely unnecessary. He polished his shoes before he went to bed, so why on earth he needed to take a cloth to them again in the morning was quite beyond her.

He finally gave Daphne a peck on the cheek. She foolishly wondered when it had changed from being a proper kiss, but it was so long ago she couldn't remember. When they were first married, he had insisted on bringing her tea in bed every morning. She'd stretch out in their lovely big bed, marvelling at her attentive husband. Did familiarity inevitably change everything, she wondered, or were some couples as much in love at fifty as they had been in the first flush of their relationship?

She didn't even wait to clear away the breakfast things, which was unheard of, as she wanted to find the diary. She knew it was the only way of conveying to Fran what had really happened, or, if she were honest, the only way she could possibly deal with it. To stand in front of Fran and form the words to tell her would be totally beyond her emotional capabilities.

She had first started writing a diary in her early teens. It had begun as a small act of independence. She could fill the empty pages with all her inner-most thoughts and ideas, without the prospect of being slapped down by her mother. When she started dating boys, her private thoughts were penned secretly at night, often under the bedcovers by torchlight so her mother wouldn't walk in and demand to see what she was writing. She'd continued to write her diary even after she was married, but on the day Fran was born she'd stopped. She had placed her last diary with all the others, up in the attic in an old wooden chest she'd had since she was a child. The chest was secured with a small, heart-shaped padlock. It had kept her brother's prying fingers away from her most treasured possessions. After her diaries were placed in it, the padlock kept her secret safe.

She went into her bedroom and pulled out the bottom drawer of her dressing table. At the back of the drawer was a small mother of pearl jewellery box that lay amongst bigger boxes containing some of her less valuable items.

She took the key out of the box and placed everything neatly back. Upstairs, the loft ladder was easy to release and she climbed carefully up it and pulled open the trap door that led to the large roof space above the house. Many years ago, before they'd bought it, initial preparations had been made to create another bedroom in the attic. There were floorboards across the whole length of it, and a small window that allowed a chink of light into the musty darkness.

She found what she was looking for under a pile of old suitcases. She briskly placed the key in the padlock, opened the chest and, without looking at any other items, pulled out one diary from amongst a whole pile of them. She had no problem identifying the one she wanted as it was bright pink, whereas all the others were in various shades of soft blue and green; for some long-forgotten reason, she had abandoned her usual custom and bought a bright pink one that year. She held the diary in her hands. Embossed in small gold print in the top left hand corner was the year: 1973. She knew this was a harsh way of doing it, but what other course of action could she possibly take? She opened the diary and found the page where it had all begun. Fran would probably understand, but whether she could ever forgive her would be quite another matter. She knew she couldn't have found a worse time to tell her, but her hand had been forced. She had absolutely no choice.

≪

The bedroom shouted a welcome at her the moment Fran walked into it after the short drive back from the hospital. On the dressing table were two of her mother's expensive vases, bearing flower displays that Fran thought looked as though they should be standing on pedestals to celebrate a wedding. Daphne had arranged them to perfection and Fran knew she couldn't have done better herself.

'These, darling, are from Daddy and I,' Daphne said, fiddling with one of the displays, 'and the others arrived this morning from Annabel.'

Fran went across and read the small card from Annabel. It just said: *Keep your spirits up! Much love, Annabel.*

Fran held the note in her hand and said, as casually as she could, 'I'm going back to Warbleton tomorrow. Don't say I won't be well enough to drive because I'll be fine. I want to get back to Tom.'

She looked down at her hands and waited for the explosion. When it didn't come, she glanced at her mother. Her composure was disconcerting; she would normally be coming out with curt, sharp expletives, but on this occasion she simply said she'd make them both a cup of tea and walked out of the room in her usual brisk manner.

She returned barely five minutes later with a cup of tea in one hand and a little pink diary in the other and announced, 'I don't think, darling that it would be a good idea for you to go back to Warbleton at the moment.'

Daphne placed the cup of tea on the bedside table and handed Fran the diary, which had a book mark in it. 'I want you to read this from where I've marked it. I'm afraid I'm taking the coward's way out,' she said.

'For God's sake, Mother, what on earth is all this about?' Fran felt intensely irritated. 'Why are you giving me this diary to read?' She threw it petulantly onto the bed. 'If I want to return to Warbleton today, tomorrow or whenever, you can't stop me.'

Daphne sat down next to her on the bed. 'This is frightfully difficult for me, I wish beyond anything else that I'd told you years ago,' she said.

Fran noticed that her mother was very pale and there seemed to be a glimmer of tears in her eyes.

'Told me what years ago?' she said, more gently.

Daphne stood up again and walked towards the door, then paused briefly and said, 'I promise to answer all your questions when you've read the diary. Please try and understand when you read it, and don't be too judgemental. I've only ever had your best interests at heart.'

With that, she hurried out of the room.

Fran felt her heart begin to thump as she looked at the small pink diary in her hands and wondered what it was that her mother so anxiously wanted her to read. She had never known her mother to behave in such a way. She was almost apologetic, yet Daphne was a woman for whom the word 'sorry' didn't exist. She opened it at the page her mother had marked.

May 19

I dropped Simon off at playschool this morning and managed to avoid having to talk to any of the other mothers. They always want to get so intimate and I really don't feel I need to sit with other women drinking coffee and talking about children. Bought a dress to die for in Harvey Nichols. I'll wear it to the next office function of David's. He was late back from work again. I rang the office twice but he wasn't there. When he did turn up, it was past nine and he said he'd been for a drink with Roger. I wish he could understand how much I look forward to him getting home. I said it would be nice if he could put Simon to bed occasionally, but he didn't seem very enthusiastic. If he carries on like this, Simon won't even recognise him.

May 20

I suggested over breakfast that we go to Warbleton for a few days, as the weather's so mild and it would be lovely to be together as a family for longer than our usual weekend. He spends most of it on the golf course, anyway. Of course, I didn't say that to him. I didn't want to put his back up. He said he'd think about it, but he didn't seem very keen. I wonder sometimes why he bought the house, as we so rarely go there. Another boring day, although I did meet Katie for lunch which brightened things up considerably for a few hours. Thank God Mum dotes on Simon and likes having him. I never dreamt she'd take on the role of grandmother so well.

May 23

We're not going to Warbleton, but David has got to go to Jersey on business. I tentatively suggested I go along too and told him Mum would love the chance to have Simon for a few days, but he said he'd be too busy. He's changed so much from when we first married. He wanted to be with me all the time then. It's almost as though he doesn't even see me any more. If that's the effect a baby has on a marriage, I wish I'd never had one.

Fran put the diary down and wondered what all these words were leading up to.

So far, it just seemed the typical sort of boring diary that anyone might keep, a mixture of thoughts and frustrations that normally played around in one's mind, but never went any further. She picked it up again. The next few days were blank and then she read:

May 28
Had lunch again with Katie. She seems to have it all. Sexy, adoring boyfriend, successful career, loads of money from her own achievements (how satisfying would that be to have money that you'd actually earned yourself!). Well, at least I've got money even if it is David's. Sometimes I look at Katie and wish I was her. I actually wish away Simon and David. I grasped marriage as though I was drowning, but I'm not clever like Katie. I could never have had this brilliant lifestyle without David. At least I get to drive a Porsche. Even Katie hasn't got that.

May 29
The flight from Jersey was due in at seven forty but he rang to say it had been cancelled because of fog. I put the phone down and knew he was lying, but what was so strange was that it was such a stupid lie. I would have expected him to come up with something better than fog. I immediately rang Gatwick airport and asked if any flights from Jersey had been cancelled, and they told me emphatically that there were no flight delays or cancellations. I then did what all women suspicious of what their husbands are up to do. I looked through the pockets of his suits. There were all sorts of odd bits of paper that didn't tie up, car park tickets in places I'd

no idea he'd been to and, of course, a dinner bill with the name of a hotel clearly emblazoned across the top. We'd certainly never been there. I'm writing all this calmly, but my mind is racing down all sorts of horrendous avenues. I have to assume he's being unfaithful to me, but the thought makes me so angry that I can barely confront it.

Fran felt all the distressing emotions of a few weeks ago hit her again. The horrible doubt, and then sudden awakening as to what was really going on. So, her mother had experienced this too. She could barely read on, knowing without doubt that history had repeated itself.

May 29

I came out with it almost as soon as he walked in the door. He poured himself a larger than usual whisky and I asked him if he was being unfaithful to me. His initial response was anger, how could I possibly think that of him, he said. What was almost clinically interesting was how indignant he managed to sound. I threw my small pool of evidence onto the table and told him I knew no flights had been cancelled from Jersey.

He looked so shocked that I could almost have laughed. He made no attempt to deny anything then, he just looked at me and said he was most dreadfully sorry. He would end the relationship immediately, it meant nothing to him. I didn't want to know any of the sordid details. I refused to cry and ask him why he'd done it. I simply told him I'd be going to Warbleton because I couldn't bear the sight of his ugly, adulterous face.

May 30

I've left Simon with my mother. I know I should have taken him with me but I want to have time to myself. I'm fed up with being at the beck and call of an annoying three-year-old. I do wish I was more maternal, but I'm just not. I find children quite unbelievably annoying. Watercolour Cottage is all in perfect order, but I now feel really depressed, and wonder why I've come here as it's so empty and bleak at this time of year.

Fran flicked quickly through the next few entries. They said nothing significant until June 3rd.

I met him down by the beach huts. His dog came over to where I was sunbathing topless behind one of the huts. He was incredibly embarrassed. He apologised and introduced himself. He said his name was Jim Reeves and then we chatted for almost half an hour. He told me he was staying over at Starston Hall where his cousin lived. I've agreed to meet him for a drink in The Reed and Whistle tonight – two can play at David's little game.

Reeves… Fran's heartbeat escalated. The next three days were empty, then came the entry on June 7th.

I think he's falling in love with me. It wasn't what I'd planned at all. He is the most gorgeous man though, and sex with him is brilliant, it lifts me up to the most incredible heights. I've never experienced that with David. Jim isn't married but he has a son. He said his wife died nine years ago. His expression didn't invite questions, so I don't know why his poor wife died.

Fran scanned through the pages of the next few weeks not wanting to read the details of her mother's affair with Tom's father. However, the words on June 14th stood out:

I'm going back to London otherwise I shall die of boredom even though having an affair with Jim is exciting. I know I'm going to hurt him. I haven't told him yet that I'm married and have a child. Tomorrow isn't going to be very pleasant, but I'm beginning to miss London. The nearest shops are in Southfleet and it's a boring little place. The most exciting thing that happens here is when a band plays in The Reed and Whistle.

June 15
Today has been as beastly as I thought it would be. He came to Watercolour Cottage for supper, and I told him I was married. He was so shocked. He asked why I wasn't wearing a ring. I told him I'd removed it because I was so angry with my husband. I then told him all about David and his affairs, and I also told him that I had a three-year-old son. He told me he loved me, and if I got divorced he'd marry me. We could live on his farm down on the Romney Marshes. I said I thought only sheep lived there, and he actually managed to laugh. I couldn't bring myself to tell him there was no way I could be a farmer's wife and I'd die of boredom stuck in the middle of nowhere.

There was nothing then for over a month, and she could barely bring herself to read the next entry suddenly experiencing a terrible forboding.

July 10th
I'm pregnant and I know it's Jim's baby, but I shall have to pretend to David that it's his. I just pray it's late. David might have his faults but at least he gives me everything I could possibly wish for. He's been very attentive since I've got back. I'm just not romantic enough to follow a dream, but I do miss Jim.

Fran closed the diary.

There was, thankfully, a bottle of white wine in the fridge. She uncorked it and poured herself a large glass. She wondered if people became alcoholics because they were unhappy. It seemed a pretty obvious conclusion. The pushchair wasn't where Daphne normally tucked it away neatly in the hall, so she assumed her mother had taken Grace out for a walk.

She sat at the kitchen table and wondered what the definition of the word 'incest' was. Sexual intercourse with a close relative seemed the most likely one. She looked down at her hands and saw that they were trembling like a very old man's. Her heart was beating so fast and hard that she thought it might not be able to cope and would suddenly cease to beat at all. She pushed the glass of wine away from her and, burying her head in her hands, cried wretchedly for everything she had lost.

She had no idea how long she had been sitting there

before the sound of Daphne opening the front door made her lift her head from the table. She walked out into the hall and looked at her mother with anguished accusation.

'Please,' said Daphne plaintively, 'let me get my coat off before you start.'

'Do you know what the most unbelievable thing about all of this is?' said Fran, as though she hadn't heard her mother speak. 'The most unbelievable thing is that I've spent the last twenty-four years believing David to be my father.'

She lifted Grace out of her pushchair and gently carried her into the kitchen.

'I'm pleased,' said Daphne, 'that you're managing to be calm about this.'

Fran turned to her mother, her face awash with fury. 'I'm not calm,' she said bitterly. 'Not remotely. You have no idea what this has done to me.'

'I'll answer any of your questions. I know we need to talk about this.'

Fran turned her back on her mother and mechanically began to prepare scrambled eggs for Grace's tea. She noticed that her mother now bought free-range eggs. The yolks were an amazing deep orange.

'Did you hear what I said? I know you need to understand, to have some answers.' Daphne poured herself a glass of wine from the bottle Fran had left on the table and, took a large, unladylike gulp.

'I've got to get out of here. You feed her.' Fran thrust the bowl of scrambled eggs into her mother's hands, flung on her coat and slammed the front door violently behind her.

Afterwards, she had no idea where she'd walked. She

remembered pushing open the door of a café and asking for a coffee. She looked at the other customers sitting at tables, irregularly placed in the awkwardly shaped room. The owner had used every inch of space available. She admired his ability to conjure a café out of such poor material. Did anyone else in the room carry dark secrets, evil secrets around with them, she wondered? They all looked like such nice, ordinary people, but she looked normal, too… or did she? She took a couple of sips and had to leave. If she kept walking, perhaps the disgusting word *incest* would stop revolving round in her head. Perhaps she'd find she'd woken up from a nightmare and none of what she had read was true.

Where on earth did she go from here? She couldn't possibly see Tom herself and tell him. To watch his face when she broke the news, 'You're my brother,' would be enough to tip her over the edge. She had to hang on for Grace's sake. Annabel or Elisabeth would have to tell him. It was an almost impossible favour to ask, but she knew either one of them would do it for her. A letter would be too cruel.

She must have been walking for over two hours because Daphne had already put Grace to bed by the time she returned to the house. She was sitting at the kitchen table with a smudged face from crying, the bottle of wine in front of her almost empty. Fran tried to feel some sort of detached sympathy for her, but her anger was too fresh to allow any other emotion to creep in.

She took her coat off and sat opposite her mother.

'Where do you want me to begin?' asked Daphne.

'I feel so angry, so let down. You're my mother and, by your silence, you've made me commit incest.'

'But darling, I never dreamt in a million years that this would happen.'

'And I love him, I love my brother in a way no one is ever meant to love their brother.'

'Oh, darling.' Daphne started crying, quiet sobs that aroused absolutely no pity in Fran.

'Does Dad know he's not really my father?'

'I've never breathed a word of this to a soul, and that mustn't change. No one must know, especially not your father.'

'How could you possibly have lived with that lie all these years? And what about Tom's dad? Didn't he have the right to know he'd got another child?'

Fran stood up and paced round the kitchen.

'I suppose this is my retribution, and yours, too,' she said harshly.

'Do you have to turn this into a biblical drama?' said Daphne, with a sudden spurt of anger. 'An unforeseen set of circumstances has caused all this. If you hadn't leapt into bed with another man on the rebound from Malcolm, none of this would have happened.'

'So it's all my fault now, is it?' Fran found she was shouting. 'How could you have encouraged me to marry Malcolm? He's from the same mould as Dad, you must have seen that!'

'I realised after my fling with Jim that falling madly in love isn't always the most important thing. I'd have shrivelled up and died down on those marshes in Kent. I wanted the best for you, and Malcolm could provide you with everything you could possibly want.'

'No, no, that's not true. It was everything *you* could want. I didn't want that, but I was too weak and pathetic and easily manipulated by you and Dad to realise it. Didn't you care that Dad was unfaithful to you?'

'Of course I cared, but I forgave him. After the first time, I turned a blind eye if I thought something was going on. Men aren't meant to be monogamous, we just have to accept that.'

'Well, I can't and I never will. I pity you, Mother. You've lived a lie for all these years, and I don't even believe you and Dad are happy, you just rub along together. You let your wings be clipped and you've never flown.'

'Stop using ridiculous metaphors, I've got everything I could possibly want,' Daphne insisted.

'Materially, but certainly not emotionally.'

'Stop twisting everything I say. Do you want me to beg for your forgiveness on my bended knees?'

'No,' said Fran. She felt exhausted. 'Were you never going to tell me who my real father was?'

'No, I didn't feel it was necessary.'

'Didn't you think that it would have enabled me to understand myself better if I'd known?'

'You had everything Fran, everything.'

'I never understood why I was so different to you all. Why I hated living in the town, and saw the streets and houses as part of a prison. But it's no wonder I felt that way, if my father and his family have lived on the Romney Marshes for generations. The countryside is in my blood!'

Daphne stood up awkwardly. Walking to where Fran sat, she placed her hands firmly on both of her daughter's shoulders. 'I beg you not to tell anyone. If you do, you'll wreck my life,' she said.

Fran stared at her mother's drawn, wet face, and saw she had suddenly walked across the line from where the look of youth still lingers, to where it can never return. Had it occurred over the last few hours, or had it been touching her for a long time?

She looked at the small, puckered lines above Daphne's top lip and the deep crows' feet fanning out from her eyes. Her hands gave away her age even more than her face; there was no mistaking the appropriately named brown age spots that ravaged them. Did she ever look at those spots and mourn her lost youth? Fran wondered. She remembered so many of her friends' mothers where age had given them a grace and charm that had its own kind of beauty. Sadly Daphne would never be like that. She removed her mother's hands from her shoulders and held them, and in that moment the anger that had been eating her up turned into compassion.

'I know this is difficult for you, too,' she said gently, 'but it's got to be dealt with. Don't you think Dad ever suspected?'

Daphne let her hands remain cradled in Fran's grasp. 'I sometimes wondered, but when you were born nearly four weeks early he never questioned it. He wouldn't have thought there was any need to.'

'We'll tell him together.'

She stood up and embraced her mother as if trying to transfer some of her own strength into the crumpled figure she was holding.

'We've got to help each other through this dreadful time, and then, who knows, something good might come out of it,' she said.

They didn't hear David walk in, or see him pause in amazement when he saw the unlikely spectacle of them wrapped in each other's arms. He coughed uncomfortably to draw attention to himself.

'What's going on now?' he said impatiently as he put his briefcase on the kitchen table.

Daphne removed herself from Fran's arms, pushed her hair away from her face and asked David if she could pour him a whisky.

Fran watched her mother place the whisky in front of David. She sat opposite him and seemed to shrink into herself. The strong, vibrant woman who had been Daphne had disappeared.

'You look a mess,' he said unkindly. 'Shouldn't you go and sort yourself out?'

He took a swig of the whisky.

Fran looked at David. She wondered when she had first known that she disliked this pompous man whom Simon resembled so closely. She knew it was a guilty secret that she'd carried throughout her childhood, and into her teenage years. He had intimidated and frightened her without any recourse to physical violence. Had she been too weak and passive to rebel? At university, her friends smoked dope and experimented sexually, but she'd always stayed on the periphery of it all. Was that because of her father? She didn't think so. Maybe it was just that blowing her mind in that way didn't appeal to her. She'd experienced the biggest adrenalin rush of all out amongst the waves in a force six. Nothing in the world could beat that, apart from the two nights she'd slept with Tom. The thought was like a hard slap in her face. She walked over to stand next to her mother. 'We have something to tell you.' She stared straight into her father's hard blue eyes, then paused and glanced down at Daphne. 'Go on, Mother,' she said.

'Twenty-five years ago I was unfaithful to you. Fran is the result of that indiscretion.'

Fran looked at her mother and wondered how she could use such unfortunate terminology. It wasn't nice to have your existence described as an indiscretion.

David took another swig of whisky and gave Daphne a contemptuous look.

'Do you think I'm a complete fool, woman? When I looked at the chubby, black-haired baby in your arms who was born four weeks early, I certainly didn't imagine for a moment that it was mine.'

Fran watched him play with the whisky glass. He looked as calm and composed as if he was chairing a board meeting.

'I don't think,' he said, 'that we now need to announce to the world that anything has changed.'

'Of course it's changed.' Fran met her father's eyes defiantly. 'I know for a start.'

He stared her down.

'I've always prided myself,' he said stiffly, 'in treating you in exactly the same way as Simon. You've been positively spoilt for the last twenty-four years. I expect some sort of loyalty now for all those years I've covered up for your mother's adultery.'

Fran wanted to shout at him, 'But what about your adultery, and what about love? You never gave me any love!' But for Daphne's sake she kept quiet.

'David,' said her mother, 'you truly are the most wonderful man. Fran and I will be eternally grateful to you.'

She touched her smudged red face. 'I think,' she said, smiling weakly at him, 'that I'd better go and tidy myself up, and then I'll prepare us all a nice meal.'

Fran watched her mother's retreating figure and tried not to despise her.

12

Nipping into The Reed and Whistle for a quick lunch time pint was once again a bright slot in the day for Jack. Phoebe was back behind the bar, having given up her flirtation with both William and office work, and George was no longer the love-sick bore whose hunched figure had begun to have a depressing effect on everyone.

'I'm glad to see you two have patched things up. I'd almost decided to stop coming in here, although sacrificing my lunchtime pint would have depressed me even more than having to watch you, George, old mate.'

'I'm sure I wasn't that bad,' said George.

'Well, it's not going to be depressing any more,' chirped up Phoebe.

Even James, when he came in a few minutes later, didn't have the same hangdog appearance he'd been carrying around with him since Elisabeth had started work at the estate agents.

'So you've cheered up, too,' observed Jack. 'Let me buy you a pint. All these happy faces are worth it.'

James propped himself on the bar stool next to Jack.

'Thank goodness Amy Cooper has decided her ailing dog needs her constant attention,' he said. 'I feel as though I've had a commuted jail sentence.'

'You can thank me for that,' said Jack, handing James his pint. 'I told her she was slowly killing the poor dog off, dragging him out for walks at all hours of the day and night. Now she's got a conscience about it and will probably kill him off anyway, by nursing him to death.'

'Has Annabel been in today?' asked Jack. 'She said last night she might pop in for a lunchtime drink.'

James gave Jack a severe look. 'I hope you're not entering into a flirtation with a married woman.'

'Certainly not, but I must say I never dreamt she'd be so much fun. We played all the pub games last night and she beat me hands down at all of them!'

'I wouldn't have thought she'd be your type,' Phoebe said. 'She seems such a town girl. She always looks so immaculate with her perfect make-up and clothes.'

'I know what you mean,' said Jack. 'She looks just like one of those girls off the front page of *Vogue*, but underneath all that glamour she's down to earth and great fun.'

'I thought you never read anything other than your *Trout and Salmon* magazine?' mocked George.

Jack gazed thoughtfully into his pint. 'She's very beautiful,' he said. 'She reminds me of Marilyn Monroe, she's got that amazing hour-glass figure.'

'Amy Cooper will be reading me the riot act again if you start misbehaving,' James said, passing his empty pint to Phoebe for a refill. 'I hope you're not going to encourage Annabel?'

'I might,' said Jack, and winked at Phoebe.

For the whole of the next day, London lay darkly under a wet sky. Fran went through the motions of playing with Grace and talking about trivial things with her mother, all the time trying to decide what action to take. It had been an effort even to decide what to dress in when she got out of bed. She knew a failure to be able to cope with the small details of everyday life could be the onset of a nervous breakdown; however, she was determined this wasn't going to happen to her. She just had to face up to everything and deal with all the traumatic events of the last few days in a way that was the least harmful to everyone involved.

It was late morning when Daphne suggested they go out to lunch. They went to a smart little restaurant only a short walk from the house where she and David were regular customers. The waiter who met them at the door reluctantly allowed Fran to take the pushchair in. She felt the eyes of all the other customers were resentfully watching her progress through the restaurant with the pushchair. They were led to a table tucked away in the corner. When a smart-suited gentleman on the next table smiled at her, in a way that somehow managed to include Grace, she wondered if perhaps she was becoming paranoid. She smiled gratefully back at him.

It was easier to talk in the restaurant. The suffocating atmosphere in the house had become almost unbearable. They both ordered grilled trout with salad and a light pasta dish for Grace, who played with the assortment of little toys that Fran had tied across the pushchair, squeaking excitedly at a small furry rabbit that pinged up and down when she touched it.

Daphne ordered a bottle of Sancerre and when the wine had been poured into their glasses, she asked Fran what reason she was going to give to Tom for splitting up with him.

Fran looked at her mother in amazement. 'How can you possibly imagine that I'm going to lie to Tom?' she said. 'I've got to tell him the truth, and Jim has a right to know he has a daughter.' She waited for Daphne to start on again about how grateful she should be to David, but instead there was a deathly silence. When she looked up at her mother's face, she saw that there were silent tears running down her cheeks, and watched whilst she dabbed them away with a crisp white napkin that had been placed on her lap by an attentive waiter.

'Oh Fran…' Daphne seemed to be making a desperate effort to compose herself. 'Are you ever going to be able to forgive me for all of this?'

Fran leant across the table and touched her mother's hand. She tried to smile at her. 'I suppose I've got to look at this in a different way altogether,' she said. 'If you hadn't met Jim, I wouldn't be here now, but you do understand I can't keep this a secret.'

She looked at Daphne, and was relieved to feel that compassion had replaced anger. Carrying this knowledge alone for so many years couldn't have been easy for her mother. Daphne was suffering, too; she had to remember that.

Daphne played with the soft little curls that were just beginning to touch Grace's neck. 'I know you must tell him the truth,' she said, 'I do understand. I dread to think how David will react, but for once I'm going to have to stand up to him and be brave. I'm not as hard as you think I am.' She looked appealingly at Fran. 'I've had to harden up over the years, or David would have trodden all over me.'

The trout was placed in front of them. Fran ate small bits of the delicious pink flesh in between placing spoonfuls of pasta in Grace's mouth.

'I don't think I can see Tom myself. It would be too painful. Do you think it would be wrong to ask Annabel or Elisabeth to explain everything to him? Do you think that would be too cruel?'

'I think it would be worse for him to have you standing there in front of him, knowing that you couldn't be his.'

Fran leant across the table and once again touched Daphne's hand.

'I'll ring Annabel tonight, and then tomorrow I'm going to go away with Grace for a while. I'm not sure where yet, but I do need to be on my own to come to terms with all of this.'

'Of course you do. Now, finish your meal and we'll go home and decide where it would be best for you to go.'

That evening, after a meal beautifully prepared by Daphne during which Fran had brief spurts of conversation with David that led nowhere, she escaped to her room and called Annabel. Her father might expect her loyalty, but now Daphne understood there was no way this could be kept a secret. The phone rang and rang but there was no reply. Her mobile phone was switched off, too, which was very unlike

Annabel. She tried every half hour and finally, just before eleven thirty, she was relieved to hear her voice at the end of the line.

'Sweetie,' said Annabel as soon as she heard her voice, 'I know you're feeling dreadfully down at the moment but here's something to tease your mind and amuse you. I had rather a splendid evening last night with your friend the vet, and an even better one tonight. Nothing naughty, of course, but he's certainly fun to be with.'

It was so strange the way everything around you carried on as normal. Fran assumed that must be how bereaved people felt. The world didn't stop for your anguish. People laughed and cried and carried on their everyday lives even though your own world was collapsing around you.

'Fran, are you there?'

'I can't come back to Warbleton.'

'Whatever do you mean? Are you ill?'

Fran told her everything in a flat, unemotional voice, and asked if she could face telling Tom, and if not, then perhaps she'd ask Elisabeth to, because there was no way she was ever going to be able to speak to him again. There was a brief silence, and then she heard Annabel gasp, 'Oh, my God, you poor girl. No, of course you can't come back up here and see him, it would be too awful for you. I'll tell him. Be strong and I'll come back to London as soon as I've sorted things out here.'

'No, don't do that.' Fran could picture Annabel standing by the phone in Watercolour Cottage. She never imagined that the house would fit comfortably around her sister-in-law, but now, strangely, it did. 'I want you to stay there. I don't know what I'm going to do yet, but I'm definitely not staying in London.'

'I'll call you after I've spoken to Tom. Hang in there, Fran. The worst has already happened. It can only get better from here on.'

Fran prayed she might be right, but she certainly couldn't see any prospect of things improving even moderately in the near future. Nothing could alter this disaster.

~❧~

Annabel was tempted to go and talk things through with Elisabeth immediately as it was almost too much to take in, but the thought of James prevented her. She'd just have to wait until the morning, but there was absolutely no way she was going to be able to sleep. She thought of Jack, and his fondness for Fran, and felt a great longing to be with him. He'd asked her to go back and have a coffee with him when they'd left the pub, and she'd refused. The refusal had been an old habit from her dating years, when she'd liked to play hard to get. She had laughed at herself to find she could still behave in such an immature way.

In the moonlight, she could see Jack's Citroen looking as though it had just had a collision with some bales of hay. She knocked hesitantly, but the house was ablaze with lights so she assumed he must still be up. When he opened the door, he smiled down at her and ushered her into the kitchen. It was a true farmhouse kitchen. The room was large, with worn flagstones covering the floor and massive beams running the full length of the ceiling. In the corner of the room, a grandfather clock ticked away merrily. There was an open fire still blazing, and in front of it, on a rather grubby-looking rug, two border collies and a lurcher dozed happily.

He made coffee, not from a jar of Nescafe as she'd expected, but from a sophisticated coffee machine. She felt totally at ease in his company, sipping coffee and touching on different subjects that interested them both. He talked about Fran and her summer's in Warbleton when she'd been a child. He told her about the first day she'd turned up at his surgery, when she could have been no more than seven or eight, with a large herring gull in her arms that had a broken wing. She'd looked at him with her serious blue eyes and asked him if he could mend the seagull. He smiled at Annabel.

'I could never understand how her parents could let a little girl like that roam about so freely, although I know Warbleton is about as safe as it can get,' he said. 'But they seemed an odd pair, her parents. They hardly ever spent any time with the children.'

'I'm here because of Fran.'

'And I thought it was because you found me irresistible!'

They must have talked for over half an hour before she asked him why he had never married.

'How do you know I haven't?' he answered with a smile.

'I think Fran would have mentioned it.'

'Women are an enormous complication. I suppose I just like a peaceful life.'

'Don't you ever think about having children, and the fun you could have with the right companion?'

Jack smiled again and put his arm round her. 'Perhaps I've been with the wrong sort of women,' he said.

'You can't possibly imagine that I'd be one of the right ones,' she said.

'It could be fun finding out.'

She laughed outright at his comment, and told him she had to make an early start the next morning as she was on a mission for Fran.

'What's Fran been up to now?'

Annabel rose to go and said, 'It's complicated, I really can't talk about it at the moment.'

He stood up and put his hand under her chin and gently tilted her face up to his. Between kisses, he told her he was an early riser, and promised to kick her out of bed before six thirty the next morning!

'I can't go to bed with you,' she said. Even to her own ears she didn't sound very convincing.

Jack kissed her again and placed his hand on the small of her back and gently pushed her body into his.

A warm flood of sexual excitement rippled through Annabel, and she allowed Jack to lead her through to the bedroom.

It was just before six when she awoke to feel Jack's hands stroking the length of her body. When she went to get out of bed, he held her and said that now he was nearly forty, he felt he was ready to have a woman complicate his life!

'As you well know, I'm already married,' said Annabel, reluctantly disentangling herself from his arms, 'so you're still safe!'

'I don't think for a single moment you'd have done what we did last night if you were happily married. I don't want to pre-empt you but I have a feeling your marriage is probably over.' He gave her a searching look.

'But is my marriage any worse than most, I wonder?'

'I'm certainly unable to counsel you on the state of a marriage,' he said with a sympathetic smile. 'James thinks everyone takes their marriage vows far too lightly, but I believe there's no point in staying in a marriage that's fallen apart unless there are children to consider, and even then it's often a mistake.'

She let him pull her body close to his again.

'If you had got to know me last year when we spent a week in Warbleton, you wouldn't have liked me very much,' she said.

'Have you changed so much?'

'I was a self-indulgent, spoilt London socialite who thought of little else but fashion and lunches.'

He muttered into her long blonde hair that a London socialite seemed an incongruous partner for a country vet, but on this occasion he was prepared to make an exception to his strict dating rules!

They made love again slowly and skilfully. When she guiltily dressed and looked at the clock, it was nearly six-thirty.

She went past the gate to Watercolour Cottage and straight down onto the marsh. She was amazed at the beauty of a fresh day when it was viewed at seven in the morning. She regretted all the years when she'd lain in bed, letting the day unfold without her. She wasn't lazy, but she rarely arose before eight-thirty; it just didn't seem necessary in London.

When she reached Tom's cottage, smoke was already spiralling out of the chimney and his black and white dog was buried in muddy water, trying to drag something out of the reed beds. *Just the sort of set-up Fran would love*, she thought. It all looked rather like something from a different century but, even with her new state of mind, too off the beaten track to appeal to her.

He must have seen her because he was waiting at the open door when she reached the cottage. 'Is Fran all right?' he asked anxiously.

She told him they needed to talk.

They went inside the cottage and Annabel suddenly had no idea how to begin.

'Is Fran all right?' he asked again.

She paused and wished some wise, guiding hand would help her. When no sensitive, gentle explanation came into her head, she thought the best thing was just to come straight out with it.

'No, Tom, she's not,' she said. 'Things are as bad as they could possibly be.'

He looked as though she had struck him. He sat down heavily on the settee and ran his hands through his thick brown hair. 'She's ill? Please tell me she's not dead!'

'No, no, of course she's not dead, whatever made you think that?'

'You said things were as bad as they could possibly be.'

Annabel took a deep breath and sat next to Tom on the settee. She placed an arm round his shoulders and said, 'Well, in a way, Tom, I suppose she is dead to you in the sense that you can never be with her.'

He stared at her like a puzzled child.

'Twenty-five years ago, your father met Fran's mother in

Warbleton. They had an affair and Fran was the result of that relationship. Daphne didn't breathe a word of it to anyone until she found out that you and Fran were seeing each other.'

Tom groaned. He stood up and walked across the room to the open door, where he stood for several minutes before speaking again.

'She must have been to hell and back,' he said, 'and I so nearly told her.'

'Nearly told her what?'

'I wanted to go to see my father and ask him first. I didn't want to betray his trust.'

He paced round the sitting room. 'I had no idea my father had been in a relationship with Fran's mother, but then why should he have told me that?'

'You must see,' said Annabel, walking across to him and putting her hand gently on his arm, 'that this is the end. You and Fran are brother and sister.'

'But we're not!' he exclaimed, 'thank God we're not.'

Annabel stared at him, wondering at his mental state.

'Believe me, Annabel, what I am saying is true.' He looked at the disbelief on her face and knew he had to continue. 'I'm going to tell you something that hasn't been spoken of for many years. My mother was pregnant by another man when she and my step-father married. Dad met her before she even knew that she was pregnant. They were going to tell everyone after the baby was born. But when she died in childbirth he didn't feel it was necessary.'

Annabel smiled encouragingly and told him to go on, but her mind was already racing, anticipating the unbelievable joy this news was going to give to Fran.

'He didn't want people to question and judge something that they knew nothing about,' continued Tom. 'Not even our closest relatives knew, it was just between Dad and me. He told me when I was fourteen. He said my mother had briefly gone back to an old boyfriend, but quickly realised it was a mistake. But I couldn't say anything to Fran until I had seen him, because I felt I would be betraying his loyalty to my mother.'

'I can understand that,' Annabel said. 'Is that one of the reasons you accepted Fran's pregnancy so easily?'

'I like to think I would have done so anyway, but yes, it obviously influenced me. It was as if I'd been given what death had denied my mother – the chance to love.'

Annabel wondered how on earth Fran was facing up to the false knowledge that she'd had sex with her brother. She'd sounded calm on the telephone last night, but she would be feeling completely distraught. She wouldn't be surprised if it tipped her over the edge. If Daphne ran true to form, she'd be far too involved in her own drama to have any emotions left to support Fran with.

'We have to tell Fran immediately. I dread to think how she's coping with this on top of the miscarriage. Where's the phone?' Annabel looked expectantly round the room but there didn't appear to be one anywhere.

'There isn't one,' said Tom.

The owners of the cottage had never considered it necessary to have a phone line put in and it was one of the things Tom loved about it. He found the only way to truly escape from everyday life was to make sure there wasn't a landline or mobile phone within earshot.

'It's lucky some of us live in the real world!' Annabel said, with a touch of impatience, taking her own mobile phone out of her bag. 'I've got so used to having this that I feel quite panicky if the battery goes flat.' She tried Fran's phone but it was turned off. 'Damn,' she said, 'I really didn't want to have to speak to Daphne. Do you think it's too early to call?'

They both looked at their watches and saw it was ten to seven.

'Just ring,' said Tom, 'if they kick up it's too bad. I can't bear Fran suffering for a minute longer.'

Annabel heard the phone ringing for several minutes. She could picture Daphne and David lying in bed, still half asleep, resenting the intrusive noise at such an early hour.

'Yes?' It was David's abrupt voice at the end of the line.

'David, it's Annabel. I'm sorry to wake you but I need to speak to Fran.' He muttered something incomprehensible down the line and then she heard Daphne's voice.

'Darling, what on earth's the matter? Why are you calling at this unearthly hour, and when are you coming home? I think poor Simon's feeling quite abandoned.'

Annabel decided a quick lie was needed, and said she was coming home soon, but could she get Fran, she needed to speak to her urgently.

'But darling, she's gone. She was determined to leave at the crack of dawn.'

Annabel looked despairingly at Tom who was pacing about the room.

'Where's she gone?'

'I don't know, she's decided to take Grace off somewhere for a few weeks.'

'Daphne, are you sure you don't know where she is?'

'I think it would be the kindest thing to leave her alone, don't you?' Daphne said in a sharp voice.

'Tom and Fran don't have the same dad. I can't explain now but we must find her.'

'Don't be silly, Annabel, I know for a fact they do.'

'They don't have the same father!' Annabel repeated emphatically almost shouting down the phone.

'I really don't see how that can be the case.' Her voice suddenly lost its edge and went so quiet that Annabel could barely hear her. 'Isn't Jim Tom's father?'

'No, he's not. I wouldn't lie to you about this. Please just tell me where she is. Her mobile phone's switched off and every minute she doesn't know, she's suffering.'

There was a brief silence. Then: 'She's gone to stay in a cottage belonging to a friend of mine in the Lake District. I made the arrangements for her last night. The cottage is empty for the winter and it seemed the perfect place for Fran to stay while she comes to terms with everything.'

'Daphne, just tell me the address or telephone number,' Annabel said impatiently.

'There's no number, it's a holiday cottage, but I can give you the address.'

She reeled off the address and Annabel scribbled it down.

'Thank you, Daphne and please, if she calls you, tell her everything, and then get her to ring me.'

'Of course, darling. I can't even begin to tell you how wonderful this news is. So if Jim's not Tom's father, who is?'

'Daphne, I must go. I'll speak to you soon.'

Annabel slowly put the phone back in her bag and shut the little catch.

'What's happened?' Tom asked anxiously.

'Fran's gone. Apparently she's packed her bags and disappeared, and you can hardly blame her.'

'Oh God,' said Tom. He sank into a chair and ran his hands despairingly through his thick hair.

Annabel walked over to him and gave his arm a little shake. 'It's all right, I've got the address. Now put the kettle on, I'm in desperate need of a coffee.'

Fran drove out of London before dawn was making any attempt to break. London, she decided, looked more depressing than she'd ever seen it before. The streets and pavements were empty, and the harsh electric lights gave a stark ugliness to the bricks and concrete. Even to her eyes, a soft dawn and sunlight could mellow the sombre metropolis. She drove slowly down one-way streets and pulled up at traffic lights where, within a couple of hours, streams of traffic would be fighting to get into the right lanes. Leaving at this hour, she should be in the Lake District easily by ten. She hoped the cottage was warm and cosy. She had no idea how long she wanted to stay there, but she needed somewhere to come to terms with the turmoil that had entered her life.

For most of the journey, Tom kept forcing his way into her head. Pictures of him grinning at her with the sea bass in his hands, or thoughtfully explaining some detail to her, became more real than the traffic that she was speeding past in the outside lane. She wondered if either Annabel or Elisabeth had broken the dreadful news to him yet. She tried not to imagine how he would feel; it made her feel sick and breathless. She slowed down and pulled into the inside lane until she felt calm again. She couldn't even be his friend now, and because of their relationship she had lost the chance to know her real father. The only bright light in the whole of this traumatic situation was Grace. She was fast asleep, happy and secure. Thank heavens she was too young to be affected by all the turmoil going on around her.

The cottage was in the tiny village of Elterwater. The fells folded round it and Fran fell instantly in love with the stone cottage and its dramatic surroundings. The back door led out onto a small garden with a shallow beck running past the bottom of it. Beyond the beck rose the fells, sweeping up into the sky. A small flock of Swaledales and Herdwicks were grazing just beyond the fence to the side of the garden. They looked curiously at her and Grace, but didn't scatter in demented terror like most sheep did.

It was early afternoon when she heard a knock on the front door and opened it to see Tom standing there. She stared at him, unable to frame any words in her head.

He took hold of her hands and said, 'Jim is not my father, he's not my real father.'

Fran removed her hands from his. What he said made no sense.

'Fran, we're not brother and sister. My dad wasn't my real dad. Oh, you poor girl.' He wrapped her in his arms and let her cry.

Once inside the cottage, he told her the whole story as he'd related it to Annabel.

'It's like one of those dreams,' she said, 'when you so want it to be true, but you wake up and find it isn't, and the disappointment is quite unbearable.'

He shook her gently. 'This is real, but I just wish I'd told you sooner. I can't believe I've put you through such a nightmare.'

'Yes, it was a nightmare.' She remembered her horror when she'd read the entry in her mother's pink diary. 'If it hadn't been for Grace, I think I'd have gone mad.' Tom walked over to where Grace was playing and lifted her up so she could see the sheep that had found their way through a gap in the fence. About a dozen of them were now browsing happily on the lawn.

'What about your real father? Doesn't he know you exist?'

'My mother told him she was pregnant with his baby, but he was quite happy to have no involvement when he knew Jim wanted to take on the responsibility. I've seen him a few times over the years. He's fine, but we've nothing in common.'

'Can we go for a walk?'

He passed Grace to her and she put her in a little hooded coat. They walked out of the village onto the lower fells. The early evening sun had pushed its way through some stubborn clouds and the whole valley became rich with sunlight.

'I came to the Lake District once on a school adventure week when I was sixteen,' Fran said. 'I loved it instantly, the fells and valleys, and clusters of cottages in remote hamlets.

When I got home, I devoured all of Hugh Walpole's books which are set in the Lake District.'

Tom laughed at her. 'You're quite an incurable romantic, aren't you?'

'I was born into the wrong century, I think. Anywhere that seems to have escaped the modern world appeals to me.'

He took her hand. 'You'll fall in love with Greece then,' he said. 'Some of the islands are so beautiful they seem unreal.'

By the time they got back to the cottage it was almost dusk. Tom lit a fire whilst Fran fed Grace and then bathed her.

Later, they sat holding hands in front of the blazing logs.

'Love for you swept me away,' Fran said. 'It was like hurtling down a mountain on skis and not being able to stop.'

He stroked her dark hair that almost reached her waist.

'Is that such a bad thing?'

'No, but I know I've got to have time on my own. I need to divorce Malcolm and sort my life out.' She looked at Tom's face to see the effect her words were having on him.

'I'll wait for however long it takes,' he said. 'I'm going down to the Romney Marshes next week to tell my father about you. That is what you would want, isn't it?'

'Yes, but I'm not ready to meet him yet.'

'No, I understand. When the time's right I'll take you down there, but we have all the time in the world, there's no rush.'

In the night she woke and clung to him, sobbing.

'Shh,' he said and held her in his arms whilst she cried herself back to sleep.

He left after breakfast and told her he'd be in Warbleton until the middle of March, and then he'd be off to Pellini.

'I'm not going to call you or even write,' he said. 'I respect your decision. Just come to me when you're ready.'

He left Cumbria feeling a great sadness. It was going to be a long winter down on the marshes without even the prospect of a glimpse of Fran. He had seen her in all her different guises, mother, laughing playmate and finally lover. He certainly wasn't prepared to give her up without a fight. If fighting meant patience and waiting, he'd do exactly that.

The colours of autumn clung to the Lake District until the middle of November and then strong winds and torrential rain turned the landscape into winter. It was cosy and warm in the cottage and Fran was given the peace and solitude she asked for. Every few weeks she received a letter from her mother, and she always replied promptly. Daphne seemed to have slotted back into her normal routine and wrote about dinner parties and bridge evenings as though the traumatic few days they'd shared had never happened. She also received lovely newsy letters from Elisabeth. She heard nothing from Annabel until December. Then a short letter came telling her that Annabel was going to join her for Christmas and giving the date and expected time of her arrival.

It was a weird Christmas with just the two of them and Grace, but a very happy one. It snowed on the day Annabel arrived and then continued to snow for the next three days. She had arrived with boxes full of tasty things to eat and several bottles of champagne.

'We may as well make this a Christmas to remember,' she

said. She gave Fran a big hug and immediately uncorked one of the bottles.

Fran laughed at her and produced two surprisingly elegant champagne flutes from one of the cupboards. 'I see you haven't thrown off all your London habits,' she said.

'A girl's got to enjoy champagne every now and again.'

'I couldn't agree more,' Fran said as she sipped the champagne.

They let Grace have a tiny sip and watched in amusement as she screwed up her little nose. 'I bet when you have a baby it won't do that.'

'Sweetie, my milk will probably taste of champagne!'

When they'd cleared away the last traces of the evening meal and settled in front of the fire with a coffee, Annabel told her she was divorcing Simon. He was going to buy Watercolour Cottage from his parents to give to her as part of the divorce settlement. She wasn't making any claim on the house in Notting Hill, which was worth a small fortune, so he was perfectly happy with the arrangement. She also told Fran that she had fallen in love with Jack.

'Don't laugh,' she said. 'Who on earth would have imagined I'd fall in love with a country vet!'

'Jack's the loveliest man. I couldn't wish for you to be with anyone nicer.'

'Well, it's early days yet, but who knows? We're having fun at the moment, and I've been helping out in the surgery with appointments and answering the phone.'

'Annabel, I don't believe you!' laughed Fran.

'I knew you wouldn't, but I'm enjoying it. I can't quite believe it myself but I wake up in the morning and actually enjoy getting out of bed. Apart from when I'm snuggled up to Jack, which I have to admit is becoming more and more frequent!'

'So Watercolour Cottage is yours.'

'Almost, but sweetie, you know it will always be there for you too.'

It had been February when Fran's divorce finally came through and, despite constant urgings from Annabel, another four weeks before she appeared in Warbleton again. By one of those weird twists of fate, she had missed Tom by a few hours. He had left for Gatwick airport barely two hours before she found herself fighting with the sand-filled padlock on her beach hut.

That night up at Watercolour Cottage, Annabel was completely out of patience with her.

'Did you really expect him to wait for you forever, while you were indulging yourself in analysing your life?' she said exasperatedly.

'Don't be cruel, Annabel, I was only trying to do what was best for both of us.'

'I know that really,' she said gently, 'but I've felt so sorry for Tom over these last few weeks. 'Now, pick up the phone and book a flight out to that island that he's gone to, and book a flight for Grace and me in a week's time.'

'I can't leave Grace,' Fran protested.

'Yes, you can. Have a week of freedom. Windsurf and enjoy yourself with Tom. Don't feel guilty. I would have hoped all that soul-searching in the Lake District would have sorted your guilt problems out.'

When she still looked unsure, Annabel added, 'I've got a little secret for you. I'm six weeks pregnant. Jack's over the moon, and I think I am too.'

'Oh, Annabel!' Fran wrapped her arms round her and hugged her excitedly.

'So you see,' Annabel said, 'I need the practice. I promise I'll take the greatest care of her.'

The landing strip was nowhere to be seen as the plane circled and came down low over the sparkling water. There appeared to be numerous little islands dotted about, but none looked large enough for a plane to land on. And then suddenly, as the plane flew seemingly inches above the water, the landing strip came into view and Fran heaved a little sigh of relief. She didn't mind flying, but she always felt quite euphoric after take-off and landing.

It was the oddest airport she'd ever flown into. It was hardly an airport at all, just a strip of tarmac and a low building, and only one plane loitering uncertainly next to the building looking as though it shouldn't really be there at all.

Fran smiled enthusiastically at the air hostess, and let the warmth of the Greek sun wash over her as she descended down the steps and across the tarmac to the weird little building. Unbelievably, the odd assortment of suitcases and rucksacks were already rattling round the conveyor belt.

Within minutes, she was back out in the sunshine looking for a taxi to take her to Pellini.

It was an hour's drive to the small fishing village that over the past few years had developed into a windsurfing mecca. Some of the time she kept her eyes firmly shut, convinced that the taxi driver was a complete maniac as he lurched round blind corners, inches from the abyss at the edge of the road.

The taxi screeched round the final bend before hurtling down the hill towards Pellini. Orange and olive groves spread like so many small gardens across the wide valley that swept back inland between high, wooded mountains. It was a spectacular sight, even when viewed from the back seat of a battered old taxi and feeling slightly car sick. There were no high-rise buildings along the long curve of the beach, just a few pretty white houses within a stone's throw of the deep blue Ionian sea. The small village of Pellini fronted the harbour, where fishing boats jostled with each other next to the harbour wall. She saw canopies almost spilling over into the water, and beneath them people were eating, shaded from the mid-day sun.

When the taxi dropped Fran off outside her apartment, the strong thermal wind that came screaming down off the mountain every afternoon was in full force. It was a phenomenon the local inhabitants had lived with for years. They had never thought much about it until it began to attract windsurfers from every part of the globe, and created a lucrative tourist trade for them. A wide balcony with an attractive wooden table and chairs placed on it afforded a magnificent view of the bay, and if she leant out slightly and looked inland, she could see the olive groves spreading back through the valley to the base of the mountains. She sat on one of the chairs and looked out to sea, which was a foaming mass of white caps. Brightly coloured sails flashed across the water as the windsurfers took to the sea like so many migrating birds all flocking together. Suddenly, she jumped up from the chair. What on earth was she doing watching? She wanted to be out there, too!

When she asked at Club Pellini for Tom, no one seemed to know where he was, so she put a wetsuit on, hired some kit and went out to play in the bay.

The chap who was on duty in the lookout tower was conscientiously scanning the water for windsurfers in trouble. There were always a few every day who overestimated their abilities and gave the people in the rescue boat the chance to rev up the engine and scream out across the bay. He suddenly spotted someone who, even by Pelinni standards, was doing some pretty spectacular manoeuvres. He concentrated his binoculars on the windsurfer and saw that it was a girl, just as she performed a quite spectacular loop off the tiniest bit of chop.

'Get that!' he shouted, just as Tom walked past the tower.

'Get what?' Tom yelled back up at him.

'Out there, the green and yellow sail. Brilliant windsurfer, and it's a girl!'

Tom trained his binoculars on the dancing sail. There was something about the fluid beauty of the manoeuvres that he recognised. He'd last seen them off a windswept beach in England.

When Fran eventually came back to shore, Tom was

waiting for her. He looked at her happy face and tangled wet hair. He touched the wet curls and said the same words it seemed he had last spoken a lifetime ago. 'I suppose you think I was impressed with that little display.'

'Well, were you?' She smiled brightly up at him.

'Just a bit,' he said, and leant over and kissed her.

Acknowledgements

Thank you to my sister Sue for getting me into windsurfing, and for wonderful days spent at her beach hut where my novel came to life.

Thank you also to my children, for their ideas, love and encouragement.

Photo by Georgie Watson

M. A. MEADOWCROFT worked for the Marketing Director of a large finance company in London before having four children. She did a correspondence course in journalism and has been published in *Kent Life* and *Windsurf Magazine*. After qualifying as a windsurfing instructor she set up Rye Watersports by the Kent/Sussex coast. She spends summers at her centre and winters writing and going to windy parts of the world to pursue her love of watersports. She lives in an old farmhouse on the edge of the Romney Marshes. This is her first novel.